The Dinner

Anna Davis

SCEPTRE

Copyright © Anna Davis 1999

First published in 1999 by Hodder and Stoughton
A division of Hodder Headline PLC
A Sceptre Book

The right of Anna Davis to be identified as the Author of
the Work has been asserted by her in accordance with the
Copyright, Designs and Patents Act 1988.

10 9 8 7 6 5 4 3 2 1

All characters in this publication are fictitious and any
resemblance to real persons, living or dead, is purely coincidental.

British Library C.I.P

ISBN 0 340 71841 2

Typeset by Palimpsest Book Production Limited,
Polmont, Stirlingshire
Printed and bound in Great Britain by
Mackays of Chatham plc, Chatham, Kent

Hodder and Stoughton
A division of Hodder Headline PLC
338 Euston Road
London NW1 3BH

For Robin, my father

The Dinner

Arrival
Drinks in the lounge

Hors-d'Oeuvres
Vichyssoise
Halloumi Cheese Salad with Rocket Pesto

Main Course
Pink Trout with Almond and Herb Purée
Potato and Parsnip Galette
Green Salad

Dessert
Coconut Bavarois with Tropical Fruit Sauce

Coffee

Departure

Arrival

The door was opened by a pink glass bottle with arms and a painted-on smile.

Clarrie blinked and the bottle became a thin woman with blonde hair scraped into a bun, wearing a pink mini-dress and a red smile which sliced through the fog. It was Tilda, and the smile slipped away as the fog evaporated.

'Heavens, Clarrie . . . what are you doing here?'

'Visiting.'

Tilda's dress was made of velvet, and the velvet was the only soft thing about her – even the tendrils of hair that had been teased out to hang in front of her large ears were fixed and brittle. A red spot of agitation appeared on the powdered throat, just above the thyroid scar from last year's operation, and it grew. Tilda put a hand to her throat, concealing both the red patch and the scar, and shifted from one foot to the other.

'But we're expecting guests.'

A long-legged black spider was making its way slowly along the soft skin under Tilda's left eye, walking in the direction of her nose. Another spider was moving at exactly the same speed under the right eye. Soon they would reach the nose bridge and meet each other.

Clarrie looked away. When she looked back she saw that the spiders were Tilda's eyelashes. Tilda's mouth was pursing itself up into an angry ball.

'This is a very important evening for Alex.'

Clarrie shrugged and stared blankly.

Tilda was straining to see into the darkness behind Clarrie. Her neck stretched out and her pond-green eyes narrowed.

'Where's Morris? Has he come with you?'

'I'm alone.'

Clarrie watched Tilda's mouth intently. It was making all kinds of interesting shapes and sending out wrinkles to ripple through the thick make-up. It struggled to form some more words.

'Have you just come all the way down from Newcastle on your own?'

Clarrie nodded.

'To – *visit*?'

Clarrie nodded again.

Tilda took a deep breath. She folded her arms against the cold outside and her diamond ring glinted in the glow of the brass lamps hanging to either side of the front door.

'You could have phoned to warn us the arrangements had changed, Clarrie. I mean, we understood you were coming down with Morris in two weeks' time.'

'I'm alone.'

'Yes, so you said. Is something wrong?'

A fuzzy grey shape appeared in the hall behind Tilda. It spoke in a well-modulated gentle voice.

'Who's there, Tilly? Is it the Thackstons?'

'No, darling, it isn't the Thackstons.'

The shape became more clearly delineated as it approached the door. It was Alex, peering out at Clarrie and looking surprised.

'Good God, Clarrie, what on earth brings you down here?'

'She's visiting, apparently.' Tilda moved to allow Alex to sidle past and give Clarrie a hug.

Clarrie found her face pressed against the wide knit of Alex's cream-coloured sweater so that she could see and feel the hairy fibres. When her head was released, hot and dazed, she could see through the holes in the knit and right through Alex's body, which was momentarily transparent, to look straight into the swirling water-weed of Tilda's eyes.

'Oh, Alex darling, you haven't got changed yet.'

When he moved to one side, Tilda's hands were on her hips and her face wore the exasperated expression reserved for her husband.

'Sorry, darling, I was just about to go up when—' He suddenly remembered Clarrie's presence and took hold of her left hand, leading and then – when she made no move – tugging her in, extricating a small leather bag from her frenzied grasp. 'Look, for crying out loud, we're keeping poor Clarrie standing out here on the doorstep as though she were nothing but a stranger. What kind of family are we?'

After momentary reluctance, Clarrie relinquished her hold on the bag and allowed Alex to pull her into the house. Tilda closed the door and followed with an audible sigh.

Alex was chattering excitedly as he led the way through the golden hallway with the mini chandelier and the bare wood floor which made shoes sound like horses' hooves. 'So where's Morris? Is he coming today as well?'

'I'm alone.'

'Oh. Well, it's nice to see you anyway.'

The chandelier was tinkling and throwing reflected shadows against the warm walls. Clarrie threw her head back to look at it, but Alex didn't allow her to linger. He opened a heavy dark-wood door and revealed the kitchen, full of the most wonderful smells and steam, a table covered in green leaves, yellow sauces, peelings, walnut shells and fish innards, and a small girl in traditional waitress dress and frilly apron, stirring a large pot on top of the stove.

'Is this what it's supposed to do, Mrs Stone?' said the girl. Her face was red from the rising heat despite the fan whirling on the ceiling.

Tilda clopped across and snatched the wooden spoon from her, making fraught stirring motions. 'Oh my God, what have you done to it? It's ruined!'

'Now, now, Tilly. Calm down, I'm sure it's fine,' said Alex, running a hand through his wispy hair and placing Clarrie's bag on the polished floor.

'What do *you* know about soup, Alex! Just look at it.' In a loud whisper she added, 'It's all *her* fault.' By *her* she meant Clarrie, but the waitress clearly thought this dig was intended for her.

'I was hired to wait table,' she said, folding her arms. 'And that's what I do. I wait table.' The steam had caused the thick eye make-up to run down her cheeks, making her look like a panda.

Clarrie could see her own face reflected in the side of the shiny steel saucepan as though in a fairground mirror. As she moved from side to side it became long with an incredible chin, or wide like an all-in wrestler.

'I'm not blaming you, you silly girl. I'm blaming . . . oh, forget it. Let's just try to save this soup, shall we? Before it curdles completely.' Tilda turned down the heat and stirred slowly, muttering to herself. Was she swearing or praying?

'I'm warning you, any more of this and I'm going to charge you extra.' Pauline moved so that she stood right in front of Tilda and looked her straight in the eye with defiance. 'Cooks get twice what I'm getting, you know.'

'Yes, but a cook wouldn't have let the soup get into this state.' Tilda filled her ladle with the creamy liquid and let it trickle slowly back into the pot, as though this would somehow prove her point. 'Anyway, I won't be talked to like that by some kid barely out of school.'

'Now, now, ladies, come along.' Alex slid across the floor to prise them apart and planted himself firmly between them. His insubstantial body tried to assume an air of authority, but to little effect. 'This is just a small hiccup at the beginning of what will no doubt be an extremely successful evening, thanks to both of you, so let's all be friends, shall we?' He glanced nervously into the angry faces of the two women. Alex cleared his throat and continued. 'Tilda, I'm sure that *something* can be done with the soup—' a little snort from Tilda '—and anyway, the guests aren't really due for another half an hour or so. Hell, what's a bit of soup when we've had such a lovely surprise!'

Tilda seemed baffled as to what this lovely surprise could be, but scowled all the more when she saw that Alex was indicating Clarrie, who was now staring at the bottom shelf of the dresser which was filled with recipe books. (Was that one really called *101 Weeping Sores*? No, it was *101 Welsh Soufflés*.)

'Now, where can we put Clarrie? The blue room?' Alex had succeeded in diverting Tilda's attention, for the moment at least.

'No, the green, I think.' Her mind had moved from soup to sheets. 'The bed's already made up in the green room and I really don't have the time to concern myself with that kind of thing at the moment.'

'I'll take her up then,' said Alex.

'No you don't! You need to get changed and I'll have to find something for her to wear.' Tilda was surveying Clarrie's black T-shirt and jeans with disapproval.

'Oh, yes, clothes,' muttered Alex, and slipped away.

'Is something wrong with my clothes?'

'They just aren't right for tonight, Clarrie. I'm sure I can dig out something more suitable for you.' She turned to Pauline. 'Now would you please watch the soup for just *three* minutes? Don't let it boil again.'

Pauline sniffed. 'I hope you'll be tipping well, that's all I can say.'

Tilda turned her back and Clarrie saw Pauline's face become a gargoyle for a second as she poked out her tongue and widened her eyes.

Clarrie surveyed the partially deflated pink balloon of Tilda's bottom, waggling in front of her face as she climbed the stairs. Tilda was talking constantly but Clarrie was listening to the sounds of the house: the questioning creaks of the stairs as Tilda trod and the answering creaks as she herself moved close behind; the tinkling of a set of crystal glasses vibrating on a small table where the stairs twisted round; the distant erratic clatters from the kitchen and the steady ticking of the grandfather clock on the landing of the second floor, growing louder as they ascended. It was as though they were climbing the rib cage of a living creature. Clarrie could see the walls moving subtly in and out, and listened closely for the sound of breathing.

'I *said*, what do you think, Clarrie?' Tilda halted and turned around so abruptly that Clarrie almost bumped into her.

'Yes,' said Clarrie.

'Yes – what?'

'Yes, Tilda.'

'You haven't been listening to a word I've been saying, have you?' Tilda's hands were on her hips once more. Clarrie shrugged. Tilda began climbing the stairs again, muttering: 'I don't know why I bother wasting my breath, I really don't.'

'This is my dressing-room. I don't think you've been in here before, have you?'

Tilda pushed open a door to reveal a small room, lit by spotlights, with a mass of people standing in a queue that snaked around the walls. Some of them began to push against each other and it looked as though a fight was about to break out.

'What colour do you fancy?' said Tilda. The people were only clothes, and Tilda was rifling busily through them.

She looked up for an answer, but Clarrie was staring blankly.

'Cat got your tongue again, has it? Well, never mind. Just try not to stare at the Thackstons like that, eh.'

'Sorry.'

'I should think so. Now, you must be about a twelve, so most of these ought to fit you. What about this one?' She pulled out a red dress made of floaty material with a golden flower stitched on one shoulder, but Clarrie was scowling.

'Or this.' A purple clingy number with a low back and slits up the sides. Clarrie made no response.

No, perhaps not.' Tilda's face was now as pink as her dress, as she puffed her way through her outfits. 'Would you prefer trousers?' She held out a pair of brown silk trousers with matching cropped top.

'I don't know.'

'Actually, they'll probably be too long in the leg. Can you see *anything* you could wear? I mean, there must be *something*.' Tilda threw the trousers on the floor and glanced nervously at her watch.

Clarrie looked down at the pale blue carpet with tiny white flowers, like water sprinkled with confetti. Perhaps she could dive in and lose herself.

'Clarrie, I'm doing my best here, but you simply aren't helping in the least. Now please . . . Ah, the very thing.'

She slid from its hanger a long white dress that carried a hint of shrouds about it, and tried to hold it against Clarrie's body.

'*No!*' Clarrie wrenched the dress from Tilda's hands and threw it away from her as hard as she could, almost breaking several of Tilda's fingernails, then stood hunched up, shaking uncontrollably.

Tilda was also shaking. She looked down at her hand, as though to check that it had really happened, and then back at Clarrie.

When she spoke again there was genuine concern in her voice. 'What's the matter, Clarrie? What's going on?'

Clarrie shook her head and shut her eyes tightly, saying nothing.

Tilda moved slowly towards her. 'Has something happened to you? Is it something to do with Morris, is that why you've come here?'

Clarrie hunched over even further, turning herself into a cowering child. She opened her eyes again, and they were filled with fear.

'Look at the state of you.' Tilda reached out gently to touch her left shoulder, and Clarrie shrank away as though scalded. But now Tilda had had enough. Her patience would only stretch so far. 'Oh, for God's sake, Clarrie! Pull yourself together, can't you? There's always something, isn't there, and you just don't want to be helped.' She turned her back and started pulling dresses from the rack again.

Clarrie slowly uncurled as she watched the colours flying. There was a kind of high-speed rainbow going on in front of her and she was entranced. She was only dimly aware that Tilda was still speaking to her as she flung things onto the floor.

'I refuse to allow you to ruin the evening, do you hear me? This is Alex's big bite at the cherry, his chance to make an impression on Brian Thackston. You might not know who Brian Thackston is, but let me inform you that if he likes Alex and decides to go into partnership with him, then we'll be made. *Made*. Now, whatever you might think of me, I know you like Alex and I know you'll want the best for him, so you'll be presentable and polite, and you'll make nice conversation when anybody talks to you. Do you understand, Clarrie?'

She turned around and Clarrie noticed that bits of her hair were working themselves loose from the bun and standing on end with little static clicks. Fluff on her dress and tears in her eyes – were they real or were they made of glass?

'I said, do you understand?'

Clarrie thought about Alex's face, of the way it tried hard to look clever and calculating, resulting only in a habitual expression of puzzled friendliness. She liked him for the softness in that face. She thought of his eyes, dark and sparkling like

Morris's; of the shape of his head, his shoulders, his gangly legs. The brothers were undeniably alike, and she loved watching them when they were together. She relished the strength of the bond between them – even when they clashed, they seemed to be fighting against their differences. Clarrie didn't have a brother or sister herself . . .

'Clarrie—'

'Yes, I understand.'

Tilda heaved a sigh and dabbed at her eyes. When she looked up, her face was wearing its best bright and efficient expression.

'Right. Now choose a dress.'

Clarrie pointed randomly at the sleeping cat on top of the pile of strewn garments.

'A good choice, I think,' said Tilda. 'I can see you in black mohair,' she added as she scooped up what proved to be a long knitted dress with a low neckline and no sleeves.

'OK.'

'Come along, then. We don't have much time.' Tilda grabbed hold of Clarrie's right wrist and marched her out of the room, leaving the clothes still in their pile. She moved so fast that Clarrie didn't feel her feet touch the floor. It was like those childhood dreams where the body defies gravity and floats up the stairs, except that in those dreams your wrist isn't being gripped and painfully tugged.

'In here.' Tilda opened the third of three doors and Clarrie found herself walking into a field.

The walls were olive green, the ceiling was bottle green and the curtains and bedding were grass green covered in daisies. Tilda closed the curtains and checked there were clean towels in the adjoining bathroom.

'There you go. You'll be all right in here, won't you, Clarrie. Last time you were here with Morris, you said this was your favourite of our guest bedrooms, remember?'

'Did I?'

But Tilda wasn't expecting a response. She turned to face Clarrie and knitted her hands together. 'Now, I'd normally say feel free to take a shower, but it'll only be about fifteen minutes until the guests arrive, so I think you'd better just get dressed. There's some stuff on the dressing table that you might want to help yourself to – you know, perfume and make-up. Go ahead and spoil yourself. Anyway, be sure to come down in about fifteen minutes, and don't forget what I said: presentable, polite, chatty.' She retreated to the doorway. 'I'd better go and check on Pauline.'

Clarrie watched the door close and sat down on the bed. The mattress was very soft. Clarrie preferred a hard mattress, liked to feel the shape of her bones when she woke up in the morning. She got up, disappointed.

There was a pine wardrobe on the far side of the room. Clarrie pulled the doors open – it was empty and smelled of dust. She put her small bag inside and closed the doors again. She looked up at a poster of Van Gogh's 'Sunflowers' which hung on the opposite wall in a clip-frame. The flowers weren't flowers; they were yellow fluffy creepy-crawlies scuttling and squeaking behind the glass. The longer she stared, the more she thought she could see legs and teeth and antennae.

'Not real,' she said aloud and the creatures retreated into flowers, but still Clarrie hated the picture. She moved towards it. Perhaps she could do something to make it easier to put up with – perhaps if she turned it upside down it would look better. She grasped the picture firmly and swivelled it round so that it was inverted, but when she tried to let go, there was nothing holding it up and it crashed to the floor.

She bent down to pick it up and saw that the glass had broken. 'Shit!' She lifted the poster with its wooden mount onto the bed and stooped to pick up some of the larger shards of glass.

There was a sharp pain in her right index finger and she saw that she had cut herself. A ruby of blood appeared and grew bigger. Clarrie knelt on the floor and watched the ruby grow. She sucked her finger so that nothing was left but a murky smear then squeezed it so that another jewel emerged. There was blood on the glass too, but not in that perfect round shape. Maybe if she blew on it, it would dry and she could wear it as a ring when she went downstairs.

Downstairs . . . She had no time to be sitting here playing with her blood, she had to get presentable. But what about the broken picture? It had to be hidden so that nobody would notice it. She collected the other large shards together, careful not to cut herself again, lifted the lacy valance and pushed them under the bed. Then she pushed the picture itself under as well.

She stood up, brushing dust and dried blood from her hands, and caught sight of the empty patch on the wall where the picture had been hanging. It was very noticeable, so she pulled off her black T-shirt and hung it on the picture hook. That was better.

Now, to change. The dress was hanging over a chair at the dressing table, where Tilda had left it. Clarrie touched it and liked its softness. She stood stroking it for a couple of minutes before starting to undo her jeans. She hadn't worn a dress in a very long time, but now the idea appealed to her. It would be like being a child again, dressing up in Mum's party clothes while she was out of the house. Once the dress was on, she stood in front of the full-length mirror to admire herself, and saw that she did indeed resemble a child in its mother's clothes. Maybe she should stuff some tissue paper into her bra to pad herself out – no, she'd always despised women who behaved in that way. That was the kind of thing Tilda would suggest, along with tying back her hair and plucking her eyebrows.

She looked down at her feet in their red baseball boots. Tilda had forgotten about shoes! Clarrie sat on the edge of the bed to take off her boots and socks – she would just have to go barefoot, and if anyone asked her why she would tell them she was bohemian. Yes.

Now to the 'stuff' that Tilda had been talking about. There was a light above the dressing table, so Clarrie switched it on. The light made a hundred twinkles dance in the row of perfume bottles. It was quite beautiful. Which of the liquids actually smelt nice? Clarrie needed somebody to advise her, but nobody was available so she went for the prettiest bottle and squirted a generous amount onto her neck. Ugh – it was disgusting, like aerosol air-freshener. Better conceal it with another.

This time she chose the least ostentatious bottle. Yuk – that was vile too, perhaps even more vile, something like fly-spray. What could she do? She wanted to wash the perfume off, but Tilda had said she didn't have time for a shower; it would be far too late to start washing now. She closed her eyes and picked another bottle entirely at random. As she sprayed this last one on her neck and wrists she recognised it as a scent she had worn in her teenage years – not altogether pleasant, but familiar at least. It would do. She ran a brush through her unruly hair so that it fluffed out sideways on both sides of her head, and considered putting on some make-up – no, better not – well, maybe just some lipstick.

There were five different shades of lipstick on the table, ranging from dusky pink to a colour so dark it was almost purple. Clarrie chose a bright red which closely resembled the colour of the blood jewel that had oozed from her finger. She puckered her lips to apply it, but it smeared a little – she had never been good with lipstick. She looked around for something to blot it with but found nothing. She contemplated kissing the mirror to blot it but decided she had made quite enough mess already and stood up for a last look at herself. Her overall appearance was now quite dramatic, although she wished she had some shoes. She considered checking under the bed just to be certain that the picture hadn't run away but realised this was silly, and switched off the light on the dressing table as she prepared to go down, still relishing the softness of the mohair against her bare legs.

'More than just "a bit strange", Alex. She's completely unhinged.' Tilda poured herself a generous gin and tonic and took a gulp.

'Well, there's obviously something the matter, but you know Clarrie.'

'Exactly,' said Tilda. 'I do know Clarrie.'

'Tilly, I wish you could find a way of liking her. You must have *something* in common.'

She snorted. 'Oh, Alex, *please*. It isn't even a question of liking or disliking her. It's difficult enough just having a simple conversation with her.'

He was leaning against the marble mantelpiece in a consciously masculine stance. 'She's rather different, that's all,' he said. 'And as she is my brother's wife, I have worked hard to *embrace* her differences.'

'Stop kidding yourself, Alex.' Tilda jiggled her ice cubes. 'You don't like her any more than I do . . . Don't fiddle with your cravat, darling. It looks just fine as it is.'

Alex tried to stop fumbling. 'I look like a fool, a bloody dog's dinner.' He tugged his waistcoat, worried that it was riding up at the back.

'That's just silly. Believe me, it creates exactly the right impression.'

'I look like a golfing toady.'

'You could do worse than take up golf. I'm sure Brian Thackston plays.' She drained her glass.

'Tilly, you've never met Brian Thackston. He's a Northerner from a working-class background. You'd be more likely to find him down at the dog track than on a golf course.'

'Now you really are being silly, darling. Don't be so *Northernist.*' Tilda moved back to the drinks table and poured herself a second gin.

Alex frowned. 'Don't you think you'd better take it a little more slowly? You know what you're like.'

Tilda looked down at the glass as though she didn't know how it had found its way into her hand. 'Oh, yes . . .' She placed it on a coaster on the glass-topped side-table. 'I'm just a bit nervous. I always drink when I'm nervous.'

Alex moved across the lounge to put his arms around her. He kissed her forehead gently and played with the tendrils of hair in front of her ears. 'Darling, I know how much work you've put into this dinner party, but really the bottom line is that it won't make any difference at all to whether Brian chooses to go into partnership with me. It's just a gesture, and hopefully it'll be a relaxed evening with a few friends, nothing more and nothing less.' Satisfied that he had soothed her sufficiently, he sat down on the Chesterfield and patted the seat for her to join him. 'Shame about the Glesses, though,' he added. 'Eight is a much better number than six.' He took a sip of his whiskey.

'Yes, I think so too.' Tilda was still standing, half reaching for her glass again. 'But don't worry, I invited the Stilbournes to make the numbers up.'

Alex choked and spluttered. 'The Stilbournes! You invited the Stilbournes!'

Tilda was puzzled. 'Yes. Why not? Are you all right, did it go down the wrong way?'

Alex coughed into a handkerchief and then put it back into his trouser pocket. 'You know I don't like the Stilbournes.'

'I know no such thing.' Tilda's voice revealed how hurt she was. Her right hand went straight to her throat and the smiling thyroid scar. Her left hand contorted itself around the diamond ring. 'I thought we had a lovely time last time they came. Boxing Day, wasn't it? You've always got on very well with Clive—'

'Now Clive really *is* an unbearable toady.'

'—and I'm extremely fond of Heidi.'

Alex appeared to be struggling to raise further objections. 'Heidi's shallow,' he said finally. 'You'd do better to find some friends who've got more to talk about than flower arranging and the latest fashion.'

'Why are you being so beastly? They're our *friends.*'

'Friends who are probably going to ruin this very important evening!' Alex bashed his knuckles against his forehead. 'And I wish you'd consulted me before you invited them.'

At this, Tilda seemed suddenly to remember herself. She pointed a pink-nailed finger at her husband. 'And I wish *you'd* consulted *me* before you welcomed Clarrie into the house with open arms. I don't see how you can possibly be cross about the Stilbournes when we've got *her* upstairs.'

'She's my *brother's wife*, for God's sake, what am I supposed to do?'

Outside the door to the lounge, Clarrie paused. She had been about to knock, but was stopped by the words that drifted through the keyhole.

'She's my *brother's wife*, for God's sake, what am I supposed to do?'

The words hung in the air in front of her, like mosquitoes. She tried to swat them but they eluded her, mixing themselves into anagrams and finally disintegrating. More words were flying through the gap under the door, squeezing between the hinges, oozing through the cracks.

'Maybe we should phone Morris,' said Alex. 'Tell him Clarrie's arrived safely. Make sure everything's all right.'

'What for? Morris is in Newcastle and we're expecting our guests any minute now.'

Clarrie could trace the outline of Tilda's face in the knots of the wood. There was her nose, pointy and horrible, there was her jagged mouth and there was the dimple in her chin, that tiny mark near the handle. Could she find Alex's face as well?

'Tilda, we don't *know* that Morris is in Newcastle. She only said that she's here alone. What if something's wrong?'

'Well, if he isn't in Newcastle, then we can't phone him anyway, can we?'

'I just think we should try.'

'What if they've had a bust-up – what then? We could be opening a can of worms.'

Clarrie could see where the worms had been. The door was full of tiny holes. If she looked hard enough, perhaps some of them would come wriggling out.

'Tilda, I hardly think she would choose to come to us if they'd broken up.'

'Well, perhaps you're right about phoning Morris. But in the morning, eh? We don't have time now . . . God, I wish she wasn't here.'

'What would you have me do, Tilda? Throw her out on the streets?'

'No, of course not. But maybe she could stay upstairs.'

'Don't be ridiculous.'

Clarrie was watching the two wooden faces talking to each other – it was a bit like a puppet show. Perhaps this was the moment for applause. She raised her hands to clap . . .

'We'd better get you back on that exercise bike,' said Christina Thackston, testily, as her husband Brian puffed and struggled his way out of the taxi.

'I don't like it. It doesn't go anywhere.'

'That's hardly the point,' snapped Christina.

'Give it a rest, love.' Brian Thackston leant his great bulk against the Stones' garden wall and took a couple of deep breaths to steady himself. Christina had been in such a good mood while they were getting ready. But then her moods were about as reliable as British weather.

The taxi pulled away in a cloud of exhaust fumes that made Christina break into a fit of coughing. At least that shut her up!

'Women taxi drivers. Whatever next?' Brian's gaze followed the cab and its glamorous driver as it lurched around the corner and disappeared. He looked back at his spindly wife, who was fussing with her clothing.

'I could be a taxi driver if I wanted to,' muttered Christina.

'Darling, you can't drive.'

'I could learn.'

Brian straightened with difficulty and stepped onto the gravel driveway. 'Smart lights. We could do with something like that.' He gestured vaguely at the brass lamps positioned to either side of the front door. 'Authentic-looking. Lovely house,' he added, after a moment of appraisal. 'I'm surprised Alex has the money for this kind of place.'

'These old houses are full of dry rot,' said Christina with a disdainful sniff. 'Our house is much nicer.'

'Can't something just be nice on its own terms? Must you constantly measure and compare?' In his mind's eye, his wife held a tape measure up to Alex's front door, jotted frantically in a note book and clapped with glee.

'Oh, fiddlesticks!' screeched Christina, right in his ear.

Why couldn't she swear properly? Why was it always 'fiddlesticks', 'sugar' or 'drat'? 'What's the matter now?'

Christina was twisting around grabbing at her left leg, looking rather like an old cloth being wrung out. He wished he could wring her out. He'd use all the strength he had in his huge hands to squeeze every drop of moisture out of her. Then he'd hang her up to dry and leave her strung up on a line for a very long time.

'Can't you see?' Christina snapped. 'Are you blind or something?'

'See what? It's dark.'

'The ladder, of course. I've got the most enormous ladder going up the back of my tights. Why didn't you tell me!'

'I would have told you if I'd seen it.' And Brian still couldn't see it, try as he might. 'Maybe you did it getting out of the taxi.'

'This is *so typical*.'

'You're right there.' He kept his comment under his breath.

'I can't go in looking like this. We'll have to go back. I'll have to change my tights.' And she stamped in the gravel like a two year old.

'Forget it, Christina. Nobody's going to look at your legs

anyway.' And Brian stepped forward decisively and rang the bell.

What was that horrible clanging in Clarrie's head? It threatened to crack her skull open and come surging out; it vibrated in her ears, nose and teeth. She heard movements inside the lounge. Alex and Tilda mustn't be allowed to see her crouching on the floor. She scuttled up the stairs out of sight.

From her vantage point on the stairs she had a clear view of the hall and the front door. It was strange to be looking at it from this angle – it reminded her again of the floating dream. She heard panic in Tilda's voice.

'Alex, would you get the door? I'm all in a mess.'

Then Alex's footsteps, slow and heavy, as he came out into the hall. Clarrie could see a patch of thinning hair on the top of his head. He looked so small from high up.

Two dark shapes were dimly visible through the smoked glass of the front door, one much bigger than the other. As Alex grasped the two handles and yanked, light shone full on the doorstep couple, and Clarrie was reminded of films about aliens. They even looked rather like aliens – their faces were deathly pale, almost green. The man was pudgy and cumbersome; he probably couldn't move very fast, and his face was made of clay which somebody had forgotten to knead into its proper shape. Clarrie imagined that he had no bones, that he would move with a rolling stagger and be unable to cross his legs. The tiny woman, however, was carved from bone. Her thin face was particularly unearthly with its frame of ginger hair and the insipid grey of the eyes. Were those eyes looking up at Clarrie's perch?

Alex was wittering ceaselessly. 'Brian, Christina, so glad you could make it, lovely to see you. What do we have here? . . . Ah, South African – I'm rather fond of these new wines. Well, I suppose they aren't new over there, are they – but *you* know what I mean. Come in, come in.'

The couple were talking as well, but their voices were distant, cloudy. Clarrie tried to make out the words but it was as though her ears were full of water. As they crossed over the threshold into the house, the Bone *was* looking up, and Clarrie felt herself seen.

'Darling, it's the Thackstons,' called Alex, and Tilda emerged from the living-room, freshly spruced and radiantly pink. From above she looked like a thistle.

'Brian, Christina – this is my wife, Tilda.'

'Wonderful to meet you both at last,' Tilda gushed, as the lump of clay extended a podgy hand. 'Alex has told me so much about you,' she half-whispered, and beamed across at Clay Brian's fleshless wife. 'Now let me take your coats and Alex will get you something to drink.'

'Who's that up there?' said Bone Christina in a voice that could crack glass, and pointed so that they all turned and looked upward, their eyes like pins pricking Clarrie's skin wherever it was exposed.

'Clarrie, my dear, we were wondering where you were,' said Alex with a forced smile. 'Come down and meet our guests.'

The pins were still spiking her, and she found herself unable to move. She waited for the pins to turn back into eyes but they didn't, and she was glued to the spot.

'Clarrie, come down.' There was an unpleasant edge to Tilda's request, discernible only to its recipient and not to the guests, but Clarrie knew it was a command and worked with haste to unstick her feet and make her way down, trying to ignore the pins.

'This is my sister-in-law, Clarrie,' said Alex, with Clay Brian and Bone Christina still staring, and then he ushered them into the living-room. Clarrie was just about to follow when Tilda grabbed hold of her arm.

'Not so fast, Clarrie, not so fast,' she whispered, and closed the lounge door behind the guests. 'What have you done to yourself? You look like a circus clown.'

'Sorry,' said Clarrie, aware of the potency of the anger directed at her.

'Whatever possessed you?' Tilda dumped the coats at the foot of the stairs and reached for a tissue from a box on a side-table so that she didn't see the cut finger Clarrie was holding out by way of explanation.

'Come here,' said Tilda, as she put one hand behind Clarrie's head to hold it steady and used the other to wipe away most of the red lipstick. Clarrie was compliant – a small child in the park screwing up its face while its grandmother wipes away traces of chocolate ice-cream. 'If you insist on acting like a baby, then you'll be treated like a baby.'

The tissue was disintegrating and bits were getting into Clarrie's mouth.

'Lick your lips,' said Tilda, and Clarrie took in more of the soggy fragments.

Next, Tilda was frantically patting and smoothing the sides of Clarrie's head, trying to flatten down her hair. For a few seconds the world became muffled by Tilda's palms, but then she gave in.

'Your hair is very difficult to control.'

'Can't do a thing with it,' came Clarrie's automatic response, and in her mind her mother puffed and sweated as she struggled to plait her daughter's unruly curls.

Tilda moved back a few paces to survey her handiwork, hands on hips. 'I suppose you'll have to do. You'd better get in there – I'm going to sort out the coats and check on the food.'

'Yes. Thank you.' Clarrie opened the living-room door and passed through.

A second too late Tilda caught a glimpse of the sole of one foot. 'Shoes!' she hissed. But Clarrie was already inside the room.

It was autumn in the lounge; everything was brown, red and gold. A large rug lay in the centre of the room, of the sort that might fly if you knew the right word. There was a fire burning in the grate, but the flames were wrong – they had blue edges, and Clarrie could see the metal pipe that was the source of the heat. Clay Brian and Bone Christina were seated in prime positions on the uncomfortable-looking brown leather couch, their faces less grey in the soft lighting. Alex was doing his duty with the drinks at the far end of the room near the bay window that was hung with a large expanse of russet velvet – Clarrie could have enjoyed rolling herself up in that velvet but she was too well aware of what was required of her to attempt such a feat.

'Let's not talk business tonight, eh, Alex. We've plenty of time for that, and anyway we're here to get away from the office, aren't we.'

Clarrie was surprised at the ease with which the clay face formed words. She tried not to stare too hard.

Alex was evidently embarrassed. He cleared his throat and gave a nervous laugh. 'Quite right, Brian, quite right. Now what can I get you?'

'A Scotch, please, on the rocks as they say.'

Clarrie watched cubes plinking and golden liquid splashing over them. She remained standing just inside the door, unsure what to do, afraid of stepping onto the intimidating carpet and crossing the room under the gaze of the guests.

'And Christine, what would you like?'

'That's Christin*a*. I'd like a gee and tee, please.' That edgy voice again. Clarrie winced.

Alex was evidently struggling to function despite this second embarrassment. 'I *do* apologise,' he stumbled. 'Only I had a dog called Christine once, you see. Force of habit, that sort of thing.' And then, redder still, 'Oh, sorry.' He busied himself a moment longer and finally took the drinks across, smiling brightly.

'Ah, Clarrie.' He suddenly noticed her. It seemed nobody had heard her entering the room. Now all eyes were turned on her – the Bone was openly scrutinising her protruding toes.

'What's your pleasure?' Alex asked.

'My pleasure?' Clarrie was baffled. 'I like riding on trains.'

The Bone tittered behind a hand, but the Clay smiled warmly so that the flesh bunched up just under his ears.

'Nice riposte, my dear. I've always said people should say what they mean and mean what they say.' He nodded wisely after his pronouncement and raised his solid eyebrows at Alex.

'Quite, quite.' Alex was irritated with her for causing him further embarrassment, she could feel it. 'What would you like to drink, Clarrie?'

She shrugged.

'Come over and see what we've got,' said Alex, now back at the drinks cabinet.

Clarrie glanced at the expanse of carpet and space, and swallowed heavily.

'Well, come on then.'

She took a deep breath and held it as she stepped gingerly across the carpet, unsure what she feared, knowing only that she was frightened.

'This really is a beautiful house,' the Bone was saying as Clarrie reached the far side of the carpet and stepped off. 'How long have you been here?'

'Well, actually my wife inherited it about five years ago. It was her parents' house, you see. When Tilda's father died, her mother decided she couldn't manage it any more. She moved into a little flat, you know the sort of thing – with a warden to keep an eye on her and all that. Sadly, she deteriorated fast after that – she died last year. It was very hard for Tilda – they were close. We've done a lot to this place since then. Virtually gutted it and started again. Made it our own. You need to really, don't you think?'

Clarrie could dimly hear Alex talking, but her attention was entirely taken up by the array of bottles and glasses. It was like being back in the green room looking at the row of perfume bottles, only bigger and better.

'Gone are the days when people would take their parents in and care for them in their old age. Things aren't what they used to be,' came the Clay's heavy voice.

Was that a worm in the bottom of one bottle? Actually it was more like a green caterpillar. What would you do if it landed in your drink?

'Don't misunderstand me, Brian. It was all her choice. She would have been perfectly welcome to have stayed with us, but she still wanted her independence, a little place of her own.'

That golden one contained the sun, and the deep red one could be holding the organs for a transplant operation.

'Have you made your mind up yet?' Alex was talking to her.

Clarrie pointed at the deep red. She could see the distorted shape of her face glowing back at her in the bottle.

'I think we'll be saving the port until after dinner actually,' he said, quietly. 'Why don't you have a gin and tonic? You usually like a nice gee and tee.'

'OK.'

Clarrie watched Alex use surgical-looking tongs to plink two ice cubes into a glass and pour on the liquid. She was disappointed that it had no colour but the cold glass felt good in her hands when it was passed across to her. She sat down in an armchair close to the drinks cabinet, enjoying the smooth quality of the leather against her back where her skin was exposed, and stared into her drink. What was that black thing inside one of the ice cubes?

'Did I tell you they've hired a waitress for the evening?' Judy Marshall opened the glove compartment with slender fingers, drew out a bottle of nail varnish and snapped it shut again. 'Do try to drive smoothly, won't you, darling,' she said as she unscrewed the bottle. 'A sudden jolt could have dire consequences for your upholstery.'

'Must you do that in here?' barked Roger Marshall from under his moustache, taking a corner in a manoeuvre that was far from smooth.

'Just covering a little chip, sweetie.' Judy reached over to stroke his thigh. 'You know how you like me to look perfect.'

'You always look perfect to me,' said Roger, smiling at his wife.

'Keep your eyes on the road,' snapped Judy, like a school mistress.

'Sorry,' he muttered, and applied himself to his driving.

'Well, *did* I tell you?' She carefully touched up the offending nail.

'Tell me what?'

Judy sighed. 'Must I say everything twenty times – did I tell you they've hired a waitress for the evening?'

'Have they?' Roger said, without interest.

'Yes. Terribly pretentious, don't you think. Just lately, Tilda seems to have been getting rather above herself – she's lording it about as though she were landed gentry or something.'

Roger's bushy eyebrows collided in a deep frown. 'I thought Tilda was supposed to be your best friend.'

'And so she is, darling, so she is.' Judy screwed the cap back on the nail varnish and returned it to the glove compartment. 'It's because we are such good friends that I feel *absolutely* justified in passing comment on her recent behaviour.'

Roger braked suddenly at red lights. 'But would you actually tell her to her face that you think she's being pretentious and getting "above herself"?'

'Of *course* I would. In fact I will, just as soon as I get the chance.

You don't think I'm the sort of person to go talking about people behind their backs, do you, Roger?'

He shot her another glance. She had pulled down the vanity mirror and was applying more lipstick on top of her already immaculate first layer. He opened his mouth to speak and then decided to treat her question as rhetorical.

'Isn't it the next on the right, darling?' Judy searched about for something to blot her lips.

'Yes. Don't worry, I know where I'm going.' Roger took the right and slowed down to search for a parking space.

'Roger, I do hope you aren't going to be a dreadful bore tonight.' Judy adopted a little-girl voice. 'There's a space there, sweetie. Just behind that vulgar four-wheel thing.'

Roger backed efficiently into the space, and tried not to show the hurt. 'Bit unnecessary, don't you think, Judy?' he muttered.

'What was that?' She flipped the vanity mirror back up.

'Nothing,' said Roger, braking and switching off the engine.

Judy shivered as she got out, and waited impatiently for her husband to fetch her fur coat from the back of the car and wrap it around her. He leant forward as he did so to plant a light kiss on her neck.

'Oh, darling, you're wearing your *awful* blazer,' she exclaimed as she turned to face him. '*And* you have dandruff on your collar.' She brushed at his shoulders, but then – seeing his expression – stroked his cheek gently. 'I'm only teasing, Roger,' she cooed. 'Actually you look rather dashing.' And she tweaked his moustache affectionately and led the way up the drive – only turning back again to call out, 'Goodness, look at this dreadful bit of tat Tilda's picked up for the front lawn. What on *earth* possessed her – just look at the genitalia!'

The doorbell rang again, startling everybody, and Tilda's distant voice called out, 'I'll get it.' When two more people were shepherded into the room and proclaimed to be Judy and Roger Marshall, Clarrie was momentarily diverted from her ice cubes.

She allowed the introductions to wash over her – she was trying to work out where she had seen the man in the blue blazer before. Even his shiny buttons and highly polished shoes seemed

familiar. He had jet black hair and a military moustache. Military
. . . Marshalls . . . Clarrie remembered a man with a moustache
wearing a peaked cap and pointing a huge finger. That was it –
Your Country Needs You – the man was Kitchener from the old
war poster. Kitchener was nodding in her direction now, and
Alex was pronouncing his name, Roger, and telling him who
she was.

'So you're the girl who married Morris, eh? Heard quite a
bit about you from Alex here.' He turned to wink at Alex in a
manner that Clarrie found distinctly unpleasant. She switched
her attention to the sleek woman in fur standing near the door;
Cruella de Ville with slicked back hair, high cheekbones and
immaculate arched eyebrows. Her movements were authori-
tative, her posture perfect. Did she have a cigarette holder in
her black velvet clutch bag? The Bone was examining Cruella
too, Clarrie noticed, and with distinct disapproval. The Bone
was probably a Methodist or something, and the newcomer
was surely a pagan who would strip the fur from defenceless
animals with her bare teeth.

'What'll you have, Judy?' Alex was saying.

'Vodka and lemonade, please.' Cruella removed her fur and
handed it to Tilda, revealing a dramatic red dress that almost
swept the floor and eclipsed the hostess's. Tilda hovered expectantly before seeming to realise that Kitchener intended to keep
his blazer on for the time being. Having made this discovery she
quickly evaporated, muttering something about how Pauline
should be taking the coats: 'One wonders what we are actually
getting for our money.'

'Nothing for me, thanks, old chap,' said Kitchener. 'I'll have
a couple of glasses of wine with the dinner, but I've got the car
outside, you see. Judy insisted we drive.'

'*We* came in a taxi,' said the Bone in a smug voice.

'That's nice for you.' Cruella reached out for her drink. 'Roger
is my personal taxi.'

'Too right.' Kitchener was cheerfully resigned.

'Judy knows all there is to know about managing husbands,'
said Tilda as she came back into the room and picked up her
glass. 'I go to her for tips.'

Clarrie had returned to her ice cubes, and the black thing

trapped inside one of them. It was a tiny fly. She found herself sympathising with it, thinking about what it must be like to be frozen alive. Its wings were still immaculate, but it would never fly again.

'*Your* husband reminds me of someone,' the Bone said to Tilda, 'but I can't quite put my finger on who it is.'

'Just about *everyone* seems to remind Christina of somebody,' said the Clay, 'and she can never remember who.'

'Oh, you, that's not fair.' The Bone dug the Clay playfully in the ribs with a sharp elbow – or at least in the place where his ribs would have been if he had any. 'As a matter of fact I know exactly who Alex reminds me of. It's that actor . . . you know the one, he's really famous. Keith something – Keith—'

'You mean Kenneth Brannagh.' Alex wore a jaded smile.

'Yes, that's the fellow!' The Bone clapped her hands excitedly. 'Have you been told that before?'

'Just once or twice.'

Clarrie slurped the last drops of her drink and received a warning glance from Tilda. Her ice cubes were melting and she held her glass with both hands to encourage the process, breathing into it so that it misted over all around the inside. If only the fly would live again when the ice had thawed through, now that would really be something.

'. . . I'm in plastics actually, have been for years,' Kitchener was saying. 'Was in the Navy as a youngster, but – well, it's not really a career for a family man and plastic is far more lucrative.'

'So you have children, then?' The Bone sounded suddenly interested.

'Yes, three. One of each and an extra girl,' said Cruella, and quickly added, 'I began quite young, you see. They're with my mother tonight. In fact they're with her for the whole week. Half-term – marvellous invention. We palm them off on Granny and Grandpa for a bit of peace and quiet. Do you two have any children?'

'No.' The Clay answered very quickly, so that Clarrie looked up. 'No, we don't.' The Bone was staring into her drink.

'Brian's in the same line as Alex,' said Tilda, breaking the slightly awkward silence.

'Yes, dear, but there's not going to be any shop talk tonight,' said Alex, pointedly. 'Now, does anyone need a top up? Sure you won't have anything, Roger?'

The fly *was* moving and Clarrie was spellbound. The ice was melting fast, forming a little pool at the bottom of the glass, and one by one the fly's legs were freed – wriggling. Clarrie was so excited that she hardly dared breathe. This couldn't really be happening – perhaps it was just the movement of the water that was shifting the legs, creating an illusion. No – now the wings were moving too, ever so slightly at first, and then more definitely. The fly was shaking itself free, pulling itself out of the water. She was frightened for it – worried that the effort would prove too much, that it would tire itself out, fall into the water and drown, its determination all leading to nothing. She hoped it could hear her thoughts: *Slow down, there's no rush, take it easy,* but she knew that was silly. The fly couldn't understand, it was on its own. Finally, after what seemed like a very long time, it made a sudden leap out into the air. In an upward dive it cleared the glass and soared out into the room.

'Yes!' Clarrie was on her feet. The glass dropped to the floor.

The fly was gone and all eyes were on her. The room had fallen silent.

'Whatever is the matter, Clarrie?' Alex's voice was flat. His face was anxious.

'I just saw a frozen fly come back to life,' she said, and looked around at the faces. Tilda was pale, mouthing something incomprehensible to her. Cruella was smiling an unpleasant smile. Kitchener might have been smiling too under that massive moustache. The Bone frowned disapproval and only the Clay appeared genuinely interested.

'What happened?' he asked. 'Did you see something strange?'

'Clarrie's always seeing strange things, it's her artistic temperament,' came Tilda's voice.

'I *did* see something.' Clarrie was speaking to the Clay alone. 'There was a fly in my ice cube, and when the ice melted the fly got up and flew away.'

'I suppose we can say we're late because we couldn't get Max to sleep,' said Heidi Stilbourne, nestling in the crook of Clive's arm and trying to get comfortable against the hard plastic of the taxi seat. 'Babies make the best excuses for being late. You don't get asked any questions because nobody wants to hear the full story.'

'Mmm.'

Heidi adjusted the straps of her dress and twisted around to get a look at her husband's face. Clive clearly wasn't listening. 'Better than the truth, don't you think?' she continued, in a louder voice. 'That five minutes before the taxi was due to arrive, there was still no bloody sign of you. Where were you, Clive?'

He leant over to run a hand through her thick hair and kiss her on the forehead. 'I told you, honey, I was working. I didn't exactly get much notice that we were going to the Stones'. I had stuff to do.'

Heidi rearranged her hair where he had disturbed it. 'Tilda only called this morning. You know that – you were there.'

'Yeah, so you know what that means, don't you? We're stand-ins, reserves, B-list guests.' Clive withdrew his arm and began fiddling with a cuff.

'Why don't you want to go to dinner with the Stones?' Heidi lowered her voice, aware that the taxi driver might be eavesdropping. 'They're our friends, aren't they?'

'It's not *that*.' Clive brushed imaginary fluff from his lapels to avoid looking at her face. 'We were obviously brought in to replace some other couple who cancelled. I don't like it, that's all.'

'Oh, I see. It's a pride thing.' Heidi seemed content with this explanation. She put a hand on Clive's knee and squeezed gently. 'You don't want to go play unless you can be best friends with Alex. You big baby!'

'Yeah, sure, take the piss, why don't you?' Clive removed her hand and crossed his legs, turning away from her. 'I tell you, Heidi, those two make use of us. I can see it even if you can't. Or won't.'

'Clive, what *is* the matter?'

But the taxi was drawing up now and he was busying himself with his wallet. Heidi stared out at the Stones' large house, at the lights to either side of the door; into the living-room window, where she could just about make out the shapes of people moving around inside.

*   *   *

'A frozen fly comes back to life . . . it's a miracle,' said Cruella in a strange pitch, still smiling her cruel smile.

'Jurassic Park strikes again.' Alex forced a laugh. 'Now, would anyone like another drink?'

'It did happen.' Clarrie reached down to pick up her glass. 'I saw it.'

When the doorbell rang again, clanging through the awkward silence, Tilda and Alex both jumped up with an 'I'll get it', but Pauline's light footsteps could be heard moving from the kitchen to the front door.

'Good Lord, now that *is* a miracle,' muttered Tilda as she opened the lounge door to welcome the last of the guests.

Clarrie searched for the fly with her eyes along the picture rail which outlined the room, across the mantelpiece and on the ceiling. She looked up at the lampshade and down into dusty corners. Perhaps it had flown out of the door already, or maybe it was concealing itself somewhere, hiding in a vase or sleeping in the folds of the velvet curtains. Perhaps it had flown in a straight line from the ice into the blue-edged fire. What must it be like to survive being frozen to death only to be burnt into black dust seconds after the resurrection? Anyway, what did it really matter if she couldn't find the fly? Being able to point it out to everybody would not make them believe her. It would prove nothing except that there was a fly in the room, and Tilda would go in search of the insect spray. She knew what had really happened; it was safely recorded in her inner world, the world that none of them had a hope of understanding. She searched around the ceiling one last time before giving up and transferring her attention to the shiny man who had just entered the room.

Shiny had immaculate silver hair. (Surely he wasn't old enough to have hair of that colour? It must be some freak genetic inheritance which he was too proud to try to conceal, a disorder which could be useful in that it made him appear mature and distinguished.) He was wearing a pale blue suit with a slight sheen to it and a polka-dot tie. All in all he was a kind of cultured version of a game-show host who spoke out of one side of his mouth, allowing the occasional glimpse of gleaming white teeth. Even his voice with its faint Irish accent was vaguely shiny.

He was followed by a hammock; a woman who was what you might call 'buxom', or maybe 'curvy' was a nicer word for it. She wasn't fat by any means but she was certainly voluptuous with full lips and thick, glossy hair that hung down her back in meticulously arranged curls. Her hammock appearance stemmed from the peculiar dress; a kind of loose net of knotted rope on top of a silk under-layer. The dress came down to her feet and Clarrie wanted to tilt her head to one side to imagine the woman suspended horizontally between two poles for somebody to come and relax on.

'I hope we're not *too* late,' Shiny Clive was saying out of the left side of his mouth. 'I'd hate to be responsible for a burnt meal. I was ready to leave the house over an hour ago, but – well – Alex, Roger, you know what it's like when you're waiting for them to finish putting on the war paint!'

'Clive, you're exaggerating again.' Hammock Heidi was clearly not amused but she gave him a good spirited shove. 'He's determined to embarrass me tonight and I've no idea why.' She directed her comments to Tilda and Cruella. 'The truth of the matter is that Max wouldn't settle, and I just don't think it's right to leave him with the baby-sitter until I've got him properly to sleep.'

'Heidi, I know exactly what you mean. I felt the same when mine were small,' agreed Cruella.

Clarrie was concerned. Shiny Clive and Hammock Heidi were obviously old friends of Kitchener and Cruella. The Clay and the Bone were looking somewhat left out on their island-couch, watching the conversation rather than taking part in it, and Clarrie thought she could detect an edginess in Alex and Tilda, a slight fear that the group dynamic would not be right. She herself hoped the guests all knew what was expected of them and would behave accordingly.

'You needn't worry about the dinner.' Tilda was trying hard to take control of the situation; it was evident from her efficient tone of voice. 'You really aren't very late, and I have a helper in the kitchen who assures me that everything is absolutely fine. Now let me—'

'Do you mean that sour-faced little thing that opened the door?' cut in Shiny Clive. 'I doubt very much the poor creature has a clue about anything whatsoever.'

'I assure you that Pauline is perfectly competent – if a little abrupt.' Alex was sounding fairly abrupt himself and his neck was red. 'Now let me introduce you to the Thackstons. Clive and Heidi Stilbourne – Brian and Christina Thackston. Oh, and this is my sister-in-law, Clarrie.'

Hands were shaken and pleasantries muttered. Alex was pouring drinks again and the danger seemed to be over for the time being. The men stood near the drinks cabinet talking amongst themselves except for the Clay, still next to his wife and half listening to the conversation the women were having. Tilda was poised in the doorway, torn between her desire to make sure things were running smoothly in the kitchen and the need to keep an eye on her guests.

Clarrie felt free to wander in her own thoughts and leave them all to fend for themselves in the rocky valley of attempted conversations. She stared at the holes in the hammock-dress and began to taste sea-salt in the air and hear gulls calling out. She was sitting on a stone bollard looking at lobster pots and fishermen on old chugging boats in a busy harbour. She was only eight years old and she had a pen and a notebook – she was writing a story about the sea and the people who sailed on it, a story of pirates and treasure rather than fishermen with scowling faces and whisky breath, a story about a cabin boy lying in a hammock dreaming about being a pirate captain with his own ship and a box of gold. Her teacher would ask her to read the finished story out in class and Clarrie would stand in front of thirty resentful faces reading aloud in a halting expressionless voice, the words pelting forth like machine-gun fire. It was her special reading voice, carefully cultivated to sound like the other children in the class. When alone, she could read aloud in the voice she used for speaking, but it didn't do to be too different from everybody else.

'Haven't I met you before somewhere?' the Bone asked Hammock Heidi. 'You look incredibly familiar.'

'No, I don't think so.' Hammock Heidi was perched on the end of the couch next to the Bone, and seemed to be trying to move as far away from her as the seat would allow.

'Are you sure?' The Bone was screwing up her eyes and peering in a way which Hammock Heidi appeared to find extremely disconcerting. 'I have a very good memory for faces.'

'So do I.' Hammock Heidi's voice was more defensive than the occasion warranted, 'and I definitely haven't met you before.'

'It'll come back to me.' The Bone nodded and folded her arms. 'I'm sure it'll come back to me, and when it does I'll let you know.'

'Lots of people think they know Heidi.' Cruella was the rescuer. She leant forward and her sharp nose turned into a sword. 'She's rather famous. You may have seen her on the television, isn't that right, Heids?'

Hammock Heidi was blushing in a manner that would once have been called coquettish. Her whole demeanour was somehow of another era – when 'ladies' were 'ladies' and many things were considered vulgar that have since become the norm. 'Well, I *have* made a few appearances on telly, but I hardly think I would call myself famous. I mean, I'm not exactly known to the public at large. If you stopped people on the street and asked them if they'd heard of me, I'm sure you'd get nothing but blank looks.'

'I imagine it would depend where the street was.' Alex was spiky, almost venomous as he broke away from whatever Kitchener was saying to him. He turned to the Bone. 'You see, our Heidi is a world-class designer. "Heidi Stilbourne" might not ring any bells for you but try "Sasky Klimt". That's the label. That's what the exclusive boutiques are called, the name that rolls so easily off thousands of refined tongues the whole world over—'

'Oh, Alex, don't exaggerate. I doubt that anybody knows who I am outside of England.'

'I find it all enormously exciting.' Tilda was at her most animated when considering 'chic'. She was still lingering in the doorway, unable to drag herself away from the conversation. 'A friend of *mine* a rising star of the design world.'

Shiny Clive walked across from the drinks cabinet to perch protectively on the arm of the couch, bending over to give his wife's right leg an affectionate slap which made a dull thwacking noise and caused her flesh to wobble. 'I must say I'm pretty proud of the old girl, who wouldn't be in my position? This is one of hers, you know, this dress, brand new this season, goes for absolutely thousands in the shops. How much is it retailing for, darling, three thousand or four?' He reached around behind her to draw her towards him but she slid out from his grasp like a buxom eel, rearranging her dress to hang properly as she found her feet.

'Excuse me, sorry. I have to use the bathroom.'

'Poor love, she's so modest,' said Shiny Clive, sliding into what had been her seat as the door closed. 'Can't stand being the centre of attention. Practically unique in her line of work. Her full "seaside collection" comes out in April so I hope you'll all come to the launch. All stuff like the dress. All made of rope.'

'I've definitely seen her somewhere before, though,' said the Bone. 'It'll come back to me.'

Clarrie was muttering to herself, still half lost in her tale of adventure. The Clay, sitting nearer to her than anybody else, could just about hear her whispering voice in his right ear.

'Sing me an old sea shanty, like you did on those stormy nights as we rolled on the wide wild ocean . . .'

Hors-d'Oeuvres

Tilda stirred the soup and took a quick taste from the ladle – it was surprisingly good. She reached behind the blue teapot on the shelf for her packet of Silk Cut. A cigarette was necessary at this point if she was to survive the evening. Alex need never know – he was busy in the lounge supervising the Thackstons, the Marshalls, the Stilbournes and Clarrie. Alex was under the impression that she had given up smoking last year and she wanted him to remain under that impression. It was a crucial part of their preparations for starting a family; one of the many things which must be ready so that when Alex gave the word they would fuck furiously with no protection and a little Stone would spring forth with its body intact and free from toxins – at least until it hit the outside air. Everything else was ready; they had decided which room would make the best nursery, although they hadn't gone so far as decorating it for a child (that might be tempting fate and few things could be so sad as a room full of toys without a child to play with them). They had made inquiries about kindergartens, schools and even the healthiest ways of giving birth. Nobody could accuse them of not thinking things through properly.

Only one ingredient was missing before they could begin 'cooking' – the deal with Brian Thackston. That dull grey blob of a man could ultimately enable her to have a baby.

She found some matches in a drawer and lit the cigarette, taking a deep fulfilling drag. She enjoyed smoking so much more now that it had become an illicit activity; it satisfied her need to be naughty.

Pauline had been in the dining-room putting knives and forks out on the table, but now Tilda could hear her in the passage on her way back. She had no wish to share these precious few minutes with the waitress so she opened the back door and slipped out into the garden before Pauline could actually enter the kitchen.

It was cold outside. Spring was on the way but hadn't actually arrived yet. Tilda felt goose pimples appearing on her bare arms and enjoyed the sensation. Her shivers were close to sensual – coupled with the forbidden pleasure of smoking they made her feel sexy. The lawn was soft beneath her feet. She only wished she could be sure she wasn't stepping in something unpleasant. She sat down on the old garden bench and looked back at the lights of the house, imagining the strained conversation in the lounge. She would go back just as soon as she had finished her cigarette – she wouldn't be away long enough for anyone really to miss her.

With one hand she cradled her empty womb, while with the other she brought the cigarette to her lips. There was such a longing inside her, such a gaping hole. If she were religious she would say a little prayer, asking that the evening go well, that Brian Thackston would leave saying, 'Nice people, those Stones. That Alex – now there's a man I could rely on, a man with vision and imagination, a man with a wife who knows how to cook.' Of course she would inevitably have to befriend the dreary Christina, but that was a small price to pay.

It was all so absurd – this dinner party and all the other dinner parties they had given and would continue to give, the endless pandering to uninteresting people, Alex's constant fretting about his career. It was a party game that she wished she could abandon. The very fact that Alex found it necessary to pretend they couldn't afford to have a baby was ludicrous – it wasn't as though they didn't have money. The problem lay, of course, in his masculine pride. The money was *her* money, not his. It was money that had never been earned but was simply passed on from one lazy generation to the next. It prevented him from seeing himself as a real man.

She had to play along with it, there was no option. It was implicit in the rules that she was not to question the validity of his stance nor even to speak about it. It was necessary to conceal her conviction that a real man wouldn't allow his masculinity to be undermined by his wife's bank balance.

His frequent impotence had begun very soon after they moved into the house, and inevitably he refused to seek help from doctors or therapists. She was sure he knew why his 'thing' wasn't working properly but his attitude made discussion impossible. If pushed he would speak briefly of stress at work, saying he was sure things would get better soon, avoiding looking her straight in the eye and leaving the room as quickly as possible. She started going to bed earlier than him and pretending she was asleep when he came upstairs to save them both from humiliation. If Brian Thackston said yes to Alex, Tilda was sure she would have a sex-life even more rampant than when they first met. If Brian Thackston said no her virtual celibacy would continue and the baby would remain a dream.

Her left hand moved up to the thyroid scar and rested there – funny, she wore that scar for all to see but the biggest scar was somewhere inside where nobody would ever know about it – nobody but herself and Judy Marshall, that is, and anybody else that Judy might have told. Would Judy have told Heidi Stilbourne? No, Judy could be trusted. Tilda had known Judy for longer than Heidi and had always thought of her as the more reliable of the two. Their relationship was intimate from the outset as a result of Judy's way of dispensing with flannel and getting straight to the nitty gritty of an issue whereas Heidi tended to shy away from confidences.

'Have an affair, Tilda,' had been Judy's advice. 'And when you've finished with that, arrange another. Have two or three at once if you like, but just be careful about it, don't slip up.'

Tilda was amazed at what she was hearing. 'So have *you* . . .'

'Me?' Judy laughed in a way that suggested Tilda had said something very stupid. 'Good God, darling, you don't honestly think I would have survived the last ten years without a few light diversions, do you?' She lowered her voice and became conspiratorial. 'You've surely discovered for yourself, Tilda, that whatever it is that first attracts you to someone becomes the most hideous thing in the world as time goes by. Take Roger's moustache, for instance – there's a case in point. Please stop me if this embarrasses you, but we're women of the world, after all.

'When I first met Roger there was nothing I enjoyed more than having him go down on me. I loved the sensation of the moustache, you see. It was tickly and a little bit rough – not *too* rough. But now I loathe it more than you can possibly imagine. Night after night, year after year of this horrible scratchy *thing* nuzzling up to me. When Roger is down there doing the business, the moustache makes it impossible to forget that it's *him* – and now I'd like very much to pretend it was somebody else. So I find others – younger men with delicate hairless lips. And I'm careful.'

'But what about Roger?'

'I assume he has lovers too.'

Tilda shivered again and concentrated on the orange end of her cigarette, glowing in the dark. She looked at the hand holding the cigarette and imagined another hand closing around it, holding it firmly, a large male hand with a scar at the base of the thumb and a silver bangle on the wrist. She tried to banish the thought, hearing Judy's bubbling laugh carried out on the breeze, along with the more abrasive sound of Christina Thackston's voice. She should go back, but she wasn't ready yet – the hand was still there. There was another hand, too, and it was resting on her knee, sliding up her inside leg, under her dress. She closed her eyes.

The man had become a part of her daily routine. When Alex left for work each morning, she would go to the door and allow herself to be kissed lightly on the lips or the cheek. She would stand waving while Alex headed off across the road and got into the car. She would continue standing there as he drove away, until the car disappeared around the corner. That was the moment when she would permit herself one lingering look at the man standing at the bus stop across the road. He would glance up, catching her eye; not in a hostile manner, but with no discernible expression of any kind – as though to say, 'I know you're watching me, and it doesn't signify.' She would feel the embarrassment starting in the pit of her stomach and rising up her gullet – she would retreat into the house and eat breakfast alone in the kitchen.

That was how it happened every weekday. Sometimes there would be other people at the bus stop as well, but usually the man was alone. She didn't think about him very much, but when she went to the door with Alex every morning, she knew she was looking out for him and she knew it would bother her if he wasn't there.

It was only on the day of her conversation with Judy about marriage and affairs and Roger's moustache that she came to realise how much the stranger meant to her.

'I couldn't possibly have an affair,' she was insisting. 'Alex is the only man I want.'

'Oh, come on, Tilda.' Judy raised her arched eyebrows in her most disdainful and disbelieving manner.

Then Tilda thought of the man. She thought about his dark eyes and wide mouth. She thought about his curly black hair, the stubble on his chin, the gold sleeper in his left ear, the denim jacket which she disliked but which was somehow an essential part of him.

'Actually there is somebody I'd like to have sex with. A man who stands at the bus stop across the road in the mornings. Well, he's barely more than a boy. I think he might be a student or something. He's certainly far too young to want to sleep with someone of my age – he probably thinks I'm an old hag.'

The eyebrows were still raised. 'Don't be so sure. Most men are susceptible to a little persuasion.'

'No, I couldn't. I wouldn't know what to say. I don't even want to, not really.'

'Excuse me, do you have the time on you?' Tilda called out as Alex's brake lights showed red at the corner.

The man looked around to be sure she was talking to him. He was alone at the stop. Alex's car lurched into the traffic on the main road.

'Sorry, no.' His voice was nice – deep. He held up his wrists to show her that he wasn't wearing a watch. His wrists were nice too. He smiled, but only for a second, before unfolding the newspaper that was under his arm and immersing himself in it.

Tilda was relieved to see it was the *Guardian*. She wouldn't like to think of him as a tabloid reader. 'Beautiful day, isn't it,' she shouted.

'Yes.' He didn't even look up from the paper.

She was looking at his black hair. Was there a lot of hair on his body? She didn't know if she wanted him to be hairy. Well, perhaps hairy would be nice, provided he didn't have hairy shoulders. His body was gaunt. She dared to look at his crotch, and felt heat in her face. She liked the easy slouch of his body, the way he was leaning against the bus stop. He was so different from Alex – this man had a *body* where Alex merely had equipment.

Her feet were walking down the steps and onto the path. There was nothing she could do to stop them. She was in the road, squeezing between the parked cars, stepping over the puddle that never went away. He could hear her coming – was looking up, puzzled. She was stepping onto his pavement, standing next to him at the bus stop. He was shorter than he looked from the other side of the road. He was staring at her as though she were mad.

'What time's the bus due?' she asked.

'I don't know. Soon. I don't wear a watch.' He was trying to give his attention to the paper but her presence was clearly bothering him. 'Are you catching the bus?' There was suspicion in his voice. She obviously wasn't allowed to speak to him, to get on his bus; it wasn't a part of the routine. She was only supposed to give him a lingering look and then go back into her house.

'Yes, I am.'

'You've left your front door open.'

'Oh. So I have.' It was a problematic moment. There was no way of explaining it, but she still had to try. 'Actually I'm not going to catch *this* bus. I just thought you might know what time the buses come by.'

He looked at her feet, his gaze moving slowly up to her face. Their eyes were at the same level – they were nearly the same height. If anything she was slightly taller. His eyes were almost mean, so dark it was hard to make out the pupils.

'I thought I'd catch a bus later,' she added.

'The timetable's there.' He indicated a glass-fronted sheet of paper inside the bus shelter, before returning to his paper.

'Thanks.' But she didn't move to look at the timetable. She carried on looking at him, at his neck, at his throat just inside his open shirt-collar. She wanted to lick his throat – in just that place – inside the collar.

He tensed visibly, knowing she was still standing there though doing his best to ignore her.

'Are you a student?' She didn't know why she asked that particular question, but she couldn't think of anything else to ask, and she had to say something to break the tension.

'The bus is late,' he said without looking up. She could see that he was reading an article on the number of hours of television watched by the average British child.

'How old are you?' This question was even worse than the last. Perhaps the article he was reading was the one on the other side of the page – the one investigating the national divorce rate.

'OK.' He spoke without looking up. 'But not in your bedroom.'

Tilda noticed his hands – large without being fat. There was a scar at the base of his right thumb, and he was wearing a silver bangle. At first she didn't register what he was saying. It made no sense.

'What did you say?'

'I don't have much time and I don't want to do it in the bed where you sleep with your husband.'

She was still focusing on his hands because at this moment it was impossible to look at his face. He wore a gold ring on the third finger of his left hand similar to the one she was wearing, but probably less expensive.

They did it in the kitchen. She was overtaken by coyness as they entered the house, and thought about making some tea so they could chat. She filled the kettle with water, but while they waited in awkward silence for it to boil, he started unbuckling his belt and pulling down his trousers and pants.

They did it standing up. She leant forward against the wall and he fucked her from behind. At first she kept her eyes open, but the weekly shopping list was hanging up in front of her face, and she found she was reading it frantically: grease-proof paper, two boneless chicken breasts, fresh basil, eggs, butter, green apples, mushrooms ... It was very distracting so she shut her eyes tightly.

Seven distinct thoughts passed through her mind while he fucked her, and then repeated themselves in the same sequence.

1. I don't know his name – how sexy.
2. Alex has never fucked me standing up.
3. If only it was dark so he couldn't see my cellulite.
4. I didn't get a look at his prick before he stuck it in me.
5. Perhaps Alex *can't* fuck standing up.
6. I wonder if I will be able to come.
7. I wish he'd kissed me first.

He put his hands down in front to stimulate her clitoris and she stopped thinking altogether.

Tilda threw her cigarette butt into the flower-bed where next-door's cat frequently came to poo. She could still see and feel David's hands. His hands were what she remembered best – perhaps because on that day last year when they fucked in the kitchen she eventually opened her eyes to look down at the hands as they worked their magic on her. Maybe that was the best part of it: watching her own body being stimulated. Of course, his name wasn't really David – or it might be, but was just as likely Keith, Wayne or Clifford. Afterwards she had named him in her head, and it was better than knowing what he was really called. This way she was acknowledging that what she yearned for was the person she had created, not the person she had once had sex with in her kitchen.

And it *was* only once. When he had finished, he left. They didn't even have a proper conversation. At the time that was how she wanted it, but afterwards the yearning was bigger than ever. The next day, she went to the door to see Alex off to work with a pounding in her chest, but he wasn't there. She waited on the door-step for some time, and then sat in the living-room to watch for him through the window, but he didn't come. He didn't come the day after either, or the day after that. In fact, he never came back. He must have found a different way of getting to work.

And then, of course, Tilda found she was pregnant. It didn't surprise her. She had taken risks with Alex on a number of occasions, knowing that she would have quite liked a little accident, but on the day she screwed David the question of contraception hadn't once entered her head. She turned to Judy through a haze of nausea and neediness, and spilled out her problems.

'Do you want it?' Judy asked.

'More than anything.'

'So what's your problem?'

'Alex has been impotent for about four months.'

'Can you tell him about the man?'

'Good Lord, no.'

'Then you can't have it.'

Tilda felt herself freeze. Her body was locked in a kind of paralysis, and for several minutes she couldn't move and was unable to do anything but listen to Judy and nod occasionally.

'You have money, don't you? Well, there's no problem then. I'll arrange it for you. Don't worry, you'll be fine. In a couple of weeks' time it'll all be over and everything will be the same as before.'

Judy said something else too – a phrase that remained in Tilda's head. She thought she could remember a glint in Judy's eyes; a fleck of blood on her teeth – or perhaps it was only lipstick.

'If it happened to me I'd do just the same – I'd have it sucked out.'

Pauline appeared to be in a state of heightened tension. Her face was a vibrant purple and she was puffing and blowing like a horse for no apparent reason.

'Where've you been, Mrs Stone? I've had Mr Stone in here asking for you. He wants to start. It's all ready, you know. More than ready.'

'I'm sorry,' said Tilda. 'I didn't mean to leave you on your own. We *will* be giving you some extra cash, don't worry about that. Now, give me a hand with the halloumi, if you don't mind.'

The ingredients were spread out all over the table: a plate full of grilled halloumi cheese, a bowl of watercress and rocket, a dish of shelled walnut halves, a dish of pesto (prepared earlier) and an array of brightly coloured bottles – walnut oil, sunflower oil and balsamic vinegar.

The panic left Tilda at the sight of these assembled components. There were many things for which she could be criticised, but she could certainly create a good starter. It always felt something like witchcraft – delving among leaves, blending oils and vinegar for the dressing. Perhaps she should cast a special spell for the success of the evening. Maybe she should add a mystery ingredient to ensure the return of her husband's potency. While Pauline placed small chunks of halloumi in the centre of the plates and spooned on sizeable dollops of pesto, Tilda breathed into her salad dressing, trying to transmit her mental picture of Brian Thackston smiling at Alex, whispering in his ear and patting him on the shoulder, and Alex's penis growing erect so that his smart trousers bulged at the crotch and he looked ridiculous in a manly kind of way.

Tilda tossed the rocket and watercress in the dressing, and took bunches of leaves to spread out around the halloumi and pesto, forming green circles on the plates. She was just placing walnut halves here and there in the arrangement when Alex appeared, his penis far from erect and his hair in some disarray.

'Tilda, where the hell did you get to? I started thinking you must have thrown down your apron and buggered off.'

'Calm down, Alex.' Tilda was refreshed, unruffled. She placed a hand against his bristly face. 'Did you remember to shave earlier on?'

'Of course I did.' He looked like a petulant schoolboy in his irritation. She secretly liked that expression.

'Can you give me some idea of how long it's going to be? I mean, are we going to get through the entire contents of my drinks cabinet before we sit down?'

Tilda ignored him and turned to Pauline. 'Perhaps you could start taking the plates through. Are the soup bowls already out?'

'Yes.' Pauline seemed relieved that she was finally going to start the job she was paid for. She picked up a tray, piled several of the plates on it and adopted a poise which until this point had been absent as she left the room.

Alex looked bothered. 'Are you all right, Tilly?'

'Just fine, darling. Your hair is everywhere, though. Come here a second.'

She moved so that her body was close up to his as she smoothed the fluffy tangles. Sometimes he was like a baby. She couldn't resist the impulse to reach her hand down to his crotch to cradle him, wanting to feel him grow hard, but he pulled away, embarrassed.

'Tilda, what on earth's got into you? Stop that.'

'I want you.' She hadn't quite intended to say that. 'I haven't wanted you like this for ages.'

'D'you want the soup taking through now?'

Pauline was back. Tilda wanted to grab her nose and twist it, or poke the sharp fruit-knife into the hairy pimple on her left cheek.

'Just wait a couple of minutes until we've seated the guests and then bring it in,' she said.

Alex had taken advantage of the opportunity to leave the room.

Clarrie walked through the doorway into an array of red and gold. The walls were scarlet with a gold picture rail. The curtains were golden velvet and a portrait hung over the black marble mantelpiece of a smartly dressed grey-haired couple. The man stood behind the seated woman, his hands on her shoulders. Clarrie thought she saw him wink at her, but his expression was so stern that afterwards she knew she must have imagined it. Her attention switched to the huge round table, covered in a white table-cloth. She fought to resist her impulse to sweep aside the tall candles, silver cutlery, crystal glasses, plates and condiments to spread herself out on the table facing downwards with her arms and legs stretched to their full span. If only she could go with the urge, feel the hamstrings in her inner thighs pull taut, arch her back and start the round table-top spinning. She could spin and spin and her dress would fall away so that she would become a mighty whirlwind, sucking all of the guests into the great vacuum at her centre and dumping them in the Land of Oz.

She shook the fantasy away. She had rushed into the dining-room ahead of the other guests, and now they were oozing in behind her. She swiftly moved to a chair, positioned so that she could look up at the entertaining double-portrait while she was eating, and was gratified to see the Clay blobbing across to the seat next to her. She quite liked the Clay.

Tilda had always favoured round tables as being more conducive to a lively group atmosphere than the conventionally shaped dinner table, and several years ago Alex had bought a round oak table worthy of King Arthur. Even so, Tilda had intended to place her guests in specific seats to avoid difficulties. She had even drawn up a seating plan earlier in the day. She had mentally revised the plan on Clarrie's arrival so that Clarrie would be placed squarely between herself and Judy where she could be supervised.

In the event, Tilda didn't get a chance to put her plan into action. Before she could stop them, the guests surged past and began seating themselves in a haphazard manner. To her horror, she saw that Clarrie had positioned herself between Brian and Christina Thackston, with Brian sitting at quite some distance from Alex, and leaving Tilda herself totally unable to exert any kind of control over Clarrie. It didn't bode well.

'Who's for soup?' asked Tilda, as Pauline entered the room, bearing a steaming vat. 'It's Vichyssoise.'

'Tilda's a marvellous cook.' Clive Stilbourne smiled his gleaming smile across the table as he sank into a seat between Alex and Tilda. 'I'd never turn down one of her invitations.'

'Oh, Clive, it's nothing special. I'd be lost without my recipe book.' Tilda tried to force an expression of coyness, beginning to realise why Alex found Clive so insufferable.

Alex was circling the table like an agitated fly, a bottle of red wine in one hand and a bottle of white in the other, reaching through gaps and muttering as he filled glasses.

'What is this?' said Christina Thackston through the scrapings of chairs and polite murmurings.

'Vichyssoise,' repeated Tilda.

'No. This.' Christina jabbed at the halloumi with a fork.

Tilda tried to force a patient smile. 'Grilled halloumi with pesto, a rocket and watercress salad and walnuts.'

'Sounds wonderful,' said Heidi Stilbourne, adjusting the straps of her rope dress, and reaching for a piece of bread.

'I'm allergic to nuts,' said Christina.

'That's right, she is.' Brian spoke with a full mouth. In a matter of seconds, he had shovelled down half his halloumi and was eyeing the soup hungrily.

'Oh, really? What happens to you?' There was devilry in Judy's eyes.

'I'd rather not say. Just the thought of it could quite take away my appetite.' Christina reached for her wine as a restorative measure.

Tilda narrowed her eyes. She was going to have to befriend this abominable creature! What a dire thought. 'Perhaps you could pick the walnuts out and eat the rest,' she ventured, gently.

Christina was peering at her plate, sniffing at it in a way that Tilda found quite rude. If Clarrie sniffed her food in that way, she would receive a sharp kick under the table.

'Is there a dressing on this salad?' Christina turned her searching gaze back to Tilda.

'Naturally.'

'And does it have nut oil in it?'

'Ah, sorry. I didn't think.' Tilda indicated to Pauline to remove the offending plate. 'Perhaps you could try some soup, Christina. I can assure you that nothing even vaguely nutty has gone anywhere near it.'

They're like children, all of them, thought Tilda as she watched Pauline ladling soup into bowls. They're all clamouring for food, fretting that there might not be enough to go round. They're like pigs at the trough.

She glanced over at Clarrie. Strangely, her sister-in-law was behaving in a more courteous manner than any of the others at this moment, since she seemed wholly uninterested in the food. She was nibbling at a piece of halloumi whilst staring fixedly into her wine glass.

'Do you work at all?' Brian asked Clarrie, as the table settled into gentle slurping.

Clarrie paid no attention.

'Clarrie!' hissed Tilda. 'Brian is asking you a question.'

'Oh, sorry.' Clarrie looked up, smiling brightly. 'What was that?' Tilda felt herself tensing. If only she wasn't sitting *there*.

'I was wondering whether you work?' he repeated.

Clarrie seemed confused. 'No, not really.'

'Tell him about the art, Clarrie,' said Alex from his seat on the opposite side of the table. 'She paints,' he added.

Alex, what are you doing? thought Tilda.

'Oh, really?' Brian appeared to be in awe of artistic activity. Tilda reflected that he was probably the kind of man who knew nothing about art and would pay somebody to buy paintings for him, stipulating only that they be large and expensive. His house would be full of Lowry copies and dreadful landscapes in heavy gilt frames.

'What kind of things do you paint?' asked Brian, his question reinforcing Tilda's opinion.

Clarrie transferred her attention back to her glass of wine. 'Red things,' she said.

'Red things?' repeated Brian.

Tilda's fork froze half-way between the plate and her mouth, and a piece of watercress dropped onto her lap. She hoped that Brian's level of ignorance would mean he would ask no further.

'Red things?' Judy's voice was pensive. Tilda felt like throttling her. She should know better than to continue with this topic. 'What are these red paintings like then, Clarrie? For example, when I think of red paintings, I think of Rothko. Are you something of a Rothko devotee?'

'Who?' said Clarrie.

Clarrie *must* cease to be the focus of attention as soon as possible, thought Tilda. A glance at Alex told her that he was thinking the same thing.

Alex cleared his throat. 'Clarrie studied art in Newcastle,' he explained. 'That's how she met my brother, Morris. He runs a small gallery now. Occasionally he exhibits one or two of Clarrie's paintings, but mainly she paints for her own pleasure.'

'Oh, really. So your husband is a dealer of sorts?'

Why was Brian so persistent in directing his questions and remarks to Clarrie?

Clarrie's expression suggested that Alex had described a life which had nothing at all to do with hers. 'No.' Her reply was slow and hesitant. 'He doesn't do anything.'

Fortunately Brian was too absorbed in his own situation to want to find out much more about Clarrie's. 'Christina and I were thinking about having somebody come in to paint us,' he said. Somehow he'd succeeded in devouring all of his soup and salad while speaking and was looking around for Pauline to see if there was any more to be had. 'I've been admiring the picture up there. Who are the people?'

Tilda had been wondering, not for the first time that evening, whether Clarrie was in fact in the throes of some kind of breakdown. She tried not to let her relief at the change of subject show through too much.

'They're my parents. They had the portrait done about fifteen years ago. Lovely, isn't it.'

'It doesn't exactly aid the digestion to have one's in-laws staring down like that, day after day and year after year. Still, better to have them hanging here than in the bedroom, eh?'

Alex was joking, but nobody laughed. He scanned the sur-rounding faces, waiting to be rescued, but nobody was interested. He blushed and played with his soup spoon.

Tilda felt wounded. Why was he being so cruel? Why did he always have to make digs at her in front of people? And this one was so embarrassing. He blamed her for everything, and he blamed her parents. Poor Mum and Dad – what harm had they ever done him?

Clarrie looked down at her soup. It was so *yellow*. She didn't think she could cope with eating something so yellow. Red, now that was no problem for her, but yellow was another matter entirely. She was dimly aware that the Clay was talking a lot. At first he had been talking to her, but now she felt the pressure lift and she was alone with her food. She quite liked the halloumi and salad – it was very pretty on the plate and it seemed a shame to disrupt it just for the sake of eating, but Tilda would be annoyed if she didn't eat anything. She took a mouthful of the cheese. Its texture was rubbery. The rubberiness came as something of a surprise but it wasn't unpleasant. She dropped a piece of the halloumi into the soup by accident and looked up quickly to see if Tilda had noticed. No, Tilda was staring at Alex. She looked vaguely upset, but Clarrie had no idea why. Tilda was quite neurotic, really.

It seemed to Clarrie that the dinner was going well. Everybody was behaving themselves and there were lots of compliments about both the soup and the cheese. Alex was looking irritable – he kept clearing his throat and fiddling with his spoon. Clarrie hoped it was nothing to do with her. She sensed that all was not as it should be between Alex and Tilda, but she'd always thought that was what marriage was all about. Cruella was being suitably flamboyant. Her lower lip was stained with red wine, but somehow that didn't matter. She knew how to grab a person's attention and hold it. Was she trying to flirt with the Clay or was she taunting him? It was almost impossible to tell. Cruella surveyed the other guests as though they were part of the meal, and Clarrie was quite sure she was capable of devouring them all.

Her husband, in comparison, seemed ill at ease, but maybe it was just his general demeanour. The straight-backed Kitchener probably didn't know much about small talk. He would leave all that to his agile wife, preferring to listen until the conversation turned to something he felt confident about – such as the recruitment of young men into the armed forces, for example.

The Stilbournes were another matter entirely. The Hammock had barely uttered a word since she made her rapid exit from the living-room. She appeared to be listening hard to the conversation, but Clarrie instinctively knew that her expression of intense concentration was a mere curtain, hiding whatever was actually going on in her head. Clarrie felt a momentary kinship with the Hammock for she too operated a similar curtain when necessary. The flamboyant partner in that particular pairing appeared to be Shiny. He was slipping in quips that were supposed to be witty, whenever the opportunity arose. Sometimes there would be no suitable opening for him, and then he would interrupt the speaker rather than miss his moment. Nobody seemed especially interested in his comic asides, but he continued with them nevertheless.

The Clay was revelling in the attention being lavished upon him. He wasn't the kind of man who would usually sparkle in a group, but tonight everybody was interested in what he had to say. His face had become very red with his efforts to eat, speak and breathe all at the same time. Occasionally he would laugh so hard that Clarrie thought he would have a heart attack and crash forward into his soup bowl (now filled for the third time). The Bone seemed entirely preoccupied with searching through her food. The halloumi, of course, had been entirely abandoned, and the soup had fallen under suspicion. Every spoonful was scrutinised carefully, and sometimes the Bone would allow its contents to trickle back into the bowl. Clarrie had no idea what she could be looking for. Maybe something was alive in her dish. And, after all, Clarrie had to agree that it was quite amazingly yellow.

Clarrie was swimming in her soup. She'd never swum in anything so yellow before, and it was so thick that it made her arms and legs move in slow motion. The piece of halloumi which had fallen into the bowl was bobbing around, a kind of island. She pushed hard with her arms and legs to try to reach it, but the dense liquid was resisting her and it required twice as much effort to go forward as swimming in water. She coughed and spluttered as her nostrils filled with soup. She was inadvertently drinking the yellow stuff, and actually it wasn't at all bad, although it was quite difficult to breathe with thick soup clogging her air passages. Finally she was able to get one arm over the cheese island and pull herself out of the goo. She sat on the edge of the rubbery lump and looked down at the yellow coating on her skin. The mohair dress was ruined beyond redemption. Had she let them down? Had she spoiled the evening?

From where she now sat, the dinner party appeared like a stadium concert. The sound was all around her, ringing in her ears. If she tilted her head back, she could see up the Clay's huge nostrils and examine all the chunks and hairs lurking there, following the red passages right up to the place where they turned a corner and twisted away. She turned to the portrait. The figures were dark and ominous when seen on this scale. Their faces were mean and knotted, their eyes glinted unpleasantly. Alarmed, she swivelled around on her cheese to look at the comforting visage of Alex.

Alex's face was full of holes. She had never noticed his

problematic skin when full-size, but now she could imagine how it would have looked in his teenage years – a mass of red blobs which had their tops sliced off each day when he shaved. She wondered if he had been sent to a skin specialist who had prescribed lotions and pills, or whether he had just grown out of it, carrying the memories forward into adult life of the days when no girl would kiss him, and the insecurity of having spent a number of years unable to look at his own reflection in the mirror without hating himself. Poor Alex.

Cruella was telling a story about childhood, and her wine-stained lips were something of a spectacle as they shaped and reshaped themselves around her words. Clarrie could see tiny fragments of chapped skin that would usually be hidden beneath a heavy layer of lipstick. There was something in their texture and in the loose flaps of skin which reminded her of the wings of butterflies as they fluttered around the speech. Her voice boomed in Clarrie's tiny ears.

Cruella reached the punchline and laughter broke out all around the table. It was probably only a generalised polite chuckle, but it whipped up a treacherous wave in the soup bowl, and Clarrie clung to the edges of her cheese to avoid being swept away.

'I remember locking myself in the toilet when I was about two or three,' chipped in the Hammock. Clarrie glanced up at the tanned flesh appearing here and there through the hammock-holes. She could see slender hairs fighting their way through the fabric.

'I wasn't supposed to lock the toilet door, but it was all a part of my game. I can't remember what the game was, but I had to lock the door. I'd done it loads of times before but this time I couldn't get the key to turn, and then I started panicking and screaming. I was in there for hours, or at least I think I was. Time moves differently when you're a child, after all. It was very frightening. Almost as frightening as the fog-horn.'

'How did you get out?' Alex asked the question impatiently, as though he wanted to get past the main body of the story and reach its conclusion in one sweep.

'I don't remember how I got out. I only remember the fear.'

*   *   *

Yes, it must have been frightening. Being small, stuck in a very small room. And the screaming must have made it difficult to breathe. A little child would start to hyperventilate, and on the other side of the door its parents would be panicking too, trying to get it to calm down and try the key again, wondering why they had never taken it away altogether. Or perhaps there was nobody outside the room. Perhaps the child was screaming and screaming with nobody out there to hear while the parents laughed and drank tea in another part of the house.

Something big made of dull metal was descending above Clarrie's head. As it came down she could see her face reflected in its convex shape. It was a gigantic spoon, held in the enormous gnarled hand of the Bone. Clarrie could see her wrinkled stringy neck overhead, could hear her chomping teeth. The spoon was moving lower and lower, and Clarrie's distorted reflection was bigger and bigger. Why was the Bone eating Clarrie's soup?

Realisation flashed through Clarrie's mind. She was in the wrong soup bowl. She didn't know how she had got there but she was in the wrong bowl! And she was in danger of being scooped up and eaten any second now.

The cheese flipped over as the spoon plunged into the soup, sending a great yellow tidal wave washing over Clarrie's head and sweeping her into a whirlpool. Her lungs were filling up. Any second now she would either drown in Vichyssoise or be eaten by a Bone, mistaken for a *croûton*. Had it really all come to this?

Clarrie had broken into a fit of coughing, and Brian was bashing her on the back. Tilda couldn't understand what was wrong with her. One minute she was slurping away quietly and insignificantly, and the next she'd begun this peculiar laboured breathing. It was as though she were about to have an asthma attack, although Tilda couldn't remember ever being told that Clarrie was an asthma sufferer. She had tried to ignore the breathing for a while. Clarrie was probably only doing it to get attention. But it had gone on and on and on, so that she couldn't think straight or pay any attention to the story Heidi was telling about being locked in the loo as a toddler. The breathing grew louder and more frenzied. The guests had become silent and distressed and she had been forced to send Pauline for a glass of water, wondering if she could ask Clarrie to go upstairs and lie down. Then the coughing began. Clarrie's face contorted into a wrinkled ball as the wheezing and panting transformed itself into noisy spasms, and blobs of spit flew all over the table. What on earth was the matter with the silly girl?

Brian's bashing was having little effect. He looked as though he wanted to loosen her collar, but since she didn't have one, he was unable to. The guests were semi-standing now. Nobody was exactly doing anything but everybody looked as though they thought they should be, and she saw that Alex was staring at *her* – as though it were solely her responsibility to ensure that his brother's wife remained intact.

'What do you want *me* to do?' she blurted, and he merely gave her a look of contempt.

Judy was now pushing Brian out of the way to get to Clarrie.

'Maybe she has something stuck in her throat,' muttered Heidi Stilbourne.

'Don't be ridiculous, she was eating soup,' said Alex.

Judy was now sitting in the seat beside Clarrie and putting one arm around her while trying to bring a glass of water to her mouth with the other.

'Do you think she's ill? Do you think we should call a doctor?' asked Christina Thackston, but everybody ignored her.

Under her husband's cold stare, Tilda felt compelled to move to Clarrie's side, pushing the Thackston woman out of the way perhaps a little more roughly than was absolutely necessary. Clarrie's spasms were now dying down as she lolled back into the capable arm of Judy Marshall, but she still seemed to be unable to speak.

'I think we should take her upstairs for a while,' said Judy.

Tilda felt relief, not only that Clarrie was to be taken from the room, but that it was Judy who had made the decision. Had she been the one to suggest it, Alex might have interpreted it somewhat differently. As it was, he nodded silently. It had all been a little too much for him, the poor darling.

There had been so many occasions over the years when Tilda was lumbered with Clarrie. God, that hateful gender thing – Alex and Morris going off together to the pub, lounging in front of a football match on the television, or even, in the early days, heading off to a snooker hall – while 'the girls' would be left together to talk about 'women's things'. It wouldn't have been so bad if Clarrie had actually understood *how* to have girl-talk.

'Well, isn't this nice?' Tilda had said on one of those days, her heart sinking to the very ends of her toe nails as the front door thudded shut, leaving her trapped with Clarrie. 'What say we put our feet up with a little gee and tee?' She adopted her most sisterly smile, and wondered if she should actually try to link arms with Clarrie and chum her along to the drinks cabinet, but Clarrie was busy staring into the tank of tropical fish (long since disposed of) and holding her finger up as if she believed she could actually touch the mouth of the enormous fish that was industriously sucking algae off the side of the tank.

'She's quite like you, isn't she,' said Clarrie, turning her oh-so-innocent gaze on Tilda.

Tilda felt as though she had been slapped in the face. 'What?'

'Well, she is, isn't she.' Clarrie returned her attention to the fish tank.

Tilda decided to ignore her, and crossed the room to pour out two gin and tonics. How long would Alex and Morris be? One pint, Alex had said to her stony face. Only one – just a little time for the two brothers to be alone together, was that really too much to ask? Except it wouldn't be just one pint. It would be four or five and Alex would come home red-faced and loud, lurching about and knocking oranments over. Of course Tilda had to agree to stay with Clarrie. How could she not? And almost more dreadful than the idea of being alone with Clarrie was the prospect of Alex making his usual hurt plea: 'But can't you try, Tilly, please? For me? She can't be that bad, *surely*.'

Oh, but she was that bad. Tilda took a slug from her glass.

'Does she have a name?' came Clarrie's vacant voice.

'Who? What are you talking about?'

'The suckerfish, of course. Does she have a name?'

Tilda sighed. 'Oh, Clarrie, do come away from there and have a drink. No, it doesn't have a name. It's just a fish.'

'In that case I'm going to call her Tilda,' said Clarrie. 'After you.'

Tilda could have screamed. 'Why do you do this, Clarrie? Why do you put on this gormless innocent act? You might be able to get away with saying whatever insulting thing you like to Morris and Alex, but it doesn't wash with me.'

Clarrie's face assumed the expression of a spaniel that has just been kicked. 'I'm sorry,' she said. Then, a second later, 'But, Tilda, what did I do?'

'Give me strength,' she muttered, and grabbed Clarrie by the shoulders. 'On this particular occasion, Clarrie, you compared me to a fish – a slimy, grey, fat, ugly fish. That's what you did this time.'

'Oh.' Clarrie looked down at her feet. 'But that's not what I meant.'

Tilda searched the puppy dog eyes for signs of subterfuge, but found none. She let herself be drawn back to the tank, where Clarrie pointed at the foul creature.

'Look how hard she works while all the other fish are just floating around doing nothing,' she said. 'She's keeping everything clean, eating up all the crap so the others can swim around and have fun in water that isn't full of rubbish. That's why I want to call her after you.'

Tilda softened in spite of herself.

Clarrie opened her eyes slowly and was dazzled by a bright light. She closed them, and remained in darkness for a minute or so, trying to work out what was going on. She was lying in a warm bed and she had been asleep, this much was clear. She stretched out her right arm, searching for the familiar warm mass of Morris, but found only an opening in the duvet, leading to cold air.

She turned her face so that she could open her eyes again without looking up into the blinding light, and then gradually eased her lids upward, as though she were a snail emerging from its shell. A small man in a black coat was suspended five feet above the ground. He had no head, but Clarrie didn't think he intended any harm, his presence wasn't threatening. Her pupils adjusted themselves and the man became her black T-shirt, hanging on the wall. She twisted her head round and saw green curtains covered in daisies. So it was true.

She was in the green room at Alex's house. Tilda and Cruella had put her to bed. She remembered hands undressing her, careful to rob her of her comforting layer of mohair before letting her slide between freezing sheets. How long had she been asleep?

She could see through cracks in the curtains that it was night. The dazzling light was only a bedside lamp that had been left on, by which she could make out the details of the darkened room. How long had she been lying here? Had the guests all gone? Was she the only person awake in the house? Maybe she had been asleep so long that night and day had passed and night had arrived again. Well, there could be no way of knowing for sure without getting up and having a look around. She pushed back the duvet and sat up, feeling slightly giddy. Her throat was dry and scratchy – it must have been caused by the coughing. She swung her legs round and put her feet down on the carpet, soothed by its softness. Her sleep hadn't left her feeling refreshed and revitalised – her head was heavy, as though it were made of solid wood; pine perhaps, or oak, like the big table downstairs. She imagined the group of guests gathering around her in a circle, eating their dinner from the top of her head, clattering their knives and forks too loudly so that her ears rang.

She shivered with the cold and looked around for something to put on. She was wearing only her knickers. She couldn't find the mohair dress and couldn't bear to remove her black T-shirt from the picture hook, leaving the gaping space where the Van Gogh print had once hung. Rubbing her arms to stop the goose pimples, she searched the room with her eyes and noticed a white towelling bathrobe hanging from a hook on the door. She reached up for it and slipped it on, instantly warmed.

Clarrie moved to the door, holding the smooth brass knob for longer then was strictly necessary, warming it with her hand, and then letting herself out, grateful that the door didn't creak too loudly. She was surprised to find the third-floor landing light on. Somehow she had expected darkness. Perhaps they had been worried she would go wandering in the night and fall down the stairs. Very thoughtful. She moved past two doors to the top of the stairs, put her hand on the varnished wooden banister, and walked slowly down to the second floor, trying not to make any noise in case she woke Tilda and Alex.

The second floor was in darkness. Clarrie could hear the deep ticking of the grandfather clock, but it was too dark to see what time it was proclaiming. She felt around the walls for a light switch, but couldn't find one. Where was she headed for? She wasn't exactly sure. Perhaps there would be some food in the kitchen, left over from the meal. She was beginning to feel hungry; she hadn't felt any interest in food for a long time now – this hunger was good. But maybe it would be rude to help herself to food without first checking with somebody. It wasn't her house, after all. It wasn't her kitchen, or her food. The food belonged to Tilda. And Alex, of course. If they were still awake, she could ask permission. Which door was their bedroom? Which keyhole should she try to peer through, and where should she listen for the sounds of snoring and contented sleep-breathing?

What was that? Voices? It was Tilda's voice, Clarrie was sure of that. So they *were* still awake, and she *could* ask permission to go delving around in the kitchen. Maybe Tilda would come downstairs and heat something up for her. Maybe Alex would make her a mug of hot milk with a spoonful of honey, just like Morris did when she woke out of nightmares and couldn't get back to sleep. A mug of hot milk would be so good now. She could pretend she was still at home with Morris.

'Have I ever told you how absolutely wonderful you are? Have I?'

Clarrie pinpointed the right door. It was open just a crack and she could see a shaft of light. She felt a twinge of guilt – maybe she was about to eavesdrop on an intimate love scene. Perhaps Tilda and Alex were about to ease the tensions of the evening and find peace in each other's arms. Maybe they were about to—

'Yes, darling. Many, many times. Still, it's always nice to receive a little adulation.'

—but that wasn't Alex's voice. That was a woman. Cruella. Why was she still here – in the bedroom with Tilda?

Clarrie put her face up to the crack of light and peered in. It wasn't the bedroom at all – it was a bathroom with a white marble floor. Everything was white and sparkling, almost as though the interior were made of ice. Cruella was sitting on the edge of the bath, smoking a cigarette, leaning over to tap ash into the sink. Tilda was temporarily out of sight. No, now she was moving into view, stepping forward with a fag in her mouth, bending for Cruella to light it. Tilda straightened and inhaled deeply so that Clarrie half expected sparks to come flying out of the end of it. When she took the cigarette from her mouth, she exhaled audibly, and although she had her back to the door, Clarrie was sure she was smiling.

'We'll have to open the window and put the fan on when we go down,' said Tilda. 'Alex will go mad if he smells it.'

'For heaven's sake, Tilda, it's only a cigarette.'

'It may only be a cigarette to you, Judy, but it's a whole lot more than that to me.'

'God save us from caring husbands!'

Tilda turned around and half perched herself on the edge of the sink. This meant that she was looking straight out of the door and into Clarrie's eyes. Clarrie squirmed silently, but Tilda appeared not to have seen her.

'Do you think she'll be all right?' said Tilda. 'I mean, I know I'm not exactly delighted to have her here, but she seemed pretty rough. Maybe that Thackston woman was right. Maybe we should call a doctor.'

'Just let her sleep. She was as peaceful as a baby when we left her.'

'I worry, though. And then there's Alex to think about.'

'What *about* Alex?'

'I don't know. I just worry, that's all.'

Tilda's hand had gone up to her throat as she said her husband's name. Clarrie had seen her do that a number of times during the evening. Tilda had a neck like a chicken. At the moment it was the neck of a young free-range chicken, but as she grew older, it would come to look more and more like a very scraggy underfed battery hen.

'Stop your worrying. Alex is on top form, and as for poor little Clarrie – well, we've only *just* left her. Let her be.'

Only just? But if they had only just left, then . . .

'Something's very wrong with that girl, Judy. She's . . . well, let's face it, she's *weird*.'

'You've told me that before. Every time she and Morris come down you start going on *endlessly* about how weird she is and how you can't understand what he ever saw in her.'

'Yes, I know, but this time it's *more* than that. It's different.'

'How is it different? *Every time* she and Morris come down—'

'Well, that's a start. Where *is* Morris? She always comes here with him, *never* on her own.'

'And? What else?'

'Judy, you only have to look at her. She's in another world, entirely. I think she might be hallucinating all the time. It's in her eyes . . . It's like she's on drugs or something.'

. . . So they'd *only just* left. She had only been asleep for a matter of minutes – *seconds* even . . . They were still wearing their evening dresses, Cruella's mouth was still stained with wine and Tilda was pink and frazzled. The dinner was still going on, and they hadn't even begun the main course yet. Tilda and Cruella had brought her upstairs and put her to bed and come here to the bathroom to have a furtive cigarette. They had tricked her into thinking she was safe, and now they were talking about her.

People were always talking about her – always closing doors and whispering, thinking she was too deaf to hear or too stupid to understand. Even Morris joined in sometimes – muttering away with Alex and Tilda when he should have been outside listening with her.

'Just how well do you know that girl, Morris?'

'I love her.'

'But what do you really *know* about her?'

'I know enough.'

'Have you met her parents? What are they like?'

'What's your problem? What are you getting at?'

'Maybe something happened to her . . . when she was young. You know.'

'Oh, I know what you're saying. Clarrie's father is not a child abuser. You've been watching too many TV movies.'

'They don't wear badges pinned to their coats, you know.'

'And neither is her mother, come to that.'

'But, Morris, *something* must have happened to her. When she was at an impressionable age.'

'And neither are her teachers or her baby sitters.'

'Do you actually *know* her teachers and her baby sitters?'

'You're pushing it, Tilda. You're pushing it too far.'

'Some sort of trauma, that would probably do it. Something she's suppressing. Has she ever been in a mental hospital?'

'No.'

'Does she suffer from depression? Clinical depression – manic even?'

'No.'

'Judy Marshall knows this great therapist. He works wonders with deep trauma. Perhaps you might think of—'

'*No.*'

Clarrie didn't like it one little bit when Morris was part of the whispering.

'Speaking of drugs, my dear, I might just have a *little something* here to take your mind off your mad sister-in-law and your Victorian husband . . .'

Cruella was reaching inside her dress, into her cleavage. What was she doing? Was she going to pull her breasts out and shove them in Tilda's face?

Tilda wasn't paying attention to Cruella's chest; she was busy putting her cigarette out in the sink and throwing the butt out of the window.

Cruella now produced what looked like a small piece of screwed up paper from between her breasts. Clarrie was relieved that the breasts remained safely inside the dress, but disappointed that Cruella hadn't conjured up something more interesting – a dead fish, for instance – that would make the whole scene appear like a Surrealist painting. Or maybe a dead cat – that would be more macabre – or a dead Dalmatian. That might fit her personality rather well.

Tilda had picked up Cruella's cigarette butt and thrown it out of the window as well, and now she was trying to wash away all traces of ash, scrubbing at the sink with the palm of her hand, and muttering, 'Why don't I keep some decent cloths in here . . .'

'Tilda, my sweet,' cooed Cruella, 'have a look at what your

bestest, bestest friend has brought along for a special, special treat.'

'What?'

She turned around, flustered, peering down at whatever it was that her bestest friend was carefully holding.

'Judy . . . Judy, we can't!'

'Why ever not?'

Clarrie's face was pushed as close as possible to the crack in the door. She knew there must be something more to see, but she just couldn't get the right angle to look down into Cruella's cupped hands. It was the most frustrating situation – like going to the cinema and having a large section of the screen obscured by a tall person sitting in front of you. The section in which a vital part of the action is occurring.

'Judy, I'm *supposed* to be holding a dinner party. I've got to go back downstairs to see that Pauline doesn't make some dreadful unholy mess of serving the second course. I've got to stop Alex from throttling the Stilbournes, I've got to be the perfect wife in front of that boring hideous blob. I've got to chat with *Christina Thackston*, for crying out loud. How the hell am I going to manage all that if I'm *out of my tree*?'

Tilda was all worked up. Her hair was spidering out of the bun again and her hands were darting around – first up to her throat, then back down to twist frantically around each other, then up to the head to make feeble attempts at smoothing the hair. Her eyes had gone boggly and her lips had become so small and tight they had virtually disappeared inside her mouth. She didn't seem to know whether to stand or sit or leave the room altogether. Clarrie wondered if she should run back up the stairs out of sight, but something stopped her. Somehow she knew that Tilda wasn't going to leave the room, not until she had consumed a substantial share of whatever Cruella had in her hands. Cruella seemed to know it too – she was unruffled by the display of frenzy – she was smiling seductively.

'Darling,' she began, and her voice was like golden syrup. 'There's no need for all this panic. I'm not going to make you do anything you don't want to. But look at yourself, Tilda, you're getting into a complete state about nothing. Now I hardly think a nice line of dear old Charlie is going to make matters any worse

– not unless you intend to go back downstairs with powder all around your nostrils. In fact, I think it might make you feel a whole lot better, Sweet-pea. Auntie Judy knows best.'

Cruella had won. Clarrie knew that Cruella knew she had won. Perhaps even Tilda knew – she was already relaxing, perching on the edge of the sink again.

'But we'll have to go straight back down . . . Alex will realise, I'm sure he will.'

'Rubbish. We can stay up here for quite a bit longer. We're looking after your ailing sister-in-law, remember?'

'She's not *my* sister-in-law. She's *Alex's* sister-in-law.'

Tilda looked like a sulking child whose parent won't give in to it.

'*Alex's* sister-in-law, then. What's the difference when all's said and done?'

Tilda was moving out of sulking mode and into meekness mode.

'Well . . .'

'This stuff is very good, you know, Tilda. I had some yesterday with Molly.'

Tilda was crumbling. She was already leaning forward greedily, straining for a better look. And like a teasing lover, Cruella shifted away slightly.

'Perhaps just *one* little snort.' Tilda was a schoolgirl, maybe twelve years old. 'How much have you got there?'

'A gram. Enough for both of us. After all, it is just a dinner party. We can't be leaping around the room like we did in Brighton that time, now can we?'

Tilda appeared to crumple – it was like watching a piece of paper fold in on itself.

'Judy, I'm so unhappy at the moment. If Alex doesn't get this partnership . . . well . . . I just can't bear it. I think about the baby all the time. You know, the one that I – well, and the ones that I *want* to have. It's just that my life feels so horribly empty all the time, and – well, I can't seem to fill it, I can't seem to . . .'

'You don't have a credit card handy, do you, Tilly? Or something else that's small with an edge?'

Clarrie felt a pang of sympathy for Tilda. She had never felt sorry for her before, but at this moment she glimpsed a sad human being inside the brittle pink shell. It was all very distressing and Cruella was apparently oblivious to it, absorbed in her little parcel of powder.

'Ah, that'll do nicely.' She detached a small card which had been blu-tacked to the wall.

The card had some words on it. Clarrie struggled to read what it said but the writing was too tiny from her vantage point. She was pleased when Cruella started to read it out in a singsong voice.

'"If you love something, set it free. If it comes back it's yours, if it doesn't, it never was." Good God, the old hippy adage. Can't think where and when I first read it. How can you sit staring at *that* while you're taking a shit every day!'

'I rather like it,' said Tilda. 'And anyway, Alex was being ironic when he put it up. It was supposed to be funny.'

'Ha bloody ha.'

'Well, it's pretty useful now, isn't it.'

Cruella was busily scraping powder into lines on top of the cistern. She rolled up the card into a narrow tube. 'Shut up, Tilly, it's play-time now.'

They had twisted so Clarrie couldn't see their faces. Cruella bent low over the tube and sniffed long and hard. Tilda bent over her, watching impatiently. Clarrie suddenly felt cold and sad – it was the sadness of the observer, the eavesdropper, the outsider. It was a sadness she experienced frequently. Then Tilda was speaking again, in a wheedling voice.

'Judy . . . I know this is a stupid question, but I can't help asking it – you didn't . . . *tell* anybody . . . about . . . well, about the *thing*, you know – David and the baby and everything . . . I mean, I want it to stay our secret. I don't even want Heidi knowing, or . . . well, *anyone*.'

'You're right,' said Cruella, curtly. 'It *is* a stupid question. Jesus Christ, the bloody door's open. Lock it, will you? We don't want any intruders.'

And then there was darkness.

Main Course

Alex was drumming on the table with his fingernails in the distracted nervous manner of somebody who isn't fully in control of his actions. A muscle in his left cheek was twitching and trembling. He was trying hard not to stare at his watch, but kept inadvertently glancing at the large Rolex adorning the hairy wrist of Roger Marshall. They had been gone over twenty minutes now – how long did it take to get a delirious young woman to lie down on a bed and close her eyes, for God's sake?

He had the strangest feeling that Judy Marshall was up to no good. He didn't trust her – never had done. It was as though she were sneering at him all the time. He knew Tilda considered Judy her best friend, and this made him all the more uneasy. He was sure Judy knew things about him that he'd rather she didn't know. He didn't actually think she would be indiscreet – oh, no, Judy was far too sophisticated to run around telling stories – he just didn't like the idea that she knew of his failings. When Judy was around, he felt emasculated. And at this moment, he couldn't shake off the suspicion that she and Tilda were off in one of the bedrooms – or even his study, God forbid – giggling together and gossiping about him.

He glanced across the table at Roger. Poor old Roger, there was something pathetic about him, always had been. Perhaps the years of being married to Judy had worn him down, taken away his confidence and left him only with that ridiculous moustache. He liked Roger, though. You could rely on him – he was absolutely straight, which was more than could be said for Clive Stilbourne. What must it be like being married to Judy Marshall? Making love with her must be like having sex with a metal clamp.

Roger had little patience for nervousness. Essentially it was a public display of cowardice and panic, and a good sense of internal discipline should prevent its ever becoming visible. During his years in the Navy he had forged nerves of steel for himself. It was his military training that had given him the temperament he needed to survive in the business world. And he had survived until now, hadn't he? No matter what the future might hold, nobody could take those ten years away from him; they were stored safely in the past. And that was what life was all about – the safe accumulation of memories. When your life is held in the past, people can't get their grubby mitts on it.

'I hear Herriot is on the verge of going under,' he said, dredging up the first topic that came to mind. It was as though speaking lightly of somebody else's failure would reinforce his own successes.

'Dear Lord – poor old Percy!' Brian Thackston was suddenly jolted into animation and the blood rushed to the broken veins in his cheeks. He had spent the last twenty minutes in hungry contemplation of the empty plate in front of him, and the only discernible noise from his direction had been the subdued gurgling of his stomach. 'I can't say as I was ever that fond of the old codger, but we go back a long way. Strange, I saw him not three months ago and he *seemed* to be doing very well. It just goes to show – you never can tell, can you?'

No, thought Roger to himself, you certainly can't. And his thoughts flickered briefly around his own financial predicament before he dragged himself back to the here and now and the bumbling slob sitting in front of him. 'I think there's been a bit of confusion,' he said out loud. 'I was talking about *Michael* Herriot. I assume you're referring to Percy Herriot of Herriot, Frick and Palmer?'

'Oh, right, I see.' But Brian had now gone off on his own tangent. 'Actually, Percy isn't with Herriot, Frick and Palmer. He works solo – doesn't believe in partnerships. That's probably why he's doing so well, now I come to think about it.'

'Funny, I thought we were talking about James Herriot, the popular television vet.' Heidi Stilbourne spoke in a voice that was quiet and steely while she sat staring blankly into space.

'I wonder if everything's all right upstairs?' muttered Alex.

'Perhaps I'd better go and check on them.' He stopped drumming on the table for a moment while he visibly weighed up the consequences of leaving his guests alone, and then, having decided to do nothing for the time being, began drumming again in a rhythm that was more syncopated than the previous one.

Clive Stilbourne was dimly aware that Christina Thackston had begun a fresh topic of conversation, one that was her own form of solo venture, not requiring contributions from anyone else at the table. Her ceaseless wittering bounced off the surface of his brain rather than filtering through into his consciousness. His thoughts were concerned with his elegant wife, who was still staring at nothing.

She knows.

The phrase filled his field of vision, rang like a clanging bell in his ears and caused his heart to thud in his throat so that he had to swallow fast. *She knows, she knows, she knows.*

Clive's mouth was parched and his wine glass was empty. He looked anxiously around for Pauline who was hovering near the window, seemingly waiting to be of service but in fact immersed in a world of her own, as became apparent when he tried several times to catch her eye and failed, finally procuring the desired top up only by flicking his glass so that it pinged, jolting her into action.

When had Heidi realised? Just now, sitting at the table? Had the truth finally dawned on her over the hors-d'oeuvres? She must have been suspicious for a long time. After all, she wasn't stupid.

He took a large mouthful of wine from the newly replenished glass and forced himself to look at his wife. She had stopped staring into space and was now focusing her attention on her glass, toying with the stem. Her face had lost the awful hollow expression it had been wearing just seconds ago, but she was still pensive, distant. *She knows.* What was that comment she had just made, the one about James Herriot? So sarcastic, and Heidi was *never* sarcastic. She had been pensive and quiet all evening. And so touchy – she had even left the room earlier on when they were talking about her clothes designing. When had she ever objected to people talking about her designing? She usually relished it, loved every second of the attention. *She knows.* He imagined her knowledge crystallising all through the evening until it formed a hard shiny whole with that comment about the television vet. It wasn't the words themselves – he glimpsed another layer of meaning behind them.

The game is up, Clive. I know everything, you bastard.

What would happen now? What would become of them when they left this place later tonight?

He had never seriously considered giving up the boys for Heidi – they were as necessary to him as food or drink. Nevertheless, his marriage was sacred – no boy must ever be allowed to interfere with his family life. Heidi must be protected from knowledge of his activities and shouldn't be exposed to any kind of risk in the form of disease. He'd thought it through very carefully before getting married. He had never paid for sex in his life but affairs were messy and risky – it would be far better from now on to engage in business transactions – that way everybody knew where they stood.

Rule number one was that he would never bring a boy to the house. This rule was the very foundation of his double life – the boys *had* to be kept entirely separate. He had a regular place in a quiet location, and cash-in-hand guaranteed the absolute discretion of the proprietor with not so much as a raised eyebrow. Clive would go to meet with a boy two or three times a week. He liked to have five or six regulars who understood his requirements, and every few months or so he would tire of one or another and take on a new one. He ran his liaisons smoothly without a single hitch for the first five years of his marriage. He could proudly and truthfully say that he believed he made his wife entirely happy, and how many men could say that without nagging doubts at the back of their minds? Heidi had a beautiful home, a successful career, a healthy bouncing baby and a loyal and attentive husband who would frequently come home early from the office to make love to her. What more could a woman want?

It was when Clive met Saul that everything changed. Saul was a dream boy, a honey, a blond Australian surfer with puppy eyes and the body of a Greek god. Saul was the only boy who had ever made Clive melt inside. First Clive began breaking the *little* rules. After fucking they would lie in bed together for hours, stroking each other and whispering. They would shower together and Saul would wash Clive all over very tenderly. They would leave the hotel together and go walking in the park nearby. Sometimes, if there was nobody around, they would hold hands. One time they stood under a tree in the rain and kissed each other for a long time – Clive had suddenly found he was sobbing like a child and Saul had licked his tears away. Clive didn't see the other boys as frequently as before – it seemed that nobody else could satisfy him. Saul told Clive that he loved him, that he didn't want to be paid any more, but Clive insisted on paying Saul more than ever so that he wouldn't have to share him with anybody else.

It was all rather worrying, and so completely unexpected. Clive had always seen his activities with the boys as impersonal. They did things for him which Heidi could never do, and they were distinguishable from each other only in that one might give an excellent blow-job, another might have lots of appealing orgasms, another might have a nice penis or pert buttocks or be good at talking dirty or being passive or commanding or biting without leaving marks. He had never been in love with a boy before, and found it hard to believe that he could be in love with Saul.

Saul was invading his inner world. He would lie in bed with his wife, thinking about being with Saul. He would get up to see to Max if he was crying in the night, and find himself staying up long after the baby had fallen asleep again so that he could be alone with his thoughts. At the office, he was distracted and couldn't apply himself to his work in the way that he had previously. He began to toy with the possibility of installing Saul in a flat, but the idea also filled him with fear.

Once Saul had been installed in his new flat, he began to realise how powerful he had become. He would phone Clive at work – something which was strictly forbidden – in order to tempt him, drawing him away from the office at times crucial to business. He would tantalise and torture Clive, bringing him to the edge of physical ecstasy and pulling back to make him get on his knees and beg. Clive was gradually being reduced to a nervous wreck, and Saul knew that he could have anything he wanted.

And Saul wanted to be let into the sacred part of Clive's life.

Clive selected the time for Saul's visit to the house very carefully. Heidi had gone off to Paris for five days to meet with buyers. It was mid-winter which meant it would be dark early and Saul could be brought into the house without any of the neighbours seeing. Conveniently, Max was in a phase of falling asleep at around seven o'clock in the evening and sleeping right through till morning.

It was impossible for Clive to enjoy Saul's visit. As he watched him running his hands over the furniture, nosing into cupboards, peeping in at the sleeping Max, he felt as though something was tearing inside him. What would Saul ask for next, a three-in-a-bed with him and Heidi?

They made love in the marital bed – it was what Saul wanted. He made Clive promise not to wash the sheets before Heidi's return, but they both knew he would. Saul wanted the maximum violation, wanted Heidi to smell the presence of another man in her bed. It was all getting a little too much for Clive to cope with.

Thankfully, Saul didn't ask to stay the night. He had had his pound of flesh for now. Clive went downstairs to see him out, fetching his wallet from the pocket of his overcoat.

'Don't,' said Saul, as Clive pushed a wad of notes at him.

'You have to eat, for God's sake.'

'I know, but—'

As the front door opened, everything froze – Clive's extended hand holding the money, Saul's flushed face and stance of refusal – and Heidi, who stood in the doorway with her key and her suitcase.

Clive thought his fixed smile would split his face in two. He realised that he was still holding out the money, and hastily returned it to the wallet. 'Hello, darling. You're back very early. I thought you'd be away until Wednesday.'

'It didn't go very well.' Heidi slammed the door behind her and turned back to face them. 'They didn't like my stuff. I'm tired.'

'Here, let me take that.' Clive reached for the case, but Heidi was reluctant to let it go.

'No, it's OK, don't worry. Who's this?'

Clive tried to formulate an explanation, but nothing would

come. He was too busy reeling at his colliding worlds to be able to speak.

'I'm Adonis,' said Saul with a brilliant smile. 'Nice to meet you, Mrs Stilbourne. I love your hair.'

Clive was horrified. He opened his mouth and gulped at air, trying to locate his old survival instinct which seemed to have vanished.

To Clive's amazement, Heidi giggled. She seemed revitalised. 'Why, thank you,' she said to Saul. 'So, Clive, who is this charming young man with the mythical name?'

'It's not his real name.' Clive's voice was flat, devoid of expression.

Heidi was removing her coat, squeezing past them to hang it up. 'Have you ever done any modelling, Adonis? You'd be absolutely perfect,' she said, easing off her shoes.

'I'm from Sydney, Australia,' said Saul, avoiding eye contact with Clive. 'Adonis is the name I use for entering surfing competitions. I've been in England for six months now and I'm kinda missing the old surf.'

'I bet you are.' Heidi smoothed her hair. 'It's summer there at the moment, isn't it? God knows why you're choosing an English winter over those wonderful golden beaches.'

'Ah, well, it's love that keeps me here, isn't it, Mr Stilbourne.' Saul flashed him a look that was blatantly provocative. Then he seemed to decide to stop the torture. 'I've been boring Mr Stilbourne with my life story, you see. My real name is Saul, and I've been baby-sitting your adorable little boy for the evening. He's been real good. I think he'd sleep through just about anything.'

Relief surged through Clive's body, energising him. How he loved Saul at that moment – and Heidi too. He loved the whole world.

'So what's wrong with Carolyn Wilson?' asked Heidi. 'Why did you need to take on a new baby-sitter?'

Words were coming easily again. 'Well, you see, darling, I went out to play squash with Alex last night and Carolyn came to sit as usual, and . . . well . . . she brought that boyfriend of hers along, you know the one, and . . . look, I don't have any proof or anything, but I'm sure they've been *in our bed*. I haven't had time to change the sheets yet so you can go and take a look if you like. Anyway, I got on to an agency today and they sent Saul along. He comes highly recommended.'

'Gosh, and I always thought Carolyn was such a nice girl. Still, you never can tell, can you? Nice to meet you, Saul. I hope he's paying you well. I'm going up to run a bath now so I'll leave Clive to see you out. I expect I'll see you again soon.'

Does she know? Clive took another mouthful of wine. Even though he had been hit by this same fear thousands of times since Saul had infiltrated his house, its impact hadn't lessened. If anything, the fear had grown. Here he was, sitting around the table of the man who had until recently been his closest friend, terrified yet again that Heidi had discovered his secret – while Saul lounged comfortably in the Stilbourne family home, watching television and diligently listening out for any sounds of distress from baby Max.

Gradually he started to calm down. He reminded himself again of the number of times he had felt this panic. And after all, what had happened this evening that would have told Heidi anything new? Nothing. His trauma had been generated by one uncharacteristically sarcastic comment – no more, no less.

'What is the name of your cat?' asked Christina Thackston.

'What cat?' Alex was perplexed, but then Alex was always perplexed, or so Clive thought.

'*Your* cat.'

Alex stopped his infernal drumming. 'We don't *have* a cat.'

No, of course not, thought Clive. Alex wouldn't keep a cat because cats have bad habits, no sense of decency and no shame. Alex Stone had an incredibly well-developed sense of moral outrage for someone who was essentially a kept man, desperate to crawl to some fat old git and his shrew of a wife for the sake of advancement. What were the exact words Alex had thrown at him that day when they sat in the bar together after playing squash?

My God, Clive, where the hell is your sense of decency? Where is your shame?

Was that the way to talk to a man who had just broken down in front of you? When your best friend starts sobbing into his pint and tells you something he has never told another living person – wrings his anguish out of his miserable fucking soul and spreads it out like a carpet – do you sit there like some smug vicar and tell him he has no sense of decency, no shame, no morals? Alex had refused to hear any more. He had just got up and left.

'But there was a cat under the table earlier. It was rubbing against my legs! It was a little black cat.' Christina was indignant.

'I'm sorry, Christina – I don't know what was rubbing against your legs but we simply don't *have* a cat.' Alex was peering at Roger's Rolex again.

Clive smirked quietly to himself – the Thackston woman must have been rubbing legs with Alex's idiot sister-in-law. He couldn't quite work out how Clarrie had extended her legs so far under the table, but it *must* have been her with her odd mohair outfit. Aloud he said, 'Alex, old chap, we really must fix up a game of squash some time soon. I've been missing our weekly sweat sessions, not to mention our man to man chats.'

'Yes . . . well, the thing is—' Alex began.

'Goodness gracious!' Christina Thackston put a hand to her head to signify shock and pointed towards the open door.

Everybody slowly turned their heads to see what she was looking at, some of them half expecting the elusive black cat to come padding into the room. But it was Clarrie, standing hesitantly in the doorway, wearing a white towelling dressing gown.

Clarrie took time to look around at the circle of faces, trying to gauge the general mood, but each person was somehow in their own unique space. The Bone was staring aghast as though at a ghost, while her husband simply looked hungry. Kitchener's glare was disapproving – his eyes told her that he thought her manner of dress inappropriate. Shiny seemed amused – he smiled with his lips slightly parted so that his gleaming teeth were visible – while the Hammock didn't bother looking up. She was far more interested in her wine glass.

Clarrie avoided Alex's face for as long as possible. She had a feeling that he would not be pleased to see her. But when she looked across at him, she didn't see the anger she was expecting

– merely confusion and dismay. He plainly couldn't understand what was going on.

'Where are Tilda and Judy?' He sounded as though he needed to clear his throat.

Clarrie thought about the bathroom door closing, about Tilda's state of general distress and Cruella reading the poem aloud in a scathing voice: *If you love something, set it free.*

She shrugged.

'Aren't you supposed to be sleeping, dear?' The Bone spoke in a patronising manner. Having been caught off-guard she was determined to re-establish her superiority.

'I've done my sleeping.'

'But, Clarrie, I don't quite understand – where are Tilda and Judy?' Alex wore a perplexed expression very well. It was as though his features were specially constructed to look like that.

'I thought I'd been asleep for a whole night and a day,' said Clarrie.

The Clay chuckled to himself. 'I have to agree with you there. It *does* feel like a good twenty-four hours have passed since we had our starters.'

'I'm terribly sorry, Brian.' Alex was overtaken by embarrassment. Clarrie remained hovering in the doorway, temporarily forgotten, while he called to Pauline to begin serving the main course. 'I'm sure my wife will be back in a moment. I suppose they must have got caught up in girl talk, you know how it is.'

Pauline pushed sulkily past Clarrie, giving her a look of, *Which planet did you spring from anyway?*

'What happened to your dress?'

Clarrie didn't realise at first that Alex was addressing her again – he wasn't looking at her while he spoke. But, after all, everybody else was dressed in the clothes they had been wearing all evening. She was the only one who had changed. She looked down at the dressing gown, thinking that it actually suited her a lot better than the mohair dress.

'What happened to your dress, Clarrie?'

'I couldn't find it when I woke up.'

'Leave her be, Alex.' The Clay was leaning back in his chair, smiling warmly. 'The poor girl's had a hard evening, haven't you, love. We don't have to stand on formality, do we? We're all friends here, after all.'

Alex managed a watery smile. 'Quite so, quite so. Sit down, Clarrie. Don't worry about the dressing gown.'

Clarrie felt wary and vulnerable, as a person might who was walking through an unknown place in the dark, or a small animal edging around a trap. Something in the atmosphere of the room had changed since she was taken upstairs. It was different now, more threatening. Even the Clay with his kind words seemed more sinister than before. As she moved around the table to get to her seat, she kept as close to the wall as she could, wanting to remain out of reach of anybody at the table. They didn't seem to notice what she was doing anyway – they had become immersed in a new conversation. She arrived at her seat and sat down, grateful that nobody was watching her very closely.

Something was still wrong. Clarrie put out her tongue and tasted hatred, but was uncertain from whom it was coming and where it was directed. There was a pungent loathing in the air that lay somewhere behind one or more of the smiles. It made her shiver.

'Hello, darlings.' Cruella was entering the room, followed closely by Tilda. They were clearly in high spirits, and as they resumed their seats it was as though something heavy lifted up and dissolved high above the table. 'I'm sorry we've been such a dreadfully long time. You'll have to forgive me for kidnapping your hostess.'

'Clarrie! Why aren't you upstairs in bed?' Tilda's eyes were bright and her pupils were huge.

'I woke up.'

'Yes, so I can see, you naughty girl.' Tilda wagged a finger playfully at Clarrie and flashed a beaming smile at her husband. 'Why, darling, how sweet of you to wait for us. Let's get back to the dinner, shall we.'

Can I really eat something with a head? Clarrie asked herself, contemplating the large fish laid out on the white plate in front of her as though it were awaiting the attentions of a surgeon or an undertaker.

'Trout – how marvellous.' The Clay rubbed his hands with glee as Pauline placed his dish in front of him.

'It's grilled pink trout in a paprika butter,' said Tilda. 'We have a friend who supplies us with wonderful fish – extremely fresh.'

'She's right, you know,' said Shiny. 'I've eaten trout here before and I'll swear it's the best I've ever tasted. Can't get the name and address of the chap who supplies them, though. Heidi and I haven't been allowed into the exclusive circle of people who've been introduced to the fish-man.'

'What rubbish, Clive. You know very well why I won't give you his number.' Alex turned pointedly away from Shiny. 'You must understand, Brian and Christina, that this man *isn't* a fishmonger, and it isn't a question of exclusive circles – he's just a very generous friend, that's all.'

'Oh, Alex, don't get so het up.' Tilda passed a bowl containing a green mushy substance to the Bone. 'Clive's just having a little joke, aren't you, Clive?'

'Am I?'

'What's this?' The Bone held up a dollop of the green mush on the end of a serving spoon, as though it were some specimen requiring a special examination by experts.

'It's almond and herb purée.' Tilda had a new chemically assisted patience which was obviously helping her to deal with the Bone.

'I can't eat almonds.' The Bone dropped the spoon with disdain and averted her face while passing it on to her husband, as though the very sight of the substance would make her swell up like a balloon. A second later she seemed to realise that her reaction might appear ungracious. 'I don't wish to seem rude, but I'm used to being able to *see* what I'm eating. In my house carrots look like carrots, peas look like peas and potatoes look like potatoes. Now what on earth is this?' Pauline had placed another plate in front of her, on which sat something resembling a baked brown flower with many petals.

'That's a potato and parsnip galette.' Tilda was clearly trying to suppress laughter.

Clarrie was wondering whether dead things feel pain as she fixed her gaze on the glaring yellow eye of her fish. Certainly dead people couldn't express themselves but did it necessarily follow that they were incapable of feeling anything? She thought some more. How easy and convenient it was to make the assumption that a dead person had ceased to *be* a person. That meant they could be burned up or buried underground. They could even have their organs cut out of them to be given to somebody else. But after all, how crowded the world would be if nobody got rid of all those silent stiff people.

She looked down at her fish and muttered, 'Sorry.'

'That's all right, dear,' said the Clay, as he reached across the table to grasp a bowl of green salad that Clarrie really should have passed to him.

'Now that we're all back round the table and fighting fit, I'd like to propose a toast.' Kitchener was brandishing his glass of wine as though he were about to pull a pin out of it and throw it at somebody. 'To our very kind host and hostess.'

'Yes, to Alex and Tilda,' echoed Cruella.

'May God bless them and all who sail in them,' added Shiny in a low voice.

Glasses were raised and clinked. The high-pitched ting of glass on glass caused a sudden sharp pain in Clarrie's head. The ringing of the glass and the accompanying pain went on and on, long after it should have ended. The diners sipped from their glasses, placed them back on the table and picked up knives and forks, but the excruciating sound reverberated on, making Clarrie want to scream. It was clear that nobody else could hear the sound that was threatening to split her skull. And yet she felt that the din was coming from somewhere outside of herself. She twisted around in her seat, bewildered, searching for the source of the hideous noise.

It was Shiny. His face had somehow become transparent, like glass. His features had vanished altogether, and Clarrie was able to see that his head was full of bells; big bells, little bells, church bells, sleigh bells, cow bells and the bells from alarm clocks. There were so many bells crammed into the cavity that they took up every millimetre of space. The visual effect was of a dense metal chaos. The aural result was pandemonium.

The clanging and ringing was becoming louder and louder, and yet nobody but Clarrie seemed able to hear it. As it ascended to a level at which she thought her very ear-drums would burst and her world would fall into silence, she shut her eyes tightly.

The noise ceased. It was as though it had never happened. Clarrie opened her eyes to find that the bells were all gone and Shiny's face was firmly in place again. The aftershave was as strong as ever but the room was quiet once more. She breathed out her relief slowly and tried to expel the incident from her mind and fix her attention back on her dinner.

'I do believe you're a lucky young woman,' boomed the Clay's voice in Clarrie's left ear, jolting her out of her stupor. 'To have Alex and Tilda among your nearest and dearest, I mean. You were ill and they looked after you – were concerned for your well-being, even in the middle of a dinner party.' And his stomach gave out a strange low sound like a moan, as though it were trying to contradict him.

Clarrie tried to smile in response, but her facial muscles became confused and instead she found she was squinting, viewing the room through the dense veil of her eyelashes.

Still squinting, Clarrie observed them all cutting into their pink trout. None of them had any problem dealing with the head. She supposed that if any of them was secretly worried about the staring yellow eyes they would nevertheless preserve an outward calm for fear of showing themselves to be unsophisticated.

They fell quiet, focusing on the food. The air was heavy with the force of their concentration. Small noises of appreciation were being made but the only other sound was the rhythmic clicking of Tilda's jaw as she chewed. Clarrie suspected that half of the concentration in the air came from the private thoughts that were masked by enthusiastic eating, while the other half radiated from Tilda's unsuccessful attempts to will her jaw to be quiet. Clarrie would have liked to tell her not to worry too much about the jaw – the sounds were comforting, like the ticking of a clock. In fact, as she looked around, she could see that they had all begun eating in time with Tilda's jaw, munching and shovelling with mechanical regularity. If Tilda's jawbone were to stop its cracking, time itself might grind to a halt. Concentration was rippling in reverse, moving inward in concentric circles from the diners to collect at the centre of the table with the condiments and candles. Clarrie would have liked to be able to gather it up and save it for later. Her own energy and enthusiasm for the meal were flagging badly.

'Are you feeling better, Clarrie?' The Clay spoke with his mouth full and received a warning glance from his wife. His teeth were covered in the green purée so that he looked as if he were digesting a Martian.

'Yes.'

'Are you prone to these attacks?' asked Kitchener, spearing a substantial chunk of fish and wedging it into his mouth with some difficulty.

'I don't know.'

'I seem to remember Morris talking to me once about your little turns,' Kitchener continued. He looked something like a lopsided hamster, having used his tongue to push the bolus into his left cheek.

'I've been told I'm very excitable,' said Clarrie, attempting a piece of the galette and carefully avoiding her fish.

'I think that's something of an understatement,' put in Tilda.

'Now, now, darling,' muttered Alex.

'How's the gallery going?' asked Kitchener. 'I can't think of Morris as a businessman, but I've heard he has the beginnings of a success on his hands. Christ, it's been *years* since I last saw the old bastard – oops, excuse the language!'

'It gets bigger,' said Clarrie. 'He knocks down walls and it gets bigger.'

'Does Morris still have that dreadful beard?' asked Cruella. 'I don't mean to be rude but it was *awful*.'

Clarrie looked down at her fish, half hoping it would answer the questions for her, but it just lay and stared.

'Do say he's shaved it off,' insisted Cruella. 'If he hasn't, then you must *make* him do it.'

'He shaved it off,' said Clarrie.

'Thank heavens!' Cruella put her hands to her heart in a theatrical gesture.

'And then he shaved off all his hair as well.'

'I'm sure Brian and Christina can't be very interested in my brother's hair-style, never having met him' said Alex, prising the skeleton out of his trout.

'I quite like hearing about people's families,' said the Bone.

'Finding out about family sometimes gives one an added perspective on a person. I remember when I first met Brian, I was just *dying* to meet his parents.'

Alex scraped his knife against his plate loudly. 'Yes, well, some people are totally different from their families, aren't they. And fond as I am of Morris, I don't think we have a single thing in common.' He cleared his throat loudly to end the discussion.

And it was true. Alex and Morris had nothing in common – not any more.

A sudden odd twinge in the big toe of Alex's left foot made him wince, and pushed a memory to the front of his mind.

He was lying on his bed, wearing his Flintstone pyjamas, crying quietly. Morris had hold of Alex's left foot and was peering anxiously at his bleeding toe.

'I think you're going to lose that nail, bro.'

'It hurts,' sobbed Alex, and reached up for his big brother to hug him.

'I know, I know.' Morris held Alex tightly, stroked his hair. 'I'll see if we've got something to bandage it up with. Then you'll be a real wounded soldier. Now come on, no more crying.'

Alex struggled to control his tears, not wanting to be a baby. 'I hate it when they argue,' he said.

'Yeah, so do I.'

'I could hear their voices. Dad was shouting at Mum. But I couldn't hear what they were saying.'

'So you went to listen at the door.' Morris kissed his hot forehead softly.

'Yes. And then they opened the door and . . .'

'I know. It got your toe. Let's have a look for that bandage, shall we?' Morris made to get up.

'No, don't leave me!'

Morris sighed and took hold of his brother's hands. 'Don't worry, Alex. Whatever happens with Mum and Dad, you'll always have me. Understand?'

Alex did lose the toe-nail. And in spite of everything Morris had said, he felt he'd lost his brother. Over the years, Morris had gradually changed into someone else. Ironically, his parents had weathered the storm and slipped into a placid old age together.

'You aren't eating your fish, Clarrie,' said Tilda. 'Is something the matter with it?'

'I don't know,' said Clarrie.

'And *you* aren't eating at *all*, Heidi.' Tilda was glancing at everybody's plates, one by one, like an anxious mother. 'Are you all right?'

'She's fine,' said Shiny quickly, and then more softly, 'Aren't you, darling?'

'Absolutely,' said the Hammock in a voice that shook. 'I just have a few things on my mind, that's all.'

What does she have on her mind? Clarrie wondered. Does she clang and ring and trill like her husband? Each person around the table seemed to be concealing rather than conveying something whenever they spoke. Their faces were like shields being held up to protect what lay behind. Perhaps people always did this and she had just never noticed before. Perhaps communication was really concerned with warding off rather than opening up. Maybe all these people were caught up in a chain of social events that required them to employ elaborate defence tactics, drifting from cocktail party to dinner to business lunch, wanting only to curl up in a corner and be left alone. Again, she thought about the clanging chaos she had discovered in Shiny's head and found she was blushing. It was almost as though she had seen him naked.

'. . . It was *so* funny,' Cruella was saying. 'I'd never been on the Underground on Valentine's Day before. It was rush hour and the train was pretty full, and there was me with my little bunch of tulips that I'd bought in the station because I thought they were pretty. The response I got was incredible! There were some people who were looking at me with envy and bitterness, seething with hatred in fact – obviously thinking, *That lucky cow has somebody who loves her enough to send her flowers when I'm going home to an empty house and a microwave meal.* And then there were others who looked at me as though to say, *She's in love – how sweet.* And it made me want to say to them, 'You've got it wrong, all of you – I bought them myself, you fools!' But do you know what was even funnier – there were five or six women with these absolutely *huge* bouquets and they were looking at me too, and they were obviously thinking, *My flowers are better than hers*. Can you imagine – *my flowers are better than hers*! And they were looking at each other as well. And I could see their minds ticking over, thinking, *Mine are red roses and she's only got spring flowers*. Or, *Mine are silk so they'll last forever while hers will be dead in three days*. Or just, *Look at the poor cow with the tulips!*

'And do you know what the funniest thing of all was – I started playing the game too. I was thinking: *My tulips are beautiful in a simple minimalist way and your flowers are all so gaudy and tacky – I'd much rather have someone tell me they loved me with a nice bunch of tulips*. Yes, I really thought that. And in the end it made me want to shout out to the whole carriage: "Yes, I know my flowers are small and cheap, but who needs flowers on Valentine's Day when your husband's bought you a brand new white GTI and parked it outside the front door, with a pink sash tied around it and a little card under the windscreen wipers that said: *For the only real woman in the world?*"'

'Why do you want to go telling everybody about that?' Kitchener's words to Cruella were almost coy and his embarrassment didn't ring true.

'Why shouldn't I?' she cooed. 'I don't see why I have to be ashamed of having a very romantic and very *rich* husband.'

The Bone emitted a strange little sound that was somewhere between a snigger and a hiccup. Clarrie thought she saw her fingers tighten on her knife and fork, squeezing and gripping until her knuckles showed white.

'Your story was told to amuse,' she forced out, her voice accompanied by a little jet of spit that shot into the air and dropped, to settle in a bubbly blob in the middle of the table. 'But it serves to demonstrate what I have long believed – that Valentine's Day is the most ridiculous, commercial and meaningless day of the year.'

'Perhaps a little harsh, dear,' the Clay half whispered.

'Not so commercial as Mother's Day, surely?' said Shiny.

'And what about Christmas?' added Cruella. 'What could be more meaningless or commercial?'

'You'd better leave that one well alone, Judy,' said the Clay, chortling and dabbing at his mouth with a napkin. 'If you get my wife started on Christmas, there'll be no stopping her . . . she'll be bending your ear for the rest of the night, won't you, dear?'

The Bone smiled weakly and took several large gulps from her wine glass. 'Don't worry, I have no intention of boring you all with my ideas and opinions,' she muttered, and gulped at the glass again.

Clarrie found she was staring at the Bone, gazing so intently that a wave of dizziness and nausea swept over her. She stared and stared as the Bone's features seemed to move and slide, slipping and melting away until all that was left was a space where the face had once been, a space that began to take on a form of its own, slowly evolving into a perfect representation of the corner of a room – a room in the house of an old person. It was all done out in mustard tones with a brown swirly carpet that was somewhat threadbare, and had faded wallpaper that must once have been patterned but was now drab and mottled. There was a dark wooden corner table with a lace doily on the top and two silver photograph frames, which were empty. Light drifted into the scene from a window that Clarrie was unable to see. Dust particles were floating through the airless air. A large bluebottle buzzed in from somewhere and started to throw itself against the mottled walls of the room, hitting them with such force that Clarrie thought it would splatter itself.

She blinked and the Bone's face returned – all pinched and agitated, aware that it was being stared at. The Bone's shrewish eyes darted an edgy glare at Clarrie, and for a moment she thought she caught another glimpse of the bluebottle, bashing itself against the glassy exterior of the Bone's right eyeball. Then she finally stopped staring and looked back down at that other unsettling eye, the yellow eye of the dead trout on her plate, believing for a moment that it had just winked at her.

The trout remained intact. Clarrie speared a piece of galette and then used her knife to smear some of the almond and herb purée over it. After checking to see that Tilda wasn't looking, she allowed herself the pleasure of licking off the purée as though she were eating an ice-cream, holding it in her mouth and blending it with her saliva to get the full fragrant flavour, before finally swallowing. She imagined the bright green colour trickling down her gullet and dyeing the contents of her stomach. She liked to extend the pleasure of eating in this way – by imagining the internal processes that followed. After all, chewing and swallowing were only a tiny part of it. It was important in many ways to gain a thorough understanding of what happened on the inside. Glancing once more at Tilda, Clarrie popped the piece of galette into her mouth and attempted to suck it into a pulp without using her teeth, letting the sweetness of the parsnip seep slowly out. She tried hard to ignore the ugly downward curve of the trout's mouth.

'. . . I used to work as a lifeguard at the local baths every summer when I was home from university,' Alex was saying, as Clarrie tuned herself back into the conversation. 'It was a good job, I didn't have to do very much – just sit about and tell people not to run around and all that sort of thing. Once in a while I had to dive in and pull an idiot out of the water, but not very often . . .'

Clarrie was pleased to see that everybody was listening to him – whether out of politeness or genuine interest it was difficult to ascertain, but they were paying attention at any rate. Alex was in his element and Tilda had a dreamy expression on her face.

'. . . Anyway, Tilda used to come in twice a week – Tuesdays and Thursdays, I think it was . . .'

'Mondays and Thursdays,' Tilda put in.

'. . . Sorry, *Mondays* and Thursdays.' Alex was irritated at the interruption. 'I didn't know her then, of course, but I used to watch her swimming up and down, up and down. She always came alone. She'd just do her lengths – very businesslike – and then go again. She used to wear a swimming costume in pale blue and her hair would stream out all around her in the water. I thought she was the most beautiful thing I'd ever seen.'

The wistful expression made him look younger. He was back there by the pool, watching his lady swim up and down.

'How terribly romantic! How did you approach her?' asked Cruella, obviously wanting Alex to get to the point.

'Oh, it took me a long time,' he said. 'All through the summer I thought about talking to her, wondered what I could say, wondered if she'd ever even noticed me. I began to call her my little mermaid.'

'How sweet!' cried Cruella, clasping her hands together. 'You never told me that, Tilda.'

Tilda was blushing and clutching her thyroid scar, eyelids lowered bashfully.

'So I thought and thought,' said Alex. 'And in the end fate intervened. I was wandering past a bookshop one day and happened to see a rather fine illustrated version of the Hans Christian Andersen fairytale "The Little Mermaid", just sitting there in the window. I'd never actually read the story, but I was sure it must be romantic. I bought the book and I wrote on the flyleaf, "A gift from your secret admirer who watches over you while you swim". I slipped the cloakroom attendant a couple of quid to put the book in the locker where Tilda left her clothes, and waited to see what would happen.'

'And she came across,' said Shiny, out of one side of his mouth. 'Not bad, not bad at all, Alex. I'd never have thought a square like you could do something as stylish as that.'

'Don't be mean,' said Tilda, coquettishly. 'It's the most wonderful thing anybody has ever done for me.'

Alex looked young while he was telling the story – the years seemed to fall away, the worry lines on his forehead and around his eyes vanished, and Tilda found herself looking into the eyes of the awkward, stammering twenty year old from the swimming pool. Or was that just the after-effects of the cocaine?

It had been romantic, and it was the romance that had swept her off her feet – not the boy himself. She had barely noticed the gangly lifeguard until the day the book appeared in her locker. She had read an article in a magazine, not so long ago, which put forward the idea that the basis of attraction is not so much the way one views the other person, as how the other person enables one to view oneself. Tilda had considered this theory at length, and found it to be true. Alex had made her feel like a princess – exciting and desirable. He enabled her to reinvent herself. The problems began when Alex's fairytale vision of his young wife began to disperse – living together day after day, month after month and finally year after year, their relationship inevitably took on the mundane colours of domesticity. Tilda needed Alex to look at her as he once had, so that she could see herself in that dazzling light again. She was losing him, she could feel it. She was clutching on in desperation to something that was slipping away forever.

It was as though they had been two entirely different people – two wild youngsters who had swum naked together after the pool was closed for the night and made big hungry love on the pool-side, dripping wet. How remote it all was. She found she couldn't even remember the last time they had been swimming together, let alone the last time they had made love.

'Christina and I don't have any great romantic story, not like yours,' Brian was saying now, with a hint of regret in his voice. 'Our parents knew each other. We've always known each other, for as long as I remember.'

Tilda imagined a fat boy with grubby knees and a thin girl with pigtails and socks down around her ankles, playing conkers in a crowded school playground.

'He had other girlfriends, lots of them,' said Christina, cheeks pink with pride or wine. 'I don't think he even noticed me until one day when he and his mother came for dinner at our house.'

'We haven't looked back since,' concluded Brian, and the arm he slid around his wife was proprietorial.

It was a dull, passionless picture, thought Tilda, and yet it was permanent and enduring. This was a relationship that was based on solid reality, rather than a flimsy, watery vision. Brian and Christina would never have suffered from the shattering of a dream, because there wasn't a dream to shatter.

'Romance is neither here nor there,' pronounced Clive. 'Romance is something invented by writers and artists. It doesn't exist.' There was sweat on his neck, making him even shinier than usual. He reached up to loosen his collar.

'Oh, don't say that!' Tilda gripped her fork desperately, not wanting to hear her own fear spoken aloud. 'Please don't bring everything down to the level of hormones and chemicals, Clive. There's more to life than that.'

'Is there?' Alex chipped in, glancing sideways at Clive. 'I'm not so sure.'

'Why, Alex, what a strange thing to say after your wonderful romantic story,' cried Judy in mock horror. 'Your little mermaid is still here, you know, sitting just across the table.' And Tilda felt a blush spread down her neck, the deep pink creeping past the thyroid scar and sweeping across her chest to merge with her dress.

Clarrie could see a hill in Tilda's head – a steep hill with trees dotted here and there. The sky above was dark and rain beat down relentlessly. She gazed into the rain, wondering whether it ever stopped. Certainly the grass was very green. The wind was howling too; there was a creaking and a groaning of branches. One small tree stood apart from the others, higher up the hill, and was buffeted more than the rest. It was so thin and frail that Clarrie wondered how it remained upright. Its branches were bare where the other trees had abundant leaves. Funny how even with all that rain falling, this tree seemed deprived of any sustenance; bare and dead. There was a moon somewhere behind the thick clouds, but it couldn't quite make itself seen.

Tilda could feel Clarrie's eyes on her, piercing and pressing. She met the gaze with her most fierce look of disapproval, but it was like trying to stare out a dead person. She had noticed that Clarrie was staring at the guests, and it was difficult to know what could be done about it. If only Clarrie had never come. If only she didn't exist. Her mouth was gaping open and, there were traces of food visible inside. Her dressing gown was also gaping at the neck, and Tilda tried unsuccessfully to drop hints to her.

A piece of galette fell from Clarrie's suspended fork, and was lost somewhere under the table. Fearing for her carpet, Tilda bent down and searched about in the dark jungle of human and wooden legs, before realising that Brian Thackston's heavy foot had already done the damage. She swore under her breath and the blood began to rush to her head.

'Darling, what are you doing down there?' called Alex from above, and Tilda resurfaced, dizzy, trying to extricate herself from the tablecloth, which had somehow got caught up with one of her earrings.

'Nothing,' she muttered. 'I thought I'd dropped something.'

Clarrie had now switched her gaze over to Heidi Stilbourne, and Tilda was released, somewhat relieved but desperate for a cigarette, or perhaps some more of Judy's cocaine. Maybe another opportunity would present itself later in the evening . . .

Munch, much, munch. A number of moths, five or six of them in all – big ones with thick brown bodies and lurid yellow wings. They were gnawing away at an expanse of lace. The lace was delicate, probably costly. In fact, Clarrie thought it was the most beautiful lace she had ever seen – not too surprising really, to find fabric inside the head of a fashion designer – and the moths were slowly destroying it. Systematically, they ate their way through the beauty; there were large areas of lace that had already disintegrated, leaving gaping holes. The Hammock, however, was eating nothing.

'D'you know – I'd just like to say what an absolute joy and pleasure this evening is.'
Brian's words came from nowhere, just as the conversation had turned to the refurbishment of the Opera House. Tilda glanced up at his open smiling face. Did he really mean it?
'I believe that people should say what they mean and mean what they say,' he continued, while darting a covetous look at the still intact fish on Clarrie's plate. 'It's just wonderful to be able to share a beautiful wholesome meal with a group of pleasant, honest people.'
Tilda knew she should be happy, but it was almost impossible to believe that this could really be Brian's perception of the evening – one so utterly different from her own. She could see that Alex, too, was having trouble digesting Brian's words, along with the piece of fish he was clearly having difficulty swallowing.
'I spend so many pointless evenings in the company of stuffed shirts at posh restaurants,' Brian continued. 'People so practised in social polish that they aren't able to express anything they're really feeling. But here . . . Well, I must confess that I thought this was going to be another one of those evenings . . . I thought I'd be subjected to dull talk about business and golf . . . that both the food and the conversation would be bland and the portions small.'
Tilda could hardly cope with this outpouring. Her mouth

silently formed the words, 'My cup runneth over,' and then she found she was nervously looking about to see if glasses needed filling. No, the glasses were full. Pauline was doing her job, efficiently and inconspicuously. Even now, she was topping up Christina Thackston's glass and then retreating to stand in a corner. Were things actually going well?

'And here we are,' concluded Brian, 'talking about things that really matter – about love, romance, childhood . . . and there's evidence of care and of family values here – there's a person at this table who has been ill and who has been looked after and welcomed back to the table, no matter that she's wearing a dressing gown . . . and I'm eating the most delicious trout I've ever tasted. I'm sharing this with you all because I believe that honesty is a virtue and people should express their true feelings.'

He's drunk or loopy or both, thought Tilda.

Clarrie saw a pair of brown animal eyes staring out of the Clay's face. She saw a dog – a mongrel by the look of things, certainly not an animal of any noticeable pedigree. The dog had only one ear – perhaps it had lost the other in a fight. Its pink tongue was lolling out of its mouth as it lounged on somebody's floor. It had a red collar around its neck with a metal tag. There was some writing on the tag but Clarrie couldn't read what it said.

Now a leg appeared in the scene – a woman's leg with a pink fluffy high-heeled slipper perched at the end of it and five toes sticking out at the front with red varnish on the nails. The dog was lying at the feet of its owner. Clarrie would have liked to be able to see who the slipper-wearer was but she could only see halfway up the calf. The dog too seemed to be trying to gaze up into the face of its owner. After a while, the floppy tongue lolled forth again and the mongrel began to lick at the toes – subtly at first and then lapping wetly. The toes wriggled with pleasure and the dog licked all the more hungrily. Clarrie looked away, repelled, and when she looked back, the Clay's blubbery face was back in place, and he was grinning broadly.

'I do take your point about honesty, about its being a virtue and

all that,' Clive was saying now to Brian, while gesticulating somewhat wildly with his almost-empty wine glass. 'But wouldn't
you agree that even at a dinner party such as this one, there
are certain limits to honesty, certain paths on which one dare
not tread?'

'I don't quite follow what you're saying,' said Brian, brow
creasing with the effort to understand.

Tilda thought Clive was being quite loathsome, was disagreeing just for the sake of disagreeing and for no good reason. His
smile was crooked, his posture menacing.

'I think that what Clive is trying to say—' began Alex, nervously.

'What I'm saying—' cut in Clive, '—is that we are all honest
when it suits us to be honest. It's easy to talk with honesty
about how wonderful the food is when the food actually *is*
wonderful.'

'Which it is,' put in Brian, smiling warmly at Tilda in an
effort to reassure her that he really was being honest, in spite
of anything Clive might be about to say.

'But what if it wasn't? What if it was awful and you were
fighting the urge to retch every time you tried to swallow?'

'Steady on, old man,' muttered Roger.

Tilda found herself looking across at Heidi, who did in fact look
as though she were fighting the urge to retch.

'What would you say in those circumstances, Brian? Or what
if you found that among your fellow guests there was someone
to whom you took an instant instinctive dislike? Would you
still be talking about the pleasant company, the wonderful
conversation? Would you be honest enough to tell the cook
what was wrong with the meal and tell your unwanted dinner
companion exactly what you thought of him?'

'Well, I . . .' Brian spluttered slightly.

Tilda found she couldn't speak. What on earth was wrong
with Clive? Why was he so determined to stir up an argument
when all had been so pleasant?

'Clive, my dear, I feel you are making mountains from mole-
hills.' Judy's voice was easy, relaxed. She had taken control. 'You
are quite obviously talking about the need for tact. And of course
we all see the importance of good manners, of social etiquette –

we express our true feelings when it is appropriate to do so. It is wonderful when we are able to talk freely of what we feel – and Brian is merely expressing his pleasure in finding that he is able to do so in our company this evening. Isn't that so, Brian?'

'Well, yes, of course,' Brian nodded.

Tilda felt herself relax. She glanced at Clarrie, who seemed not to be listening to any of this and was staring very hard at Roger.

'But, Brian, your honesty goes deeper than that, you know it does.' Christina Thackston looked dishevelled. Her cheeks held little patches of red and her forehead was sweaty. She gulped from her wine glass. 'Sometimes you are almost painfully honest about things.' She turned to Judy. 'I don't think he's ever been too bothered about tact and diplomacy. He means what he says and he says what he means.' She gulped again.

'That's a bit unfair, love, saying I'm not bothered about tact and diplomacy. Although it's true that I like to be direct both at work and at play, as it were.'

'We all like to think of ourselves as honest,' said Clive. 'But we only ever speak our minds up to a point. I'm sure none of us here would like to continue the dinner with a discussion of what is really going on inside us, what is troubling us deep down. And if we were really honest and direct, that is what we would be doing.'

'But, my dear, this is a dinner party, not a group therapy session.' As Judy laughed at her own quip, a general titter broke out around the table.

Clarrie was busy discovering the interior world of Kitchener. To begin with, she had a little trouble seeing into his head – his moustache kept getting in the way, and she had to resist the urge to reach across the table and pull on it. Finally the moustache seemed to skulk away and Clarrie was able to peer into Kitchener's large skull.

She saw a small boy with an anxious face and a severe side-parting in his black hair, wearing shorts and a grey synthetic shirt. He was very smart except for the white socks falling down around his ankles and the scuffed shoes with laces undone. He was clutching a colourful piggy bank to his chest as though it contained something precious, and he stared hard – not at Clarrie, but at his reflection in a full-length mirror that was propped up somehow in the dark space around him. In fact, the boy himself had his back turned to Clarrie, and she found that she was gazing at the reflected boy rather than the real one.

And then Clarrie could see that there were hundreds of little boys, all identical, lined up one behind the other in the mirror. She was mesmerised, at first unable to make sense of what she was seeing, before realising that there was a second mirror behind the child, and that the two mirrors were reflecting back to each other endlessly, creating a long snaking trail of small boys that stretched into eternity. She felt that just as she came to understand what she could see, so the little boy had become aware of his own endless potential. His odd face broke into a broad toothy smile and he clutched the piggy bank still tighter to his chest.

'Mine, all mine,' said the child, and the lips of the infinite reflected children moved in unison. 'Mine,' said the boy again, and a moustache began to grow under his freckled nose, becoming large and thick, and bristling as it grew. In a matter of seconds it covered the boy's whole face, concealed the infinite reflections and grew back into the moustache of Kitchener.

Once again, Clarrie was tempted to pull on the moustache, but she knew she shouldn't and instead she struggled to pay attention to the conversation. Shiny was speaking again. Clarrie had been dimly aware that he was talking quite a lot – his voice was loud and abrasive, occasionally breaking into her thoughts.

Louder still was his aftershave. Clarrie had never liked heavily scented men – she was suspicious that they wore aftershave to conceal poor hygiene. But this was unlikely to be the case with Shiny; he was the kind of man who wore aftershave to make himself more noticeable, to make his presence felt. Shiny wore aftershave as a kind of substitute for charisma.

'When I was a child,' said Clive, playing absent-mindedly with the prongs of his fork, 'I suppose about eleven or twelve, my parents took my younger sister and myself along to dinner with some friends of theirs, a couple who lived nearby. I hated having to go places with my parents, but sometimes one simply couldn't get out of it. This particular couple had always taken a great interest in my sister and myself – Meccano for Christmas, all that sort of thing.

'So, anyway, the evening moved along as smoothly as usual, and my sister and I were finding the whole thing quite tedious – until the conversation suddenly turned to the business of learning to drive. I don't know why they were talking about learning to drive but my father launched into an anecdote about the first time he had given my mother a driving lesson in his car. Well, before we knew what was happening, she was screaming and shouting: 'How dare you? You've only brought this up to humiliate me. You love to show me up in public and make me feel small,' and so on and so forth.

'And then it got worse. Quite out of the blue, or so it seemed, my mother began accusing my father of having an affair – shouting right across the dinner table in front of me, my sister and the two friends! Well, as you can imagine, my sister and I didn't know where to look, what to say . . . it was all so unreal, so shocking. I vividly recall my feelings. My biggest worry was *not* that there might be some truth in my mother's accusations – instead I was worried about the way my parents were making a show of themselves in front of their friends. In short, I was worried at the way they were washing their dirty linen in public.'

'You poor thing,' said Christina to her wine glass.

'But that wasn't the end of it,' Clive continued, looking slowly around at his audience. 'Just as my parents were reaching the crescendo of their argument, the two friends suddenly joined in. Maureen (that was her name, you see) launched in with, "Don't you look so bloody smug, Derek – I know what you've been up to all these months with Fiona from number 42 . . ." And all hell broke loose. They began taking turns to argue – first my mother and father, then their friends, then back to my mother and father – until they began to intervene in each other's arguments.'

'Good heavens, what did you and your sister do while all this was going on?' asked Judy.

'I seem to remember that she eventually fell asleep with her head on the table. And I went in search of the cat so I could get away from them all.'

Clive paused for effect. 'The point of this story is that we are very seldom honest about what we really think and feel. And that when we *are* honest – well, that's when disasters happen.'

There was a dull clunking sound as Christina Thackston's full wine glass toppled and fell. Tilda watched helplessly as red wine seeped across the table-cloth and splattered onto Roger Marshall's lap.

'Pauline—' she began, jumping to her feet. Before she could stop him, Alex had upturned the salt cellar and salt was streaming out, blending with the spilt wine in a pink pulpy mass.

'Alex, no.' She had always hated this particular method of dealing with spilt wine.

'Salt – just the thing – soaks it up or something,' he was muttering.

'So sorry,' said Christina, untouched by the spillage, free from even the smallest splatter.

'My trousers . . .' Roger was on his feet, dabbing with a napkin.

'Pauline, do something,' said Tilda to the helpless waitress. 'Take him out to the kitchen.'

'Ah, yes, white wine for a red wine stain, that's it,' said Alex, grabbing a nearby bottle.

'Alex, *please*.' Tilda clutched helplessly at her thyroid scar as he doused the mess of red wine and salt with white wine.

The heavy door swung to behind Roger and Pauline.

'I do hope his trousers aren't ruined. I'm not sure quite what happened,' said Christina.

'Not to worry.' Tilda smiled brightly at the mess that was her dinner table. 'There's always at least one spillage in an evening. It's only to be expected.'

'It's always me, though.' Christina looked sadly down at the stain. 'I don't know what happens – I come over all clumsy.'

'Not to worry,' said Tilda again. *Do I really have to befriend this awful woman?* she thought to herself. *Pious and religious one minute – drunk as a skunk the next.* 'I'll have Pauline change the cloth in a little while,' she concluded, and caught Judy's eye which gave a special glint of sympathy.

'In the meantime you need some more wine, Christina,' said Alex, reaching for a bottle. 'I shan't have you going thirsty on account of a moment of clumsiness.'

'Any expense caused . . . well, it goes without saying that I'll . . . dry-cleaning, new trousers, whatever . . .' Brian mumbled incoherently.

'Much appreciated, Brian,' said Alex. 'Everything'll be fine though, I'm sure.'

'Absolutely,' said Judy, staring at the door. 'Ghastly pair of trousers, anyway.'

Beautiful, beautiful red. The salt had tainted it, turned it pink, but essentially it remained red. Red was at its heart.

Clarrie used her eyes like a camera, blinking to freeze in her mind the moment when the red hit the table, flashing out, soaking in, taking hold. She ran the spilling sequence backwards so that the wine leaped back into the glass, leaving the table-cloth a perfect white. Then she played it forward again, savouring the moment when the wine hovered in mid-air, not touching the glass, not touching the table – hovering, like a red rain cloud ready to pour forth. Beautiful, beautiful red.

Other red – a mass of red in front of her, red beyond the wine. There was a red person across the table and that person was Cruella. Red dress, and somehow something red inside her – something strange that Clarrie sensed but couldn't actually see. Was she also taking pleasure in this red moment?

Cruella was remote in her redness. While everyone else at the table flapped over the spilt wine, Cruella remained motionless, untouchable. She was not human somehow – a red that was cold. What is the difference, after all, between something that is boiling hot and something that is freezing cold? Both will burn, both will cause pain. Clarrie looked levelly at Cruella, stared into her glassy eyes, and was not surprised to see a third eye, huge and unblinking, occupying the whole of the interior space of Cruella's head. The white of the eye was translucent, almost blue – but within the white was a cornea of pure vibrant red. The pupil expanded and contracted, growing and shrinking rhythmically, almost as a heart beats.

She has no heart, thought Clarrie to herself. *Only this red eye that sees everything and feels nothing.*

Roger's crotch and left leg were soaking wet. He had been soaked by the wine and then he drenched himself again with a wringing wet cloth, in a futile attempt to remove the deep stain from his expensive blue trousers. In the dining room he had dabbed ineffectually with his napkin, before being whisked off to the kitchen by a strangely enthusiastic Pauline. She bore down on him with a wet towel and succeeded in shoving it straight at a rather private part of his anatomy before he managed to shoo her away and take charge of the cloth himself.

'Are you sure you don't want a bit of help?' she asked in a voice that was an alarming combination of feminine wiles and practicality.

'No!' he snapped, nervous and startled. 'I can manage quite well by myself, thank you,' and twisted around so that his back was turned to her.

'I think you should take your trousers off,' came her voice from behind him. Was she genuinely eager to see him in his underpants or was it merely concern?

'I expect Mr Stone has a pair of trousers somewhere that you could borrow,' she continued.

'I don't really think you're in any position to start offering me Alex's trousers,' he snapped, straightening up.

'Please yourself. I'm only trying to help,' she huffed, and abruptly returned to the dining-room, leaving him alone with his cloth and his wet trousers.

He sponged on for a couple of minutes, now confused as to which patches of stain were wine and which were water. Finally he gave up, feeling foolish. It felt as though he had pissed in his boxer shorts. How could he have been so vain as to think the waitress was yearning to see him out of his trousers? What would a young thing like that want with someone like him? What would anyone in their right mind want with a washed up has-been like himself?

He straightened up and walked across the kitchen towards the hall, trousers clinging to his left leg, genitals cold and damp. Damn and blast that ridiculous Christina Thackston.

This awful indignity was something he could really have done without. It wasn't even his fault, damn it – not like the rest of his humiliations, which sadly could be blamed on nobody but himself.

Thank heavens for Judy. Where would he be without her? And to think that earlier this very evening he had tried to cast her love aside – her love that was his only sustenance, his salvation.

'I'm leaving you,' he had said, without knowing why he said it, without quite intending to.

With great precision and no discernible hesitation she threaded the spike of a large silver ear-ring into the hole in her left ear lobe. She didn't seem to have heard him.

'I said, I'm leaving you.' Roger meant it a little more this time; was irritated at being ignored.

'Would you zip me up, please, darling?' She stepped into her long red dress and hiked the straps up over her shoulders.

He stepped forward and fumbled obligingly until the zip complied.

'Now, how do I look?' She turned to face him, her appearance as dramatic as ever, chest white above the low-cut front, earrings glinting.

She hadn't put on her make-up yet. He always thought she looked younger without make-up. Her bare face had a vulnerability that vanished entirely once she had applied artificial colour. Nobody else saw her without make up – it was one of the privileges of being her husband.

'You look stunning. You always do.' He sat on the edge of the bed, fiddling with his cuffs, noticing what looked like a cigarette burn in the carpet – strange, since neither of them ever smoked in the bedroom. Perhaps it was the cleaner. 'I'm trying to tell you that I'm leaving you.'

'Such a silly phrase.' She had turned back to the mirror and was cleansing her face with bright blue lotion. She threw the used cotton wool pad into the bin across the room, aiming perfectly. 'And not one that I ever thought I'd hear from you. Much better to say "I'm going to leave you". "I'm leaving you" makes it sound as though you are actually in the process of going, while in fact you are sitting on the bed fussing with your clothing.'

'Judy—'

'Then after you've gone, you can say "I have left". Or should it be "I left you"? Or maybe simply "I went"?' She was moisturising now, spreading a rich white cream evenly into her cheeks, across her forehead, down her neck. She still wasn't looking at him.

'Judy, listen to me.' His voice was thin and pathetic. He cleared his throat, hoping to regain his usual gruffness.

She screwed the lid onto her jar of moisturiser and reached for the foundation. '*Must* I, darling? It does rather seem to me that you've chosen a particularly inconvenient moment to have whatever crisis you're having. We're going to a dinner party in half an hour, and I don't think I can bear to have you facing me across Tilda's dinner table all smouldering and preoccupied. Can't you put it out of your head until we get back, or preferably until tomorrow or next week?'

'I do wish you'd take me seriously.' Nowhere near gruff enough, no hint of the authority he wanted his voice to have.

She smeared peachy foundation across her face until her skin acquired a plastic quality. She sighed. 'Very well. If you absolutely insist, we'll have the discussion now. You believe at this moment that you're leaving me, much as I hate the phrase. May I ask why you believe this? Do you have a lover who is pressuring you, for example? Have you been given some kind of ultimatum? Because I warn you, Roger, it would be very rash to start making sacrifices for some fresh young thing you'll tire of in a couple of months.'

'No. It isn't like that.' He was flustered. How could she be so like a surgeon – slicing, dissecting, all blades and cold professionalism.

She narrowed her eyes at the mirror, and applied black liquid liner to her eyelids with a steady hand. 'Try to be a little more precise, Roger. Do you mean that your lover *isn't* pressurising you? Do you mean that you *won't* tire of her?'

'I don't *have* a lover.' This much he was sure of. If only he could be so sure that *she* didn't have one.

'Pity,' she said in clipped tones. 'These things are so much easier to understand when a third party is involved. In that case, I suppose we are dealing with some kind of mid-life crisis – some sort of fear of approaching forty with so many things left undone, a reluctance to acknowledge that you have three children who are growing up quickly and will soon be old enough to mock you and make you feel inadequate, an inability to cope with responsibility . . . And one of the qualities I have always admired in you is your sense of responsibility.'

'No.' Again, he found himself staring at the cigarette burn.

'Then what?' She raised her eyebrows – hard to tell if she raised them because she was baffled or whether it just made it easier to apply the mascara.

'Shame.' That word that was so difficult for a man like him to say, which nevertheless summed up the situation perfectly.

'Shame,' she repeated, thoughtfully, and pursed her lips to receive their coating of thick red lipstick. 'Shame,' she said again, using the word to blot her lips against a tissue. Was that a clatter of forceps?

He nodded, unwilling to go further. It would be easier just to leave, much as he didn't want to, much as he still loved her and needed her in spite of her infuriating coldness – maybe *because* of her coldness.

'And you are too ashamed to tell me what it is that you are ashamed of.' She twisted the bottom of her lipstick so that the red column receded and withdrew. 'You would rather tell me that you are leaving me than talk to me about this "shame".'

He nodded again, feeling heat in his face, knowing how childish he was being.

'Roger darling, there is no need for this. I know you don't really want to leave me.' She sprayed a cloud of expensive perfume into the air, and walked into it so that she would be subtly scented. He had once asked her why she didn't spray it directly onto her neck and wrists like other women did and she had merely raised an eyebrow in disdain. *Other women*, indeed.

He waited for her to continue, trying not to sneeze as the perfume cloud wafted around his face and into his nostrils, reaching the back of his throat.

'This is about your gambling, isn't it,' she said, finally turning to face him again. 'How much have you lost?'

He was so surprised that he was completely unable to speak.

How did she know? How was this possible? All this long time of silent suffering, of making excuses, inventing business trips, lying awake at night and hiding bank statements. All those hours in smoky casinos, shuffling stacks of coloured chips, staring into the centre of a spinning roulette wheel, waiting for it to slow down and stop when it just kept on spinning and spinning in an endless clattering whirl.

'Who told you?' It was lame, but it was all he could find to say.

'Nobody.' She sat down on the bed next to him and took one of his hands in hers, stroking it gently with her cool, soft fingers. 'I know you too well, Roger. You can't hide something like that from me. Now, forget all this silly talk about leaving me, and tell me how bad it is.'

He began to talk. The words were tumbling out so fast that they barely made sense. He told her about Paris and Amsterdam, about the way it gripped him, held him, wouldn't let him go until he had poured everything away, and how it gripped him still, even though there was nothing left. He told her how desperate he had been feeling, how he had hardly been able to look her in the eye for the past six months. He didn't tell her about the suicidal thoughts he had been having lately, but he told her everything else.

He found that he wanted to cry, but he hadn't cried since he was six years old and he wasn't about to start now. He had almost no dignity left as it was, and so he conquered the impulse to cry that was burning behind his eyes, and tried not to see the pity in his wife's face as she began to stroke his brow with slow soothing movements, just like his mother did when he was a little boy, before she died. Before long he had nothing left to say, and sat silently while she continued to stroke his head. And then he realised that he wanted to make love to her, wanted desperately to be inside her, but was afraid that she would reject him just when he needed her most; that she would brush him away just as you might brush away a troublesome fly, and mutter something about the dinner party they were going to, about how he mustn't smear her make up.

He was amazed, then, when she took one of his hands and placed it inside her dress against one of her warm breasts, and then gently eased him down on the bed, pressing and rubbing herself against him, murmuring in his ear, reaching for his zip.

Afterwards she became more harsh and businesslike than ever, and he realised that she had only done it to make him feel better. She left him lying in a crumpled heap on the duvet and strode naked across the room to the adjoining bathroom, switching on the light and turning on the shower, sighing at the prospect of beginning the whole exhausting process of getting ready all over again.

He lay, staring up at a crack in the ceiling that looked like a smile – or a frown if you lay the other way around on the bed. He was lost in time. He wanted to sleep, but his eyes ached when he tried to close them. Funny, that.

She emerged from the bathroom, swathed in a white, fluffy towel, stooping to retrieve the red dress from where it lay discarded on the floor.

'Everyone has secrets, you know, darling,' she said. 'Everyone has something they're ashamed of.'

He wanted to ask her what *her* secret was, but was afraid of what she might say. Instead he said, 'What are we going to do?'

'Don't worry,' she said, picking up her silk underwear and slipping her knickers on. 'Things have a way of turning out all right.'

'It's hard to see how,' he said, watching her putting on her bra.

'You leave that to me,' she said. 'I'll think of something. You need to concentrate on getting better. Sarah Manette has a very good addiction counsellor. I think I'll give him a call, get an appointment for you.'

'Mmm,' he muttered.

'Darling, do believe me, I really will sort everything out. And do stop wallowing in self-pity. It's true, you know – that everyone has secrets . . . Take Clive Stilbourne, for instance.'

'Clive Stilbourne?' Roger sat up, slightly dizzy and somewhat perplexed. Judy was back at the mirror, working swiftly on the second round of make-up.

'Yes, he's bisexual. Likes going with rent boys.'

Roger blinked. 'What utter tosh, Judy. Where on earth did you hear such a thing?'

'Oh, I have my sources,' she said, slightly distracted. 'He's in it up to his neck. Completely besotted with some blond Australian.'

'Good God!'

'Don't worry, Roger.' She smiled brightly through a new layer of lipstick. 'Don't worry about a thing.'

Clarrie was playing with the red, drawing in the salt with the little finger of her right hand. First she drew a smiley face, then a heart and then an axe. It was quite difficult to draw clearly in the salt, and all three pictures looked like meaningless squiggles. She flinched at a sudden pain in her calf as Tilda kicked her under the table. She knew she should smile a silent apology across the table but didn't feel like it.

'My poor darling,' cooed Cruella as Kitchener returned to his seat, walking strangely, his face flushed and his hands spread out in front of him in a feeble attempt to conceal the damp patch.

'Roger, you must let me lend you a pair of trousers,' said Alex, nervously running his left hand through his thinning hair.

'Nonsense, old chap. I'll be dry in a jiffy.' Kitchener ambled back to his seat and tried to sit comfortably.

'Roger has the most terrible bad luck, you know,' said Cruella. 'You can guarantee that the hand of fate will single him out in any gathering and dish out the most dreadful things to him. Do you remember last year at Cannes, darling, when . . .'

Clarrie was bored of all this talk, bored of anecdotes and recollections, jokes and theories and the clinking of glasses. She tried to close her ears to Cruella's sharp voice and gazed at Alex, who also seemed not to be paying attention to what was going on, but appeared to be deep inside himself. How different he was from Morris, how worried and conventional. Where Alex sat fidgeting and blinking, Morris would surely get up on his chair and shout, 'Boring, boring, boring! Let's all go to the beach and swim naked in the moonlight.'

Except of course they were a long way from the sea, it was far too cold for swimming naked and the moon seemed to be hiding behind dense cloud. Nevertheless, Clarrie knew that if Morris were here, he would take charge, issue a command, change everything . . . but Morris wasn't here, and Alex lacked the confidence and bearing for taking charge of things and making changes.

Clarrie strained to see into him, aware that his was now the only head her keen vision hadn't penetrated. She concentrated as hard as she could, but felt he was resisting her. He caught her eye for a moment, and she thought that in his stare she could read, *Private – No entry. Trespassers will be prosecuted*

We'll see about that, thought Clarrie to herself. Nobody stops me from coming in. She pushed hard internally, as though she were trying to have a crap, but focusing the push on her spirit rather than her bowels.

Clarrie's spirit woke instantly from its long hibernation and began trying to force itself out of her chest through the gaps between her ribs, which had served as a cage for quite some time now. She could feel an odd fluttering around her heart, as the spirit squeezed and shoved. She pushed and pushed, breathing deeply and clutching the seat of her chair with both hands to stop herself from flying into the air, propelled by the force of her exertion.

It was hard to tell how long this period of labour lasted; it could have been many minutes or maybe only a few seconds. Finally, there was a loud pop in Clarrie's head and everything went dark.

She had a brief moment of panic before realising it was only dark because her eyes were shut. When she opened them again, she discovered she was hovering above the table, level with the couple in the double-portrait who smiled reassuringly at her. She lifted a hand to wave at them and found she could see straight through it. She was invisible and weightless, drifting around the room.

This is wonderful, said the invisible Clarrie, and quickly realised that nobody could hear her. She was omnipresent.

She glanced down and saw that her physical self was still seated at the table, drawing in the salt.

Hey – look at me! called omnipresent Clarrie, but physical Clarrie remained oblivious and returned to playing with her uneaten trout.

This is great, thought invisible Clarrie. *Why haven't I ever tried it before? Is this what they mean by astral projection?*

She occupied herself briefly with flying around the room, up to the ceiling to run her transparent hand along the coving and over to the mantelpiece to perch among the ornaments, before remembering that she had projected herself out of her body for a specific purpose – to look into Alex's head.

She fluttered over to where he sat, brooding and dejected, and placed her hands firmly around his face, one hand gripping the top of his head and the other holding tight under his chin. Alex carried on sulking, unaware of what was happening. Strange to feel how familiar the shape of his face was.

His head is just the same as Morris's, she muttered.

Somehow she knew exactly what to do – she knew that if she could only twist hard enough in an anti-clockwise direction, the face could be unscrewed from its place, revealing whatever lay inside.

While Clarrie twisted and strained, Alex continued sipping his wine. The hand which held the glass occasionally got in her way. Soon she was out of breath, and the face hadn't moved at all. She wished she had at her disposal a giant version of the metal gadgets used to prise the lids off stubborn jars. She would clamp it around Alex's face and have it off in an instant. As it was, she was beginning to despair. To make matters worse, he began laughing uproariously at something Cruella had said and Clarrie lost her grip on the head altogether.

She took a moment to rest while Alex's laughter died down to a chuckle and ceased. Then she positioned her hands carefully once again and heaved with all the strength she could command.

The face finally moved, very much as the lid of a jam jar suddenly twists free – it happened so suddenly that Clarrie almost dropped it. The face was surprisingly heavy, resembling a steel frame with a dense rubber material stretched across it. Clarrie paused to examine it, and was nauseated when the eyelashes flickered against her hand and the mouth opened to cough, blowing damp air through her fingers. Alex was seemingly unaware that his face had been removed, and the face continued to function as though it were still in place on his head. Clarrie lowered it slowly, and placed it on the table where it would be safe. She spent a few moments speculating as to what Morris's face would look like from the inside, before hearing music coming from the head cavity. She turned to see what was going on in Alex's mind.

It was the sound of an organ – not a church organ – the kind that was popular in years gone by, the electric sort that was traditionally played in cinemas before the main feature began.

And there was indeed an old-time cinema inside Alex's head, complete with dusty velvet curtains and an expectant audience. Slowly, an electric organ was rising out of the floor in front of the silver screen – a little old man with yellow waistcoat and bow tie was playing 'I've Got a Luvverly Bunch of Coconuts'. The old man was smiling as he played, revealing his lack of teeth. Fully risen, he reached the end of the song and raised his shiny bowler hat to the audience as he received rapturous applause. Then he flexed his hands and began on the next number, 'She'll be Coming Round the Mountain When She Comes'.

Well I never, said invisible Clarrie as the old man raised his hat again and began on 'How Much is that Doggy in the Window'. *I would never have expected to find anything remotely like this.*

She lifted Alex's face to put it back in position on the head. As she did so, she noticed that the little old man had begun to sink back into the floor.

Putting the face back wasn't quite so difficult as removing it, but somehow it didn't seem to sit properly in position. It was slightly crooked. Clarrie tried to straighten it, but it remained askew, and soon she gave up and floated aimlessly around the room, peering into the guests' ears, trying to see down the fronts of their shirts and dresses, looking down at the tops of their heads and surveying their dandruff.

'Is something wrong with your fish, Clarrie?' she heard Tilda saying. 'Don't you like trout?'

Invisible Clarrie paused in her floating, wondering if physical Clarrie would be able to reply.

'Oh, no, he's fine. I like him very much,' said the visible Clarrie.

How strange it was to hear one's own voice as though it were somebody else's. The floating Clarrie had no control over the actions of her seated double. She found that her voice sounded slightly higher from outside than from inside her head. It was like listening to a recording – and she'd always hated the sound of her voice on audio tape. But then the sound changed, evolved, stopped being the voice of the earthly Clarrie and became a great wind, a cyclone whooshing and whirling. Omnipresent Clarrie put her invisible hands over her non-existent ears in an effort to block out the ear-splitting rushing sound, but she felt herself overwhelmed, and began to lose her balance in the air.

The room was gradually becoming vague and blurry – turning purple.

Help! shouted the invisible Clarrie, as she felt herself engulfed, sliding into a purple nothing, swallowed by her own mind, sucked into the black hole of her head like a piece of fluff whirling into the inside of a vacuum cleaner, while the diners chattered on.

And then it was over.

The room was the same as before. The stern couple still stared down out of the imposing yet entertaining portrait, the curtains were still the same voluminous expanse of gold and the candle flames still threw flickering reflections on to the crystal glasses, the silver cutlery and the faces of the seated guests. But Clarrie felt different.

She knew everything now. She knew that the Bone had something nasty bashing about in her tidy mind; that the Clay was a mass of sensual, animal experience; she knew that Kitchener was dominated by a vain and greedy child, and that Cruella coldly observed. She knew that Shiny was deprived of peace by his tormenting clanging bells and that the Hammock's soul was being slowly gnawed away; she knew that Tilda was holding out against a storm while deprived of nourishment and that Alex was going through the motions of a ridiculous empty performance, rising out of the floor only to sink back down, time and time again. Oh, yes, she knew everything now.

Clarrie felt heavy, as an astronaut might on returning to earth and the confines of a gravity-controlled existence after a refreshing spell of weightlessness. Her hands were cumbersome as she lifted her wine and sipped. She didn't want to be back in her body, governed by the limitations of flesh and blood. She couldn't recall how she had managed to step out of herself and suspected that it might never happen again.

*   *   *

None of them had any idea of what she had seen. They were finishing the last vestiges of trout, laying cutlery down, and the Clay was picking his teeth and trying to cover his belches. Tilda looked as though she was preoccupied with trying to decide whether to change the table-cloth before dessert. The Hammock was playing with a candle, much to Alex's obvious irritation. She scooped up molten wax that dripped down and watched it firm up between her fingertips, becoming rubbery and pliable. She rolled the lumps of wax into little balls and dropped them back into the flame again, an endless recycling.

Clarrie had an intuition that her trout might be trying to wink at her, but when she looked down she found instead that Tilda the little mermaid was lying dead on her plate, her hair flowing out across the remains of the potato and parsnip galette, her scaly silver tail smeared with almond and herb puree, her breasts held securely in a seashell bra and her eyes wide open, yellow and staring.

A high-pitched trill in regular double pulses – shrill and unexpected, reaching a part of the ear untouched by table-talk, tinkling glasses and clattering cutlery – woke up the diners, made a few hearts skip a beat or two and caused each person to feel a little more wide awake than was desirable.

Clarrie was thrown into confusion. Which of the dinner guests could be causing this persistent and unpleasant electronic noise? She was suspicious of Shiny because of his bell collection, but in fact the noise seemed to be coming from the table itself. She was about to put her ear to the table to listen more closely when it occurred to her that maybe the noise wasn't real – this was what happened when an alarm clock intruded into a dream and remained there while the reluctant sleeper tried hard to drive the sound away. She waited, fully expecting to wake up and find herself at home, in bed with Morris, but the dream stayed and the clock rang on like an electronic bird singing in short, rhythmic, tuneless blasts. Then she noticed perplexed expressions all around her and realised that the others could hear it too. This was no alarm clock – it was the sound of a ringing telephone, and it was coming from somewhere under the table. But why on earth would Alex and Tilda keep a phone under the table?

Clarrie spotted annoyance on the Bone's face when the Clay bent to grab her sensible brown leather handbag from under her chair and drew out his mobile phone from the back pocket.

The Bone's face became a grey rock with a protruding ledge for an upper lip while her husband barked into the receiver,

'Brian Thackston . . . Yes . . . yes . . . I see . . .'

The words, 'How – many – times—' came out like bullets, shot from somewhere behind the Bone's gritted teeth.

'Perhaps . . .' began Tilda, gesturing out of the dining-room, and her voice trailed off, limply.

'Well . . . just a moment . . . yes . . . just a moment . . .' The Clay was fully aware of his wife's rock-like exterior, and seemed to be juggling his priorities, turning away so that the Bone couldn't look at him.

'Bloody infernal thing – *everywhere* we go.' The Bone stopped as she registered she had sworn. She put a hand to her mouth, shocked at what had jumped out of it, and took a hasty gulp of her wine.

'You have my sympathy, dear,' said Cruella.

'Alex isn't allowed to use his when I'm anywhere around,' said Tilda.

The Clay was clambering to his feet, trying ineffectually to push his chair back. It began to topple and Clarrie had to reach out to catch it before it could hit the floor. It seemed to take place in slow motion, like a great sporting moment captured forever on camera.

'Yes . . . just a minute,' the Clay repeated, and put his hand over the mouthpiece. 'I'm sorry, everybody, this is most rude of me,' he half whispered.

'Yes, it is,' said the Bone.

'I'm sorry,' the Clay repeated, addressing himself primarily to Tilda. 'May I go out in the hall and finish this call, please? I won't be long.' He was anxious in his apology. 'I won't be long,' he said again.

'Be my guest,' said Tilda – which, of course, he was. She glanced at the Bone, who was twisting her napkin tightly in her hands as though she would like to throttle her husband with it.

'These things happen,' said Alex, as the Clay lumbered out of the room and closed the door behind him.

'They certainly do,' said the Bone. 'You have no idea how often. And to think – he put that dreadful thing in *my* handbag. *My* handbag! And without asking.'

There was a long silence while the Bone twisted the napkin this way and that. Everybody was fiddling with something, and the Clay's muffled voice could be heard ranting away in the hall.

Clarrie wondered if she should do something – but what? She could dance on the table or paint a smile on the Bone's face with a finger full of almond and herb purée, but what good would it do? She stared at the shaft of bright light poking under the dining-room door and wished that the Clay would hurry up with his phone call. If he was much longer about it the Bone might just screw her face up so tightly that it would turn into a fist and go flying out to punch him.

Now they were all staring at the shaft of light, all willing the Clay to come back into the room, smiling. A kind of paralysis had set in and the Clay was the only person able to break it. It was as though they were waiting for the coming of the Holy Spirit.

'Some friends of ours had this funny phase once,' said Alex, dreamily. 'They decided they had become slaves to technology – yes, I think that was the phrase they used. So they got rid of their phone and their TV and video. Chucked them on the rubbish dump, just like that.'

'And did it make them happier?' asked Cruella.

'They claimed it did,' said Alex. 'But they kept coming over to our place all the time to watch their favourite films and phone their friends.'

'Everywhere we go, day and night,' muttered the Bone.

Clarrie imagined the Clay and the Bone lying side by side in a brass-knobbed bed. The Clay was wearing a vest and reaching for his portable phone which lay trilling away between them, while the Bone, in sensible flannelette night-dress, was sobbing noisily into her pillow.

'Women don't need those things,' said Cruella, jovially. 'You wouldn't find one of *us* on the phone in the middle of a dinner party.'

'Sometimes a man needs his phone,' said Kitchener, and

the Bone narrowed her eyes to a point where they almost disappeared.

'That's absolute rot about women and portable phones!' said Alex, displaying a certain relief that they were all talking again rather than just staring at the door. 'I couldn't possibly count the number of times I've seen a woman on a train making a quick call to dear old hubby to ask him to pick her up from the station.'

'Ah, but that's different,' said Tilda, without saying exactly *how* it was different.

The Bone was heard to hiccup loudly as she drained the dregs of her glass and thumped it down on the table. Clarrie was surprised it didn't break.

The trickle of light expanded and became a flood as the Clay opened the door and shuffled back into the room, switching off his phone. When he reached his chair, he stood about awkwardly, seemingly reluctant to sit.

'Well, sit down then,' snapped the Bone, without looking directly at him.

'Yes,' said the Clay, and squeezed through to his chair, almost tripping over a trailing handbag strap as he went. His face was dejected and apologetic. He began to reach for the Bone's handbag to put the offending phone away, but received a sharp look and withdrew, laying it on the table next to his empty plate.

'Is something wrong, Brian?' Alex voiced what they were all thinking.

'No, not really, no more than usual,' said the Clay, and sat down slowly. 'It's just so difficult to find competent staff these days – well, competent *trustworthy* staff, anyway. Most people are out to rob you blind.'

'So who's been robbing you blind this time then?' spat the Bone. 'What heinous crime has been committed against the great Brian Thackston? I'm sure you're just dying to tell everyone. Never mind that you promised me there would be no business talk tonight. Never mind that you swore you'd leave your infernal phone at home. You bastard!'

'Pauline – some water for Mrs Thackston, please,' said Tilda, pink and anxious.

'I don't want any water. More wine please, Pauline.'

Pauline hovered, unsure.

'Is that really a very good idea, love?' The Clay loosened his tie and struggled with a button at his collar, clearly hot and bothered.

The Bone grabbed at her glass while Pauline was still in the act of pouring.

'I'm damned if I'll let you of all people lecture me about the hazards of excess,' she snapped.

'Nobody's lecturing you, Chrissie,' the Clay tried.

'Perhaps I could suggest a little drink in the lounge before dessert . . .' Alex said in a falsely bright voice.

'I'm not going to the lounge, I'm staying right where I am,' said the Bone. 'And so is he.' She pointed at her floundering husband with a dagger-like finger.

'Well, perhaps the rest of us could think about adjourning briefly.' There was a note of futility in Tilda's voice.

'This is just absolutely great.' The Bone was a vocal explosion. Her head disappeared behind a cloud of noise. 'You'll either spend the rest of the evening carping about some poor underpaid employee and boring everybody rigid, or else you'll sit sulking and sullen for hours on end.' She was puffing and blowing down her tortured red nostrils in a most alarming manner. 'I'd been looking forward to this evening, Brian. I haven't been out in ages. I've been stuck in the house taking your phone messages while you swan about at dinners and functions, and the one night we go out together . . . the *one night* in such a long time . . . you have to go and ruin it, don't you. You always spoil everything.' She paused for breath and took in too much air, gulping involuntarily, swallowing the next stream of vitriol.

'Steady on, old thing,' said Kitchener, forgetting perhaps that she wasn't his 'old thing' and that this was none of his business.

'Like a saucepan boiling over,' murmured Clarrie, but nobody was listening.

'Would you clear the table, please, Pauline,' said Tilda. Pauline moved forward to stack crockery, and Tilda began asking them all to pass plates down to her, perhaps to create a diversion.

The Clay's pudgy face was pale. He opened his mouth as though to say something and then closed it again.

'Brian?' Alex was worried.

'Has everybody finished eating?' asked Tilda in a high voice.

'How dare you go putting your blasted phone in my handbag?' said the Bone. 'Is nothing sacred?'

'Like a kettle bubbling and bubbling,' said Clarrie.

'A woman's handbag is the most secret place in the world,' came Cruella's fixedly bright voice. 'She keeps it a secret even from her husband – *especially* from her husband. It's even more secret than a woman's underwear drawer.'

'I'm sorry, love,' said the Clay, all weak and sagging.

'Like a balloon with the air coming out,' said Clarrie, and still nobody paid any attention.

Tilda moved quickly, carrying a stack of plates and gesturing for Pauline to follow, creating a sharp breeze as the door swung closed behind her.

'I . . . I want you to know . . .' said the Bone, seeming to struggle with her words.

'Yes, darling?' came the Clay's weary voice.

'I want you to know . . .' the Bone repeated. Her face had become white and sweaty. 'I . . . oh, dear.'

Clarrie watched, amused, as the Bone jumped to her feet, one hand clutching her mouth, and rushed for the door, very nearly taking the table cloth and everything on top of it with her. She was out in a flash and could be heard running up the stairs.

'Oh my God,' said Alex after a few seconds of silence. 'I do hope she knows where the bathroom is.'

'Excuse me,' said the Clay, grimly, as he slowly rose to his feet. 'I'd better go to her.'

He turned back as he reached the door, and mopped his brow with a large white handkerchief. 'I do apologise for this . . . embarrassing scene.' He looked at the floor as he spoke, unable to meet Alex's eyes. 'I'm afraid she just isn't very good with alcohol.' He placed the handkerchief back in a deep pocket. 'It's happened before,' he sighed. 'But not for quite a while.'

He opened his mouth as though to add something further, but then seemed to change his mind and shut it again. With a shrug, he left the room, closing the door carefully behind him. The sounds of his footsteps on the stairs were slow and heavy.

'Like a sad old bear,' whispered Clarrie.

'Clarrie dear, perhaps a little hush.' Cruella put a finger to her lips as though addressing a small child.

'It's like what a kid does, isn't it?'

Tilda started at the sound of Pauline's voice, and came back into the kitchen. She had been hovering in the hall, listening out for sounds from upstairs, trying to catch some sound of the Thackstons talking in the bathroom – even retching noises – anything would be better than this silence.

Pauline was sitting at the kitchen table, toying with an unlit cigarette.

'What?' said Tilda, fidgeting and twisting her wedding ring as she also sank onto a seat.

'You know, vomming. You'd think she'd have got past all that years ago.'

'Some people miss out on phases of life that others take for granted,' muttered Tilda, as much to herself as to Pauline.

'Eh?'

'Well, I doubt very much that Mrs Thackston has ever really been a teenager, doing teenage things like getting drunk and being sick.'

'Why not?' Pauline began searching in a pocket for something – a lighter perhaps.

'I don't know. Religion I suppose. Christina Thackston probably fell asleep one night as a child, and woke the next morning an adult – nothing in between, no fun, no heartbreak, no getting drunk and being sick.'

'Unlucky,' said Pauline, producing a lighter.

'I expect that every now and then she gets the urge to be a teenager – but it's too late for all that, and so she ends up making herself look ridiculous . . . Hey, no smoking in the house, please, Pauline. You'll have to go in the garden.'

'What, like you do?' She flicked out the flame on her lighter and dropped it on the table with a look of irritation.

'I don't know what you're talking about,' snapped Tilda.

'Yeah, right. I'm not going out there to freeze my tits off,' said Pauline. 'I'd sooner do without.'

'Fine by me,' said Tilda.

And they sat for a while, scowling at each other.

*   *   *

Clarrie wanted to help, she really did. Alex was looking as though he might cry at any moment and Tilda might *well* be having a secret cry out in the kitchen. The whole evening was geared around the Clay – this much Clarrie understood. Every mouthful of food consumed by every person at this table was for *him* – every word uttered, every munching motion of a jaw, every churning growl of a stomach. Tilda had spent many long hours struggling with shopping bags and sweating over steaming pans for him and a small fly had got itself trapped inside an ice cube to make its own unique contribution to the dinner. In a few hours, they would all go to the toilet for the Clay – and for Alex, of course.

The dinner party had failed, this much was clear. And it had failed because of the Thackstons themselves. First the phone call had broken the peace and led to their embarrassing public disagreement – and then the Bone's drunkenness had risen up like a great evil monster, making it impossible for the evening to be salvaged. What could be done now? It had clearly become a question of damage limitation. Looking around the table, Clarrie could see her own thoughts echoed in every face. Everybody was hoping that the Thackstons would emerge from the bathroom very soon, that a taxi would swiftly be called, and that the Clay would lead his wife away, muttering something about how she was feeling unwell – some feeble excuse that they could all pretend to believe in, ignoring the humiliating true cause of her 'illness.'

'So what do we do now?' asked Shiny, at length.

'We wait for that woman to stop throwing up and come back downstairs,' said Cruella, her voice revealing her impatience.

'This really is hideous, isn't it,' muttered the Hammock, dropping another globule of wax into the candle flame.

'Well, it could be worse,' tried Kitchener, somewhat lamely.

'How?' snapped Alex. 'Go on, Roger, tell me how it could be worse. I want to know.'

Kitchener shrugged. 'Just trying to look on the bright side, that's all. Trying to jolly things along.'

'Worse' was a word that Clarrie knew about – a word with a long history and an even longer future – a word that was part of some secret language which nobody quite dared speak. 'Worse' was a loaded word, and Clarrie knew all about loaded words; could spot them a mile off. She had a few of her own – words that when uttered could create and destroy worlds.

'I'm sure the day will come when we'll look back on this evening and laugh, you know, Alex,' said Shiny.

But Alex was somewhere else, staring into the wreckage: at the red wine stain covered in salt, napkins thrown down, glasses smeared with lipstick, scattered crumbs, the occasional fish bone, splatters of green purée and hardened lumps of wax that had dripped down from the candles. He could have been looking at the scene of a car crash just after the ambulance had left.

The lounge was cold and empty after the chaos of the dining-room. Tilda fussed about, lighting candles and trying to create an atmosphere, while her mind was somewhere upstairs with the Thackstons. Alex led the guests in and began pouring drinks.

Tilda moved up to him and squeezed his left shoulder but he shrugged her off.

'What do you want, darling, Gee and tee?' His voice was flat and he sounded as though he needed to swallow. He looked like a little boy whose birthday party has just been cancelled as punishment for some minor misdeed.

'Mmm, yes.' She felt the sting of rejection. It was impossible to get close to him, as though he had surrounded himself with an electric fence.

'Do you think she's a bit of an old soak?' Clive asked lightly.

'No, old soaks can hold their drink.' Judy relaxed into the Chesterfield, curling up like a cat with her shoes on the floor in front of her.

'She's probably a woman who usually keeps herself very tightly reined in,' Heidi said quietly. 'This evening she lost control, that's all.'

'She's a pain in the fucking arse, that's what she is.' Alex was still busy with bottles.

'Alex, please!' Tilda could see how close he was to losing his temper completely and taking it out on whoever was nearest – herself, no doubt.

'Well, what the fuck am I supposed to do?' He dropped the bottle opener with a dull thunk. 'I feel so helpless. No matter how much one does to ensure a successful evening, events just move entirely out of one's hands.'

'Yes, I know.' Tilda thought of the beautiful coconut bavarois with tropical fruit sauce, waiting in the kitchen. The dessert was to have been her triumph . . . now it looked as though the evening might break up before it could be served.

'It was wonderful so far as it went. The food was exquisite. They'll ask you both over very soon, mark my words. There'll be other times.' Judy attempted to soothe.

'Rome wasn't built in a day,' Clive added.

'But they *won't* invite us over, don't you see!' snapped Alex. 'This will be the end of it. They'll be too embarrassed to want to have anything to do with us again. Brian will avoid me – he'll be crossing the street when he sees me coming. He'll never be able to look me in the eye again – and all because of his stupid bloody wife!'

'Oh, come on, Alex. Surely it won't be like that? You're getting this all out of proportion.' But even as she said it, Tilda knew he was right. Alex wasn't important enough for Brian Thackston to bother to conquer his embarrassment.

'I'm getting it out of proportion, am I?' murmured Alex. 'Just you wait and see.'

'And to think,' said Tilda, 'I was worried that *Clarrie* would ruin the evening. Fate, that's what it is. Destiny and fate.'

'Where *is* Clarrie, anyway?' somebody asked.

Nobody had noticed when she slipped away. Now her absence was vaguely unsettling.

'What if she's gone to find the Thackstons?' Tilda wondered aloud. 'Oh God, as if things aren't bad enough . . .'

'No, she'll be wandering aimlessly,' said Judy, brightly.

'I don't want her wandering aimlessly in my house,' said Alex. 'You'd better have a look for her, Tilly.'

'I will not!' Tilda wanted to throw her glass at his head. 'Of all the bloody cheek.'

Alex met her steely glare. 'I don't see what's so cheeky about that – I'm busy here.' He gestured at the bottles and glasses. 'Somebody has to look after her, she's the kind of person who needs looking after.'

'Well, I've been looking after *your* sister-in-law all evening. Do it yourself.' Tilda sat on a straight-backed chair, folded her arms and crossed her legs. She closed herself up and defied him with her posture.

'All right, all right.' Alex began mumbling inaudibly as he left the room and shuffled up the stairs.

The silence was unsettling, and Clive was becoming restless. 'Do you mind if I use your phone, Tilda?' he asked. 'I think I'll give the baby sitter a quick call – just to check that Max is all right.'

'What on earth for?' asked Heidi. 'I'm sure Saul would phone if there was a problem.'

'There's no harm in checking up,' said Clive, getting to his feet. 'And I might go for a fag in the garden. I know how Alex feels about smoking in the house.'

'I'll join you outside. I could do with a breath of fresh air,' said Roger.

'He's ever so sweet, the way he worries,' said Heidi as the lounge door closed behind the two men. 'We had a bit of trouble with our last baby sitter, you see.'

Oh, dear, thought Tilda. Now she's going to start talking about babies and it's going to upset me.

'That's it, love. You just get it all out.' Brian stroked the back of his wife's head as she puked into the toilet over and over again, groaning loudly in between retching. The stroking actually seemed to annoy her and she made feeble attempts to shake him off, but he persisted because he couldn't think of anything else to do.

Now she was trying to speak. 'I saw you looking at her. I saw you.'

'Who? What are you on about, Chrissie?' But he knew who she meant.

'That Heidi woman. You've barely taken your eyes off her tits all night.' She lifted her head from the toilet bowl with difficulty, and slumped down in a heap.

He handed her a piece of toilet paper to wipe her mouth. 'That's rubbish. That's the drink talking.' Heidi Stilbourne did have a very nice pair of breasts, it had to be said. She also had a sweet little arse that wiggled when she walked.

'You always look at other women. I obviously don't satisfy you.' Her eyeballs were rolling around as she struggled to focus.

And what was the harm in looking? Of course he looked – but he never touched. 'You're imagining things, Chrissie. Of course you satisfy me. You're my wife.'

She gave a little whimper and began to cry. 'I'm not a real woman,' she spluttered. 'I can't give you . . . I can't . . .'

'That's enough.' Brian eased himself down onto the floor with difficulty and took her in his arms, doing his best, nevertheless, to keep her sour breath away from his face. 'Don't think about all that now. Everything goes dark when you've had a few too many. Everything seems worse than it really is.'

'Yes,' she sniffed into his chest.

He was rocking her slightly, as you might rock a baby.

'I've let you down again,' she moaned. 'I always let you down.'

'No, you haven't,' he lied.

'I have. I do this every time, don't I?'

'Not *every* time.' That was the truth, anyway.

'Will you look after me, Brian?' Her voice had become a whisper. 'Will you look after me?'

Alex flicked on the lamp, which cast a rectangular green glow across the photograph album lying on his desk.

'God, I'm such a fraud,' he muttered, surprising himself with the sound of his own voice as he sank into the creaking black leather of his swivel chair.

Why did I say that? he asked himself.

Because it's the truth, came his own immediate answer.

He reached for a toothpick from the china pot next to his computer and began to search for congealed food in his molars. He was obsessional about his teeth, always had been. Almost all the dreams he could ever remember having involved crumbling teeth, teeth falling out for no reason, decay on a grand scale or the discovery of vampire fangs growing where his canines had been.

I've never had a single original idea in my life, he realised, gloomily.

You only have to look around this room to see how incapable I am of thinking for myself. This chair – why, I must have seen chairs like it in hundreds of films and soap operas. J.R. Ewing had an identical one, I'm sure!

Absent-mindedly, he reached for the photograph album, noticing the sickly hue of the skin on his hand, bathed in green light.

And this lamp – how many times have I seen identical green lamps on the television? No wonder I have to go crawling to men like Brian Thackston.

He dwelt briefly on the possibility of gutting his once-beloved study and beginning again, turning it into something entirely different. Perhaps he could do it up to resemble the deck of a ship, with a wooden floor and a hammock to stretch out on when he needed a nap – blue walls with gulls painted here and there, lifebelts hung at waist height and a sound system playing gentle tidal rhythms to soothe him in his more anguished moments.

He caught sight of his green skin again and shook himself out of the reverie. It was a ridiculous idea. He'd start to hate it almost as soon as the decorating was done, and anyway it wasn't even *his* idea. He'd seen it in some catalogue or other. Such gimmicks were more Morris's style when it came down to it.

Morris . . . To think there had been a time when the brothers were inseparable, when he'd virtually worshipped the ground Morris walked on.

Alex opened the album and flipped back the sheet of paper that protected the first page of photographs.

And here they were, he and Morris hand in hand on a beach, wearing identical blue swimming trunks, hair tousled by an English sea breeze. Morris carried a plastic bucket and spade in his free hand, while the smaller Alex had a lot of sand stuck to his legs and was screwing up his eyes to keep out the sun.

Broadstairs, 1969, proclaimed the caption in their mother's round handwriting. Their father had added a further line in his spidery scrawl, *The day we lost Morris*.

Alex could remember this event clearly – he and Morris on their 'great expedition', his brother as Christopher Columbus and himself as Columbus' first mate. Neither of them was absolutely sure who Columbus was, except that he was some kind of sailor-person who discovered islands, but that didn't matter. Morris led the way as they waded into the sea together. Alex was only six and couldn't swim, so the more intrepid nine-year-old Morris was forced to restrain his urge to plunge into deep water. Instead they went in up to Alex's thighs and wandered along the length of the bay until their parents' windbreak became a distant coloured square amongst a crowd of heads and legs and deck chairs.

It was when they reached the place where the bay ended and became unknown territory that Alex began to panic. Their father had given them a stern-faced lecture earlier in the day. They were not to paddle out of the bay – it wasn't safe. Two small boys very much like themselves who had gone around the end of the bay only the previous summer had been cut off by the tide and drowned. It didn't occur to Alex to doubt his father's word – grown-ups always told the truth.

Here Morris was, trying to tell him that his father was making it up to scare them. Lying to them. How could this be? Morris was saying he had heard there was a secret cave around the corner and he wanted to see it for himself. Morris was calling him a chicken and a cowardy custard while Alex stood crying, rubbing salt in his eyes and peeing helplessly into the sea. Morris was wading and swimming away into the deep water, too deep for Alex to cope with, and Alex was stumbling back to the shore, running across the sand which stuck itself all over his feet, feeling the breeze blow cold on his wet legs, blindly treading on treasured sand-castles and falling into a hole that somebody's father had dug.

Morris was lost for two whole hours, although when he was found by the coastguard, wandering aimlessly in a neighbouring bay, he claimed not to have been lost at all. He claimed he had been playing in a magic cave and hadn't realised how late it was. Mum and Dad were too relieved that he was safe even to think of smacking him – Dad was very red in the face and Mum was actually crying. Both boys were given ice-creams, but somehow Alex felt cheated. While Morris was cavorting about in the enchanted cave, he had been stuck with their wailing, worrying parents who had kept shaking him and shouting at him. He couldn't help feeling that he had missed out on something special, that he had always been missing out.

No, Morris hadn't been lost on that day, Alex thought to himself. Perhaps he ought to cut out his father's spidery caption and transfer it to the album containing Morris's *wedding* photographs. Yes, that would be more appropriate.

'Just look at my amazing bride, isn't she wonderful!' Morris's cheeks were pink with champagne and exhilaration.

'Well, yes, of course. Very pretty.' Alex turned to regard the spindly figure in red capering around energetically at the far end of the room. A manic grin on her face, she moved in wild jerks that bore no relation to the rhythm of the music. Alex's father, who had been trying to dance with her, had retreated to the buffet table and was dodging about in the manner of a goalkeeper, clearly worried that Clarrie might lurch into the table and topple the cake to the floor.

'*Very pretty.*' Morris aped Alex's tight voice. 'Come on, Alex, no one would call her pretty, not even me. She's . . . she's something else.' He threw an arm around his younger brother's shoulder and gestured vaguely at the paintings hung at the rear of the gallery, behind the buffet table. 'Look at the pictures, little bro. Look and learn.'

Alex gazed up at the huge red canvases, and for a moment he thought he glimpsed something of what Morris was trying to show him. The pictures were without apparent form or meaning, but there was something in the red shapes; something frenzied and vivid. For just that brief moment the paintings seemed to be dancing along with Clarrie – the woman and her art were like red flames leaping up the walls and licking the ceiling. He took a gulp of champagne and wiped a bead of sweat from his brow.

'You see it, don't you,' Morris whispered into his brother's ear. His goatee tickled Alex's neck, and Alex pulled sharply away to scratch the itch.

'See what? I'm very happy for you, Morris, but you're a pretentious old sod, and you always will be.' Alex delivered the words lightly, rounded off with a laugh, but Morris clearly wasn't in the mood for jokes – he was scowling.

'Frightening, isn't it,' he said, looking Alex straight in the eye. 'My wife is, as you can see, entirely unselfconscious. She isn't a controlled person, not like you or me. Control doesn't feature in her life.'

Alex set down his champagne glass on a window-sill. The music was suddenly too loud, pounding the inside of his head and vibrating in his teeth. He sighed wearily. 'Don't draw me into this, Morris. I don't want to argue with you, not on your wedding day.'

'No, I'm sure you don't,' snorted Morris. 'Picking a fight with the bridegroom wouldn't be at all the done thing, now would it. We can't have that sort of behaviour, not at a respectable gathering like this one.'

'Why are you doing this to me?' said Alex. 'Why do you always try to ram your views down my throat? It's up to you how you want to lead your life, and it's up to me how I lead mine. I'm happy for you, really I am. Let's leave it at that, shall we?'

Now Morris was the one to laugh. 'Jesus, you do talk bollocks, Alex. You're always judging me, always trying to outdo me; undercut me. I've never known anyone so competitive as you, or so negative. What I can't make up my mind about is whether you want to be like me or whether you want me to be like you. Which is it, little bro?' He leant forward into Alex's face, so that their noses touched, and stared deep into his eyes.

'You're drunk.' Alex pulled away stiffly. 'That's all.'

'Quite right, Alex. Quite right,' said Morris, reaching for a champagne bottle. 'Top up?'

'Yes, why not.' Alex smiled, with an effort, and Morris filled his glass somewhat inaccurately.

'Coming for a dance, darling?' Tilda appeared at his side as Morris mooched off, topping up glasses as he went and jiggling his shoulders to the music.

'I hate him sometimes.' Alex spoke the words under his breath, but Tilda had heard.

'No, you don't. It's sibling rivalry, that's all. You love him to bits but he drives you nuts. That's what having brothers and sisters is all about.' She gave his cheek a playful pinch.

'I guess you're right.' Alex turned to look at his wife. She was radiant tonight, delicious in blue crushed velvet. And she moved like a dream. 'Let's dance,' he said. But as he took her hand and led her onto the dance floor, a ball of red fury catapulted across the room and landed heavily on his right foot – squarely on the toe with the corn.

'Sorry, Alex,' said Clarrie, from somewhere under her mop of curls. 'Didn't see you there.'

'Quite all right,' he winced, gritting his teeth. 'No harm done.' From somewhere across the room, he could hear the sound of his brother's laughter.

There were more photos of the Broadstairs holiday: the boys with some unknown children who were dressed in Victorian costume for 'Dickens Week' (whatever that was), Dad asleep in a deck chair, Mum paddling – apparently shouting at them not to take the picture. Then there were photos of their old house, photos of himself and Morris in school uniform, pictures of birthday parties . . . Actually, he was beginning to wonder why the album was out on his desk in the first place. He hadn't looked at these pictures in years. Was it possible that Tilda had been poking about in his study – not even bothering to conceal her nosiness by replacing the album on the shelf where she had found it?

The more he imagined Tilda searching through his cupboards and digging through his drawers, the more likely the idea became. He found he was seething with anger. How dare she! After everything she'd ever said about the importance of personal privacy and the right to keep certain things secret even from the person you were married to – all the time she was saying this she had been poking around in *his* private room whenever the mood suited her!

Alex wanted to hit someone – Tilda or Morris or the pudgy face of Brian Thackston or Clarrie's mad confused eyes or the drunken bitch who had ruined his important evening. He slammed the photograph album shut and bashed his fist against the desk with all the force he could muster, shouting, 'Damn it all to hell!' when pain shot up his wrist. He sucked at his tender red knuckles and felt tears of anger and humiliation forming in his eyes, ready to ooze down the usually mild-mannered face.

They were probably laughing at him right now, the whole bloody lot of them, huddled together around the drinks cabinet, giggling and whispering like children in a school. Perhaps the Thackstons were down there too – perhaps it was all a set-up. The minute he had left the room to look for Clarrie, Judy Marshall and Tilda had gone creeping up to the bathroom door and whispered,

'It's all right. He's gone now – you can come out.'

And then the Thackstons had come wriggling out to join in the party that was taking place behind his back.

OK, so it was all ridiculous, preposterous, beyond the realms of possibility – the kind of conspiracy theory that only a chronic schizophrenic would dare to consider – but maybe there was an element of truth in it, all the same. Maybe the Thackstons were secretly glad to have an excuse to leave such a terrible dinner party. Maybe Brian was perching on the edge of the bath at this very moment, congratulating Christina on her ingenuity in faking a drunken scene which provided them with an excuse to go home, thanking her for rescuing them from an evening of mind-numbing tedium in the company of a bunch of dull mediocrities, the worst of whom was their servile host, rather obviously acting under the misapprehension that he was an interesting person and desirable business partner.

'Alex?'

It was Heidi, of course. Heidi bloody Stilbourne, damn and blast her. She was peering around the door, too nervous to come right in. He knew this without looking. His back was to the door and he was damned if he was going to swivel around and let her see his face.

'Alex, it's Heidi.'

She was talking as though to a child, her voice unnaturally soft.

'I know who it is.'

Oh, God, he could feel those tears fighting their way through. He wouldn't be able to hold out against them much longer. For some strange reason the tune 'She'll be Coming Round the

Mountain When She Comes' was chugging relentlessly through his head. It had been all day, on and off.

'Alex, can I talk to you for a moment, please?'

To say what? What could she possibly have to say to him? Miss bloody Successful wanted to talk to Mr Failure, did she? Sasky Klimt, the renowned designer of hideously expensive dresses for the thirty-somethings, wanted a quick chat with the man who couldn't even design a satisfactory dinner party.

'Go away.'

'But I'm worried about you.'

'I just want to be on my own for a while.'

His voice was contorting strangely from the effort to sound normal. He sounded as though somebody was holding a gun to his head.

There was a moment of silence. He could hear her soft breathing and then he heard the door scrape against the carpet – she was going, after all. She was leaving. He began to feel relief, but it was a touch premature.

'I won't go until you turn around and look at me.'

Was a man never allowed a quiet moment to himself? Was he never allowed to shed a few tears in the privacy of his own home? Would nobody ever show him the respect he deserved, needed, craved and failed to get? He could smell her perfume – Chanel, wasn't it? Chanel number something-or-other.

'*Please*, Alex.'

The tears were flowing freely now. He never could stand to hear women beg – especially when he couldn't understand *why* they were begging. He was cracking under the strain, losing control. A huge sob came out of his mouth, making him sound like a performing seal. In a few seconds he would be required to balance a beach-ball on the end of his nose and clap with his flippers while Heidi blew a whistle and smiled for the cameras.

And for his next trick, Alex the amazing performing seal will make a complete and utter fool of himself – again!

And he was scrambling out of his chair, tripping over his shoe laces, gulping air and tears and phlegm and then tripping again on the steel base of the chair and almost falling on his face and coughing and grabbing at the door to steady himself and barely able to see because of all the tears and the mess and then grabbing and grabbing at her face and her hair and her breasts and pressing himself against her warm body in the ropy dress and crying some more and laughing and kissing and kissing and kissing while she kissed him back and grabbed him back and murmured something like 'Mureuemphul' – although it was obviously something else that she was saying and she just couldn't say it properly because Alex was eating her mouth.

Clarrie shifted so that her left eye was pressed to the crack in the cupboard door – the right eye needed a rest – and felt glad that she had married the elder of the Stone brothers, rather than the younger, who was not looking particularly sexy even in the midst of what would appear to be an outpouring of vast passion – the kind of passion that was worthy of a tragic hero, no less.

She hadn't intended to hide in the cupboard but when she'd heard Alex's unmistakable tread on the stairs she had panicked. After all, she was intruding in his study – a room she knew very well to be strictly out of bounds. She had been massively relieved on hearing him approach the study door, to find that the cupboard *wasn't* divided into shelves, as she had feared, and that in fact it contained nothing but a couple of jackets hanging on hooks and smelling of Alex. There was just enough room for a small Clarrie, provided she didn't need to move about too much, so she hopped inside and left the door open just a crack, like the characters used to do in those children's books by C.S. Lewis.

While the Hammock reached backwards to push the study door closed and then continued kissing with renewed vigour, Clarrie reflected that in this instance she had not intended to be a voyeur – it was a role forced on her by circumstances. In fact, she wished they would hurry up and get it over with – whatever 'getting it over with' might happen to entail – the cupboard was not exactly spacious, after all, and her neck was beginning to ache. It briefly occurred to her that Alex and the Hammock were so wrapped up in each other they might not notice her creeping out of the cupboard and leaving the room. She contemplated this possibility. If only they would move a few feet to the left she was sure she could slip past without them seeing her. Only a few feet . . .

Just as Clarrie was about to make a mad dash for freedom,

Alex broke away and sat down again in the swivel chair, leaving the Hammock dishevelled, arms still outstretched.

'Darling, what's wrong?' she asked, breathlessly.

Alex smoothed his hair and helped himself to another toothpick from the china jar. 'You're a scheming bitch, that's what's wrong.'

'I'm not. How could you say that.' She moved so that she was half standing, half sitting on the edge of his desk. Her breasts were now at his eye level, and he wrenched his gaze free of them to tilt his head up and look into her face when he spoke.

'Why did you come here this evening? You know perfectly well how I feel.' He thrust the pick into his mouth and began noisily digging at the back somewhere.

'It wasn't my decision. Tilda rang up and spoke to Clive. He accepted the invitation – what was I supposed to do!' She fussed with a shoulder strap and tossed back her hair.

Clarrie sighed quietly and switched back to the right eye. The mad dash was out of the question now. She could be stuck in this cupboard for a long time.

'You could have made an excuse – said you were ill or something. You're an intelligent woman, for God's sake.' He gestured wildly with the toothpick, stabbing at the air.

'But I wanted to see you.' Her voice cracked, she began weeping.

Clarrie reflected that the Hammock cried very prettily, a skill which few women could master. She herself was one of the majority who look hideous when crying; puffiness, red blotches, lots of snot, eyes becoming small and piggy. Most women could inspire pity or concern with their tears; certainly not desire. But the Hammock appeared to be inspiring just this – judging from the way Alex turned away a fraction and crossed his legs – trying to conceal something, perhaps? The Hammock's eyes had become huge and glassy, magnified by the tears. With each passing second she seemed more golden, glowing somehow. She was like a magnificent lioness about to make her kill.

'I've missed you,' she sobbed.

'You have no right to miss me. And stop that bloody crying.' He swivelled further around so that he didn't have to look at her.

Clarrie felt as though she were watching a soap opera – except for Alex's priggishness. A good soap opera would never have priggishness written into an emotional confrontation. Morris was occasionally priggish too – perhaps it ran in the family, perhaps they came from a long line of unbearable prigs.

'No *right*? It's a feeling. It has nothing to do with rights.' The Hammock was becoming angry now, the tears drying up.

'Then you have no right to tell me about it. You have no right to come to my house and parade yourself in front of me like a carrot being dangled in front of some poor bloody donkey, always out of reach.'

Yes, he really *was* rather like a donkey – a stubborn old donkey that wouldn't stop braying and snuffling.

'But I'm not out of reach, am I.' She bent towards him and began gently to stroke his face. He allowed this to continue for a few moments and then removed her hand somewhat roughly, but stayed hanging onto it. Her wrist looked uncomfortable in his grasp.

'You're nothing but a tease, Heidi. Just a tease.' But his voice was quiet now and he raised her hand to his mouth and kissed it softly before letting it go.

Clarrie approved of this – she thought the gesture quite gallant. Alex was recovering some of his self-control, and a touch of chivalry with it.

'You seem to have forgotten, Alex, that it was *your* choice to end it, not mine.'

He gave an incredulous snort. 'My choice! Don't make me laugh.' He jumped out of his chair, crossed the room to the window in a couple of strides and parted the Venetian blind to gaze down into the darkened garden. 'Your beloved husband's out there. Shall I give him a little wave?' He almost spat out the words. 'He seems to be engrossed in conversation with our charming waitress. Ah, how sweet – he's given her his jacket to keep her warm. Perhaps he's hoping for a bit of a quickie in the bushes in return.'

'Stop it, Alex.'

'Oh, I'm terribly sorry, my dear.' His voice was charged with sarcasm. 'How dreadful of me to cast aspersions on the good name of your sainted hubby. Ah, Roger's out there too.' He whipped around to sit down on the edge of the window-sill.

'Just leave Clive out of this, will you. I feel terrible about what I've done to him.'

'What *you've* done to *him* . . .'

Clarrie could only just hear Alex's last words, spoken very quietly under his breath. She found she was thinking about Tilda, remembering how she had looked when she was sitting in the bathroom with Cruella, remembering how her voice had sounded.

Judy, I'm so unhappy at the moment . . . It's just that my life feels so horribly empty all the time, and – well, I can't seem to fill it. I can't seem to—

'Why can't you leave Clive out of this?' Heidi snapped again.

Yes, leave him out of it, thought Clarrie. And leave yourself out of it, too. In fact, leave yourself in a room on your own somewhere until you've stopped being priggish and trying to talk like Humphrey Bogart.

But he had started again. 'Do you know how it feels to think about someone every minute of the day, to wake up thinking about them, to go to sleep thinking about them, never to have a moment's relief because they're always there in your head somewhere? Do you?' Alex jabbed at his head with the toothpick, succeeding in poking himself in the ear. His face was red and frenzied. He didn't pause to wait for an answer but continued with his monologue. 'Well, that's how I feel about you. That's why it had to be all or nothing – why I was prepared to give up *everything* for you . . . this place—' he waved an arm vaguely '—my marriage, my friends. Oh, yes, they would all have turned against me. Judy bloody Marshall would have been on the case in three seconds flat, with her poisonous gossip, getting them all on Tilda's side. But I wouldn't have cared, because I would have had *you*.'

'Did you ever tell anybody about us?' The Hammock obviously hadn't listened to a word he was saying.

'What?' He was irritated by her lack of response.

'I said, did you ever tell anybody about us?'

'No, of course not.' He seemed insulted that she should even suggest it. 'Why, did you?'

'No.' She stared down at her fingernails. 'Well, only Judy.'

Alex was so appalled that even his bottom became appalled and he almost slid off the window-sill. 'Judy! You told Judy!'

Clarrie thought about the unblinking eye and the wine-stained smile. She thought about Cruella and Tilda in the bathroom and then imagined Cruella and the Hammock in a different bathroom and then an infinite number of bathrooms with closed doors, each one containing Cruella with a packet of powder and a friend with a secret.

The Hammock was immediately on the defensive. 'Why shouldn't I tell Judy? She's my friend.' But she carried on fussing with her nails, as though she knew she had done the wrong thing.

'Why shouldn't you tell Judy ... Jesus Christ, give me strength!' Alex blustered, looking down at the garden as though looking at her would make him too angry.

'She wouldn't tell Tilda, you know. Judy doesn't operate like that.' There was a degree of uncertainty in the Hammock's voice. 'She wouldn't tell *anybody*. I know her.'

'Yes, and so do I.' The priggish tone had returned.

The Hammock picked up a retractable biro and fiddled with it, making the tip pop in and out, in and out. Clarrie found this somewhat irritating. She would have liked to open the cupboard door and confiscate the pen.

'And anyway, why should you care if she *does* tell Tilda?' The Hammock's voice was stronger again. 'A minute ago you were so obsessed with me you were going to give up *everything*, remember?'

Clarrie was beginning to like the Hammock. She had quite a neat turn of phrase when it suited her.

'Yes, well.'

Alex's 'yes, well' was the kind of 'yes, well' that doesn't actually go any further.

'Alex, it's not that I don't love you—' The Hammock's voice was tired, bored even. They had obviously had this discussion many times before.

'—you just don't love me *enough*, do you?' he cut in. 'You don't love me enough to want to be with me all of the time. You'd rather stay with your idiot of a husband – who, let me tell you this much, is not quite the man you think he is.'

'What do you mean by that?' She was startled. The conversation had taken a new direction.

Clarrie had an itch between her shoulder blades which she was longing to scratch, but she just couldn't reach it. Much as she didn't want Alex to get into trouble with Tilda, she began hoping against hope that someone would open the study door and interrupt this little tête-à-tête. Alex looked as though he was itching too – itching to tell the Hammock something about her husband, and fighting the urge to scratch.

'I said, what do you mean by that?'

'Nothing. It doesn't matter. He's just a prat, that's all – a prat who takes things for granted. And I'm stuck with a neurotic bimbo who's got about as much sex appeal as next door's cat!'

'Alex, there's no need to talk about Tilda like that!' The Hammock tried to seem shocked but was obviously pleased.

He finally got up from the window-sill and walked back over to her, taking her face between his hands none too gently so that he could look right into her eyes, exerting pressure so that her flesh bunched up and the cheek bones vanished, making her look rather unfortunately like a hamster.

'Stop playing, Heidi,' he hissed, inadvertently spitting into her face. 'Don't kid yourself about the kind of person you are. You don't give a flying fuck about Tilda – if you did, you'd never have jumped into bed with me!'

The Hammock produced a noise, an attempt to say something, but his hands made it difficult for her to move her mouth so she stopped trying.

Clarrie would never have thought Alex could be so masterful. She began to feel slightly nervous on the Hammock's behalf.

'I can't *do it* any more, did you know that?' He was trying not to shout too loudly and it was proving difficult. 'Is it common knowledge on the Judy Marshall grapevine yet?'

Was that a 'no' coming from somewhere in the hamster's mouth?

'It's all right for you women. You don't have to *perform*, do you. The worst that can happen to you is that you don't enjoy it.'

Another mumbled sound from the Hammock.

'I just can't get it up. Not with *her*, anyway.'

Clarrie couldn't see the expression in the Hammock's eyes, but she thought it was probably one of embarrassment because Alex suddenly let go of her and slumped back into the chair, his own face in his hands. He sat quietly, breathing deeply.

The Hammock touched her face lightly where he had held it. He had probably made it sore. 'Yes, well,' she said.

It was another one of those 'yes, well's. That was two in the last few minutes. How many more would there be before Clarrie could get out and scratch her itchy back? She made a decision, a kind of law – if there were three more 'yes, well's then she *had* to come out. That was the rule. She shook hands with an invisible person in her head to confirm it.

'And there's one other thing,' said Alex, letting his face emerge from behind his hands again. 'Are you really so sure that Max isn't mine?'

'Yes,' she answered without hesitation. 'I know you'd like him to be, but he isn't.'

The Hammock touched her sore cheek again and smiled. She was suddenly cool and confident after shattering Alex's illusions of fatherhood. She was moving towards him, gaining control of the situation, crouching down in front of the chair and peering up at him.

'You're right about one thing, Alex,' she began. 'I don't love you enough to leave Clive. And I'm not only staying with him for Max's sake. Your marriage might be dead but mine isn't. Clive and I still enjoy each other's company. We talk, we have fun, we have a good sex life and now we're planning a second child. Why would I want to leave all that?'

'Yes, well.'

There was the first 'yes, well'. Clarrie was only allowed another two. She was glad she couldn't clearly see the expression of hurt that must surely accompany it.

The Hammock changed her tone of voice, made it softer, more enticing. 'But that doesn't mean I don't like you, Alex, and it doesn't mean I don't miss you. Why don't you let me help you?'

'Help me?' He was puzzled.

'You know – *help* you.'

Clarrie had a nasty feeling about this. And the nasty feeling was made worse by one of the jackets behind her which was made of some kind of very scratchy material. She thought she might be allergic to it.

It became necessary for the Hammock to elucidate further. '*You* know. With your little problem.'

'Oh, God.'

'I'm sure there's nothing wrong with you, Alex. I'm sure everything would work properly with me.'

Alex rubbed at his neck. Clarrie supposed he must be getting hot under the collar – she'd never really thought about that saying before. Hot under the collar. Come to think of it, she was more than a little hot herself, and not only under the collar.

'Don't do me any favours. I'm not some cripple, you know.' His pride was wounded, the poor love.

'It isn't a favour. I want you.'

'Yes, well.'

There was another! Only one chance left. Clarrie braced herself to run.

'Let's do it now.' The Hammock was leaning closer. He must be able to feel her breath on his face.

'Now! Are you completely mad? With my wife, your husband and Judy Marshall downstairs!' Alex was embarrassed as well as shocked. His face was very red.

'Don't you want me any more?' Very little-girlish.

'It isn't that, it's just . . . well, it's downright *obscene*.'

Clarrie could hear the prudish tones of Alex's mother in the word 'obscene'. She could almost be hiding in his chest wagging a disapproving finger.

The Hammock had got to her feet with a slight cracking of the knees. She stifled a yawn and smoothed down her dress. 'Oh, well, if you're going to be boring . . . Honestly, Alex, I think perhaps you'd better get out the pipe and slippers. Shame, really, I was feeling quite horny.'

She turned and reached for the door, but then paused with her hand on the door handle, waiting. She didn't have to wait long.

'Right!' he said as he jumped out of the chair, and then 'Right!' again as he put a hand on hers to stop her turning the door handle. 'I'll show *you* pipe and slippers,' he breathed into her ear, and reached down to undo his belt.

Oh, dear, how ugly it all was. Didn't they have any sense of appropriate and inappropriate dinner-party behaviour? Clarrie shifted about to try to relieve an aching shoulder, and closed her eyes. She heard sounds of unzipping and fumbling, a giggle from the Hammock and another 'I'll show *you*' from Alex. She took a last peep and saw the Hammock's hands with fingers spread against the door and the Hammock's thick mane of red hair. They were going to do it standing up, leaning against the door, so there was no possibility of a furtive escape for the intruder in the cupboard. She saw Alex's white bottom (not wholly unlike Morris's), shirt tails flapping and trousers pushed down around the ankles as he shuffled forward and hoisted up the Hammock's ropy dress. There was a flash of white cotton knickers and the dull thwack of elastic against flesh. Just before she closed her eyes again, the reluctant voyeur noticed the discarded toothpick lying on the floor near the swivel chair. A third 'yes, well' seemed unlikely.

Dessert

'Mousy little thing, isn't she? I bet she gives good head, though.'

That's what he'd said, his breath clouding in the night air, just after Pauline had walked back into the house. Then he'd laughed, his white teeth gleaming in the darkness, and nudged Roger in the ribs with his right elbow – nudged him a little too hard – making him cough and splutter.

Clive *couldn't* be queer . . . could he? The number of times Roger had known him to pass comment on women, a more thoroughly heterosexual man didn't exist! Clive had once told him that he couldn't so much as pass a woman in the street without imagining what she would be like in the sack. Roger could remember a time when he too had felt like that, but these days he barely noticed women. With the passing of time his feelings for Judy had increased, intensified . . . he had always thought it would be the other way around; that he would become bored of her, sick of looking at her body because the mystery had gone, the thrill was over. The opposite was true. It was as though her body had grown huge, becoming godlike, expanding to fill his vision entirely. He simply couldn't imagine being with anybody else.

Alone in the garden, Roger wandered down the path, past the garden shed that smelled of creosote, down among the many rose bushes. He breathed in the night air and felt a tightness in his chest.

He knew the way he felt about his wife was unusual. Almost all of his friends were either having an affair or thinking about having an affair. One or two of them had even confessed to harbouring feelings for *Judy* that weren't wholly platonic – not that they would ever really act on those feelings, of course! It was purely a form of compliment – like telling Roger they liked his car or a new piece of furniture. It made him feel good.

Clive had told him of at least five occasions when he had been unfaithful to Heidi – two of them while she was pregnant with Max. Roger hadn't approved. It wasn't that he was especially moralistic, or even that he had any particular regard for Heidi. It was the way Clive *talked* about his conquests that offended him. There was something thoroughly slimy and loathsome in the way that he would bend his head close to Roger's, as though they were conspirators, lowering his voice to a whisper and gesturing with his hands, as he uttered a few well-chosen phrases.

'. . . it was like she was purring, Roger, purring like a sleek little cat and arching her back . . .'

'. . . insatiable, that's what she was. I had her kneeling on the floor, crawling across the room . . . *begging* for more . . .'

'. . . and you know where she wanted it? Up the arse, that's where. Right up the arse.'

Could it be . . . could it really be that all these stories were something other than what they had appeared to be? Could it be that these purring sex kittens were all *men*?

Roger had never thought of himself as homophobic. If asked, he would say it was a private matter – something that should be left to the choice of the individual – consenting adults and all that. Personally, he couldn't see why any man should want to sleep with men, but if others wanted to, well that was their business. But *Clive Stilbourne* . . .

Roger wasn't remotely attracted to Heidi Stilbourne. Large breasts, big lips, full face – far too much *flesh* altogether, in his opinion – unnecessary padding. But he knew that most men would disagree. Most men would give their right arm to sleep with Heidi. What on earth was Clive playing at?

Perhaps Judy was wrong. How did she know, anyway?

'Is there anything that woman doesn't know?' he muttered to himself, as a cat darted across the path in front of him, startling him and very nearly tripping him up.

His chest was still tight. He had been feeling vaguely bronchial all evening and had thought the fresh air might help. In fact, he felt worse than before. It was as though the night was stifling him.

*　　*　　*

Back in the house, all was strangely quiet. Pauline was reading a newspaper in the kitchen. She looked up and smiled as he came in and he smiled nervously back.

'Have the Thackstons come back downstairs?' he asked.

'Nah.' Pauline shook her head slowly from side to side. 'And I don't suppose *she'll* be wanting any dessert when she comes back down.'

She returned to her paper and Roger wandered on in the direction of the lounge.

Something made him hesitate as he was about to open the door – a sound – a kind of hiss – a loud whisper, coming from inside the room. Roger's hand closed around the cold brass door knob, and turned, slowly.

'Bitch!' came the whisper again; it was Clive Stilbourne – the same whispering voice that had told Roger of hot nights with even hotter women.

Two heads twisted round as the door was pushed open – two flushed startled faces were peering at Roger over the top of the Chesterfield, where they were sitting – Clive and Judy, alone in the room.

'Darling, I was wondering where you'd got to.' Judy's voice was sharp, quivering very slightly. She smoothed her hair with one hand.

Roger felt strange. The knot in his chest tightened still further. He walked across the room, leaned heavily on the mantelpiece, and turned to look at them.

Something was wrong, and Roger didn't understand what it was. Everything looked as it should: Clive and Judy were sitting at either end of the couch, a respectable distance apart. Judy still had her feet up on the sofa – half sitting, half kneeling, in exactly the same position as when Roger had left the room, her shoes on the floor in front of her. Clive had his legs wide apart and one arm extended along the back of the couch, seemingly relaxed in a typical slouch, a glass of Scotch in the other hand.

Something *was* wrong, though. Roger could sense that he had interrupted something. He felt as though he had walked in on a lovemaking scene . . . But there was nothing very loving in that whispered word, *Bitch*!

'So, what have you two been up to?' he said lightly, and then wished he had said something else; bit his lower lip.

'We were just having a little talk, weren't we, Clive?' Judy's composure was back but her pupils were dilated. 'There were one or two things we needed to discuss.'

'Such as?' Roger sat heavily in an armchair, crossed his legs first one way and then the other and looked around for the drink he had abandoned when he left the lounge before.

'Oh, this and that.' Judy smiled a smile that Roger didn't like very much, a hard smile.

'Judy's given me quite a bit to think about.' Clive's voice was hoarse, probably as a result of all that loud whispering.

'Really, what?' The tightness in Roger's chest had now spread up his neck. He felt as though his head were locked in one position; if he tried to move, something might break.

'You seem to be in need of a drink,' said Clive. 'Let me get you one. Scotch?' He got up and moved to the drinks table, his back to Roger and Judy.

'Just a glass of mineral water with some ice, please. I'm driving. Better not have any more.'

Roger tried to catch his wife's eye, but she seemed reluctant to look at him. 'Darling . . .' he began, and then didn't quite know how to continue.

And without looking directly at him, Judy lifted her right hand and put a finger to her lips, the familiar gesture which says, *Hush. Not a word.*

'Judy . . .' Roger said again. The gesture didn't make sense to him. It signalled that *Roger* and Judy – rather than *Clive* and Judy – were being secretive and mysterious. It was as though she were saying to him, *Clive is with us now, so we'd better be quiet*, and yet he had been the one to walk in on *them*.

'Here,' said Clive, handing the water to Roger. The glass was refreshingly cold in his hot hand.

'Clive has been an absolute darling,' said Judy. 'So generous.'

In Roger's head, Judy still had her finger to her lips. *Hush, my darling, hush.* But her eyes weren't gentle – the dilated pupils revealed excitement.

'Generous? In what way?' Roger had never thought of Clive as a kind man. *Bitch*! He heard the word again in his head, and there was certainly nothing remotely generous about it. Clive was sitting, staring into his drink, seemingly disconnected from the conversation.

'Look how coy he is – how sweet,' said Judy. She leant across and playfully pinched Clive's cheek as you might pinch the cheek of a little boy. And like a little boy, Clive made as though to brush her away – held his hand to his face, blushing and looking down.

Judy turned back to Roger. 'I was telling Clive about how we were thinking of going away for a couple of months to get away from it all – spend some time just being us.'

'We were?' This was news to Roger. He sent his mind back to the early evening, to his confession and to what she had said. She had spoken of finding him a counsellor, had told him not to worry, had said things have a way of turning out all right. That was all she'd said – there was no mention of going away together. Roger found he was irritated, annoyed that she would tell Clive such things without having discussed them with him first.

Inside Roger's head Judy still had a finger to her lips. *Hush, darling*. And now in his mind he was walking over to her, grabbing her hand, snapping that infuriating finger like a dry twig.

'Oh yes, we were,' he found himself agreeing, hastily concealing his surprise at what she had said.

'Clive has been telling me that he and Heidi are currently arranging to rent a villa in Tuscany – they're going to rent it for six months or so because Clive has so much work in Florence at the moment.'

'I hate staying in hotels, you see,' said Clive, in a sullen voice. 'Especially the hotels in Florence. Dreadful holes full of dreadful people.'

'I've stayed in some rather nice hotels in Florence . . .' Roger began, but Judy started to talk over him.

'Clive says we're welcome to go over and stay in the villa – any time we like – for as long as we like. Now what do you think about that?' She clapped her hands in glee.

'Splendid,' Roger said, trying unsuccessfully to inject enthusiasm into his voice. 'Very generous of you, Clive.'

He shrugged, smiled a smile that was more of a grimace. 'What are friends for?' He cleared his throat and took a sip of his drink.

Bitch! Could they have been having a little joke together? Was the word said in jest? Had he heard properly? After all, he had been on the other side of a closed door. No, Roger was sure he had heard right, and was equally sure that this was no joke.

Again he thought about the early evening, when she'd astonished him by revealing that she knew all about the gambling, and then assured him that somehow she had things under control. He was comforted by her unshakeable faith that things would turn out all right – but now he felt uneasy; more than uneasy. It was all so secretive . . . *Everyone has secrets*, she'd said. And she had started to talk about . . . Clive Stilbourne – Clive's bisexuality, his love for rent boys and some blond Australian.

Roger looked hard at Clive, noticing the nervous way he kept jiggling the ice cubes in his glass, the beads of sweat on his forehead and the smile that was just a touch too bright to be real.

'Where's Heidi?' Roger blurted. 'Does she know you've given us permission to invade your Italian villa whenever we feel inclined?'

'Oh, she won't mind,' said Clive, without conviction. 'She's very fond of the two of you.'

Roger nodded. 'Still,' he said quietly, 'I have a feeling my wife may have talked you into this. She's a very persuasive woman.'

'Darling, really. As if I would!'

The curl of her mouth seemed to challenge him. It seemed to ask, *What exactly are you trying to say, Roger?* while her eyes plainly signalled, *Do not say any more. Do not go further with this.*

Just how far would Judy go to preserve the life she had, the life she enjoyed, luxuriated in? How far would she go to protect her marriage, her children, her reputation . . . him? Would she lie, deceive, make threats, carry those threats through? Roger looked levelly at her, at this woman who was everything to him, and without whom he would be nothing, or worse than nothing. She was running a finger around the rim of her glass, speaking in a lilting faraway voice of Florence, Siena, olive trees and golden fields.

No. What on earth was he thinking of? How could he be so unfair to her after she had committed herself so unselfishly to staying with him? No. Any woman in her right mind would have packed her case and left him, but not his Judy. She had asked him not to leave and she had tried to stop him worrying because she knew his head was already brimful of worry. She had thought of ways to help him – like finding him a counsellor – and now she had taken advantage of a few quiet minutes alone with one of their wealthier friends to arrange a place where they could go to get away from everything and work things out. This must have been so difficult for her. She would have needed to humble herself, inadvertently revealing something of their depleted finances in asking Clive about his villa – but she would have brought into play her usual charm and finesse, made it seem as though the real issue was the friendship of the two couples and their willingness to share with each other, rather than the Marshalls' lack of money. No. He must have simply imagined he had heard Clive call her a bitch. Or else Judy and Clive *were* sharing a joke together . . . Yes, that was it. He had heard the punchline of a joke. That was all. Nothing more. Nothing secretive or unsavoury. Just a joke.

Roger set his glass down on the table and cracked the knuckles of his left hand one by one.

'I do wish you wouldn't do that, darling,' said Judy.

'Sorry,' he said. 'I fancy some dessert. Where's Tilda?'

'Oh, I think she's hovering around upstairs somewhere, trying to extract the Thackstons from the bathroom,' said Judy. She got to her feet, brushing imaginary crumbs from her lap, and stepped into her shoes. 'I think I'll go and check up on her, see if we can round everyone up and hurry things along a little. Such a drag, this business with the Thackston woman.'

Judy strode briskly out of the room, pausing at the door to give the two men a little wave. ''Bye, boys,' she cooed.

Morris once told Clarrie a story about a childhood prank. He was ten years old and Alex was seven. Their mother had been following a series of nature programmes about the behaviour and in particular the feeding habits of common garden birds. Mrs Stone was so taken with this series that she began, for the first time, to notice the birds in her own garden and to start feeding them. To begin with, she was content to scatter stale breadcrumbs on the lawn and retreat into her kitchen to watch the birds swoop down, but after a while this ceased to satisfy and she sent off for the special pack accompanying the television programme, which included colour photos and information about a wide range of bird tables available by mail order.

Mr Stone Senior was not terribly impressed by or interested in his wife's blossoming hobby, but since his general philosophy was 'anything for a quiet life' he agreed to buy the largest, most extravagant bird table advertised, provided it was delivered to the house and didn't arrive as a self-assembly kit.

Mrs Stone was delighted with the bird table, which dominated the small lawn at the back of the house. She had wanted it to be positioned in pride of place in the front garden, but her husband put his foot down, something he did only occasionally – and in this case it was for the best. After all, with the table at the back there was less activity to scare the birds and more privacy for the spectator. She could sit in the kitchen for hours on end watching the sparrows landing on the main platform and fighting for crumbs, or staring at the blue tits trying to pull seeds through the wire netting of the dangling dispenser. She was fascinated by robins splashing about and drinking from the birdbath, thrushes hopping between the special wooden rungs on the protruding pole, and blackbirds ducking in and out of the miniature thatched cottage and trying to pull out pieces of reed to build their nests with. Sometimes she even saw birds mating, but they didn't tend to do that at the table.

The bird table held little interest for Alex, who tended to agree with his father about most things. Mrs Stone was somewhat disappointed that her youngest didn't derive any joy from watching their feathered friends, but she found consolation in Morris, who appeared to be enthralled by the birds.

However, Mrs Stone was taking things too much on face value. Morris was no more interested in birds than Alex – it was the *table* that fascinated him. The bird table was like something straight out of a miniature magical world. Morris could imagine tiny people living in the cottage, washing in the bath and climbing up the wooden rungs to keep watch at the top of the pole. These people weren't fairies, exactly – fairies were for girls. Rather, they were leprechauns who had migrated from Ireland. When Morris asked his mother for food to put out on the table, he intended it for the leprechauns, not for the birds at all. In fact, he wished the birds would just piss off. They were nothing but nuisances, making a lot of noise and leaving shit everywhere with tiny bits of feather stuck in it.

But if the birds were annoying, the biggest annoyance of all was Alex. He was so boring and so lacking in imagination! He didn't behave like a little brother ought to behave, was always running to Mum and Dad with tears and moans and stories of injustices perpetrated by Morris. Kids were supposed to be in awe of their elder brothers, ready to do anything just to gain approval and acceptance, but not *this* kid. Alex even had the cheek to laugh openly at Morris when he caught him talking to the leprechauns. Morris tried to explain that he *knew* the leprechauns weren't real – that it was pretend, a game that was meant to be *fun* – but Alex just laughed at him, and so eventually Morris was forced to punch him and he ran away bawling his eyes out.

Morris's frustration with his unsatisfactory brother grew and developed until he felt he had to do something to knock some sense into the little runt, to reacquaint him with his proper role of disciple and eager follower.

An idea hatched itself, beautiful in its simplicity. When Mrs Stone was out shopping one day, Morris stole an egg from the fridge. He took the egg out into the garden and hid it in the miniature thatched cottage. And then he waited. The egg sat in its safe hiding place for almost two months, and during that time he never forgot about it – or so he later claimed to Clarrie.

Throughout the whole of the two months, the egg was nestling somewhere at the back of his mind, and he only had to think about it to feel immense pleasure. Sometimes he would go out into the back garden and reach into the cottage just to make sure it was still there and still intact – and it was.

'The egg incident was a key moment in my growing up process,' Morris told Clarrie. 'It taught me about the importance of good timing. Sometimes you just have to be patient. You have to wait for the right moment, learn to sense it. You have to let things come to fruition before you act. I let that egg mature like a good wine.'

When Morris approached his little brother with the egg held carefully behind his back, he knew the moment was right. There would be a full moon that night and, more importantly, it was Morris's tenth birthday. He was entering into double figures, leaving Alex way behind.

'What's that behind your back?' asked the small precocious one – and then let out a wail as he felt the impact, the cracking crunchy sensation on top of his head followed by the slimy oozing gunge and the most appalling stench he had ever smelled in his short life.

Morris smiled silently as he watched the greenish yolk slide over Alex's blond head and the snot-like white drip onto his hot teary cheeks. It was a truly golden moment. He had already smiled inside himself whenever he anticipated the event and would continue to smile every time he thought back on it, even after a quarter of a century had passed.

The white heart-shaped dessert in its pool of yellow sauce looked forlorn and somehow inadequate. Alex felt as though his own heart was sitting on the dish in front of him, waiting to be demolished and consumed. He wasn't sure if he could bring himself to eat it. Looking around the table, he suspected that some of the others might also be experiencing dessert difficulties. Heidi Stilbourne, in particular, looked positively queasy. Alex was glad – he wanted her to suffer as much as he was suffering.

The dessert would have been Tilda's triumph, a dish guaranteed to capture the imagination of the food-fixated Brian Thackston. While not actually unique, it was certainly unusual. The hearts were made from coconut milk, cream, egg yolks, sugar, coconut liqueur, one vanilla pod and some gelatine to help them assume their light, slippery texture and precise shape. The sauce was a mixture of puréed mango, orange juice, lime juice and passion fruit. Tilda had chosen the simple white dishes to offset the colours nicely (the green glass ones would have been a little garish with the bright yellow sauce) and had garnished the bavarois with sprigs of mint and tiny, carefully arranged curls of orange and lime rind.

She had gazed with pleasure at the hearts as she turned them out of their moulds earlier in the day and began snipping at mint with her sharp kitchen scissors. Now she gazed with irritation at the two empty places at her table. What a waste.

Although in her own house, she had felt like an intruder as she approached the bathroom and hesitated with her hand raised, ready to knock at the door.

'Try washing your face, Chrissie,' came Brian Thackston's voice from inside. 'It might freshen you up.'

'I *can't*,' whined Christina. 'My make-up will be all smudged.'

'Jesus, give me strength! Your make-up's ruined anyway, you silly cow.'

'I *can't*,' came the plaintive cry. 'I just *can't*. I want to stay here for a little while. *Please* don't make me move.'

Tilda gave two very small one-fingered knocks.

'Yes?' Brian's voice was gruff, irritated.

'Can I get you anything?' she tried.

'We're fine, thank you.'

'Are you sure? We have mineral water, lemonade – I hear that's good for bad stomachs. Andrew's liver salts, perhaps? Milk of Magnesia or whatever it's called?'

'No, thank you.'

'Well, maybe Christina would like to lie down for a little while? You could perhaps leave her to rest and come down for some dessert?'

She was interrupted by a horrible retching.

'If you wouldn't mind just leaving us for a while . . .' Brian sounded desperate. 'We're fine, just fine. Aren't we, Chrissie?'

There was no reply from Christina – merely some more retching.

The hearts quivered and wobbled as heavy-handed Pauline carried them in on a tray and whacked them down on the table one by one in front of the guests. Heidi couldn't help but notice that the otherwise sulky waitress laid Clive's dessert down more gently and gave him a shy smile as she sidled past, but perhaps her own guilt was making her paranoid. She tried to put it out of her mind.

'That girl is more interesting than she first appears,' said Clive, when the waitress had retreated into the kitchen. He picked up his spoon, dug straight into the centre of his heart and shovelled a large slimy morsel into his mouth. 'Mmm, delicious!'

'Is she really?' said Heidi, deadpan.

'She seems to know everything there is to know about D.H. Lawrence.' He went for his second mouthful.

'How fascinating,' said Judy in a tone that exactly contradicted her words. 'Remind me not to engage her in a conversation about literature,' she added, raising her left eyebrow and glancing at Tilda.

'So Brian didn't tell you how long they're going to be in there?' said Alex for the third or fourth time.

'No. She was still being sick, and frankly I'm sick of the pair of them,' said Tilda, and ate her garnish of mint and orange rind without really meaning to, grimacing as the strong flavours made contact with her taste buds.

'Darling . . .' Roger turned to his wife with a wheedling look on his face. 'I *really* fancy a drink or two. Couldn't we get a taxi home and then I'll come back for the car in the morning?'

Judy sighed loudly. 'Oh, *must* you, honey? You *know* how much I hate cabs. The driver always has BO or one of those overpowering air fresheners in the shape of a pine tree, and he always starts griping about immigration or pornography or something. Anyway, if you have a drink now, it'll make an entire evening of abstinence totally meaningless.' She consumed a dainty morsel of her heart.

'Oh, well, when you put it like that, I suppose . . .' Roger's voice trailed off gloomily and he looked at his dish so that he didn't have to see Judy's triumphant expression as she reached for her wine glass.

'I didn't really mean that I'm sick of *them* – just the situation,' said Tilda. 'I do hope she'll be OK soon. It can't be too pleasant for her.'

'Will you stop it!' Alex hadn't meant to shout but it came out louder than he had intended. He ran a hand through his thinning hair to calm himself down and tried to lower his voice. 'We've said all there is to say. Let's just forget about it, shall we?'

'Yes, let's.' Heidi seemed surprised by her own voice. She avoided Alex's eyes carefully.

'Sorry.' Tilda dropped her spoon in the midst of the pulp that was her heart. 'You've been going on about it just as much as me. Anyway, I'm sorry to bore you all, but frankly I'm the only person here who spent the whole of yesterday and most of today in the kitchen putting this little lot together. It's quite hard for me to see it fail.'

'But, darling, it *hasn't* failed.' Judy leant forward to be physically closer and tried to look compassionate. 'It just ended a little abruptly, that's all.'

Was that a smirk from Clive or was he just wiping his mouth on his napkin?

'Let's say no more about it,' said Alex, attempting an air of authority. 'Let's try to pretend the Thackstons don't even exist. Let's act as though we're just a group of friends enjoying a quiet evening together, shall we? Some of us are quite good at acting, after all.'

Alex hoped Heidi was wounded. He wanted to wound her.

'And what is that supposed to mean, exactly?' Tilda was the one to be wounded.

'Nothing. Sorry.' Alex was abashed. He tried a mouthful of the bavarois in an attempt to appease, and smiled bravely as the cold slimy pulp slipped down his gullet. He never had been much of a one for desserts.

'So what happened to our little friend, then?' Clive gestured at the third empty seat at the table – Clarrie's – and the intact heart sitting in front of it.

'I've no idea at all,' said Alex, suddenly preoccupied, having caught a whiff of himself; a gust of sex and woman's perfume rising out of his shirt. Would anybody notice? He was glad that Tilda was sitting on the other side of the table – she had always had a keen sense of smell.

'But you were searching for ages!' Tilda protested. 'And Heidi was looking around as well. The house just isn't *big* enough to swallow someone up like that.'

'I can only assume,' said Alex, 'that she didn't want to be found.'

'You mean, she's *hiding* from us?' Roger seemed amused at the idea.

'Apparently.' Alex forced himself to take a second mouthful.

'I'm not happy about it,' said Tilda.

'Quite frankly, I don't blame her,' said Heidi.

Clarrie had once told Morris a story about a childhood prank. (In fact she told the story a number of times, but on each occasion he was kind enough to pretend he hadn't heard it before.) As a four-year-old, she'd spent several afternoons a week at a local nursery school run by Mrs Greenhalgh, a large woman with copper-coloured hair who wore loose dresses that looked like tents and vast quantities of blue eye shadow. Clarrie enjoyed nursery school. She liked painting pictures and running around the garden and building walls out of life-sized polystyrene bricks. It was something of a weight off Mrs King's mind to see her daughter settled and happy at the school. Though not exactly a problem child, as such, little Clarrie could certainly be described as demanding and time-consuming, and after all Mrs King was a busy woman who benefited greatly from the occasional free afternoon.

However, although she was delighted with the nursery, Mrs King was not overly fond of Mrs Greenhalgh. It wasn't that she doubted the woman's competence and capabilities, it was simply that she thought the nursery school proprietor was a fusspot and a whiner; always collaring her when she came to collect Clarrie, with the whispered phrase, 'Could I have a little word with you, Mrs King?'

The *little word* was never a nice word, the kind of word a mother wants to hear – Mrs Greenhalgh never congratulated her on her charming, intelligent daughter. She never mentioned how well-behaved and polite Clarrie was. She always began with, 'I don't want to worry you but I'm a tiny bit concerned about Clarrie,' and continued with the day's particular gripe, such as, 'It's just that she has this rather odd way of staring at people. I think perhaps you should consider taking her for an eye test.'

Mrs King listened in silent anger to this implication that she was neglecting her daughter's health and general well-being before replying curtly, 'I can assure you, Mrs Greenhalgh, that there is nothing wrong with Clarrie's eyes. She is simply discovering the world, that's all; finding her own way of looking at things.'

On another occasion it was, 'It's just that she doesn't really play with the other children very much. She seems a little backward in her interactions.'

'There is nothing backward about my daughter,' said Mrs King, as she buttoned Clarrie's coat. 'She is an only child who isn't used to being around other kids, that's all. Clarrie is very self-contained and independent – admirable qualities in one so young, don't you think? Qualities that should be nurtured and encouraged.'

Another time, Mrs Greenhalgh came puffing up just as Mrs King and Clarrie were on their way out of the front door with, 'I know you're a busy woman and I won't keep you long – but I've been giving some thought to Clarrie's difficulties in relating to the other children and it occurs to me that perhaps her *hearing* is the problem. It's not uncommon for hearing difficulties to go undiscovered for absolutely *years*, you know.'

'Mrs Greenhalgh – I know you mean well,' began Mrs King, 'but Clarrie's hearing is perfectly fine. With all due respect, I do wish you'd stop making my daughter out to be some kind of freak. Have you ever considered the possibility that she doesn't bother with the other kids because they're just too dull and boring to be of any interest to her?' And she marched off with her perfect daughter, leaving Mrs Greenhalgh for once at a loss for words.

After this, the teacher left well alone. In addition, Mrs King had a chat with her daughter.

'Clarrie dear, do try to play with the other children at the nursery. Mrs Greenhalgh wants you to make some friends and Mummy's sick of hearing about it.'

The chat seemed to do the trick. Clarrie was enjoying the nursery more than ever, and even beginning to talk about her new friends – in particular one Dominic Lewis, who turned out to bear a striking resemblance to the Milky Bar Kid.

Then, some months later, Mrs King went to collect Clarrie only to find a pale, tired Mrs Greenhalgh asking for another 'little word'. Mrs King attempted to look patient and concerned.

'So what's the problem, then? Do try to be quick – I'm a busy woman.'

Mrs Greenhalgh's face was changing from pale to purple.

'Something must be done about your daughter, Mrs King. I simply can't tolerate this kind of behaviour in my nursery school!'

Mrs King tried hard not to laugh. 'What's she done?'

'The children have all been wetting themselves. It's been happening every day for the last week!'

'I don't quite understand what this has to do with Clarrie.' Mrs King had begun to think the silly woman had completely lost her mind.

'You may well ask . . . you may *well* ask.' Mrs Greenhalgh narrowed her eyes.

Apparently Mrs Greenhalgh had realised, while mopping up one of a number of puddles, that Clarrie was the only child who wasn't wetting herself. After interrogating several of the damp toddlers she was able to ascertain that everybody except Clarrie was petrified of the toilet, in spite of the fact that up until this week the majority of them were thoroughly potty trained and completely *au fait* with lavatory etiquette. Further questioning revealed the real reason for the toilet terror: Clarrie had told all of the children that there was a ghost in the loo which would eat anyone who went in there. Mass fear had descended on the nursery school and Mrs Greenhalgh began to discover puddles – and occasionally something worse.

'Well, at least we can now be certain that there's absolutely nothing wrong with her communication skills, eh, Mrs Greenhalgh?' said Mrs King, and took Clarrie off to Café Luigi for an ice-cream.

Clarrie stood in the doorway, looking at them all, more than a little dishevelled and still wearing the white towelling dressing gown. They seemed quite surprised to see her.

'Where have you *been*, Clarrie?' asked Tilda. 'We started to think you'd run away or something.'

'Heidi and I were searching for you,' Alex added.

'Sorry.' She shuffled forward and stood in front of the table, her head drooping and hands behind her back like a naughty schoolgirl appearing penitent before the headmaster.

'So where were you?' asked Tilda.

'In a cupboard.'

'A cupboard?' Alex was perplexed.

Shiny was clearly trying to conceal a laughing fit and amused glances were being exchanged all around the table.

'So you *were* hiding, then?' asked Kitchener. 'We were wondering, you see.'

'No,' said Clarrie. 'At least, I didn't want to hide but I sort of had to.'

'A cupboard?' Alex repeated. 'What cupboard? Where?'

'In your study,' said Clarrie, looking him straight in the face.

Alex swallowed heavily and Clarrie noticed that the colour had drained from the Hammock's pretty cheeks. He stammered slightly when he continued speaking and his voice sounded odd. 'How . . . how long were you in the cupboard?'

'A very long time,' said Clarrie, without taking her eyes off his face.

'Calm down, dear.' Tilda had mistaken Alex's mood for anger. She turned back to Clarrie. 'Clarrie you really mustn't go nosing around in Alex's study. Even *I* don't go into Alex's study when he isn't there. What were you doing, anyway?'

'Perhaps we should just let this drop.' The Hammock had recovered her composure.

'No, I want to know what she was doing up there,' said Tilda. 'What were you doing, Clarrie?'

Clarrie noticed how humble Alex had become. His face was pleading, beseeching. She felt suddenly empowered. What would she choose to do with her power? Her lips began to move but she didn't even know herself what she was about to say.

'I was looking at photos,' she said. 'Old photos of Morris and Alex when they were children.'

She saw the stiffness seep out of Alex's shoulders as he mopped his brow with his napkin. She saw the Hammock dab at a drop of blood on her lip where she had apparently bitten it. She saw, in the oblivious faces of Tilda and the other guests, how private the meaningful moment had been. And she saw gentle smiles on the faces of the elderly couple in the portrait above the mantelpiece – where formerly there were only stern expressions.

'But why were you in the cupboard?' asked Tilda, – and Clarrie saw Alex and the Hammock dragged back into exhausted tension as they realised they weren't yet in the clear.

'It doesn't matter,' said Clarrie. 'None of it matters.' With all eyes still on her, she squeezed around the table to an empty seat, and sat, pushing away the wobbling white heart in its yellow sauce.

'What are you talking about, Clarrie?' asked Cruella.

'Oh, drop it, for God's sake,' said Alex. 'We've got quite enough to think about without taking this any further.'

'It doesn't matter,' said Clarrie again. 'There are other things which matter. Things outside of this room. Things in another world.'

'What things?' Tilda snapped.

Shiny reached for Clarrie's unwanted dessert, and began to devour it in large mouthfuls.

'Nothing,' insisted Alex. 'You're talking rubbish, aren't you, Clarrie. Just trying to get attention.'

'Clive, I think we should go soon,' said the Hammock suddenly. 'I'm a little worried about Max. He was running a temperature earlier.'

'When? He seemed perfectly fine to me,' said Shiny, between mouthfuls.

'I have something to tell you,' said Clarrie to Alex. 'That's why I came here tonight. To talk to you.'

'You said you were just visiting,' said Tilda. 'What is all this?'

'I was visiting because I have to talk to you,' said Clarrie in a strangely flat voice, and then fell silent again.

'Clarrie?' Tilda was trying hard not to lose her temper.

'Aren't we the little drama queen,' cooed Cruella. 'Come on, let's get the suspense over with, shall we?'

'It's important to find the right time,' said Clarrie. 'You need to know that people are going to listen.'

They shifted in their seats, trying to find comfortable positions. Apparently the cabaret was about to begin. None of them had even the remotest idea of what Clarrie could be about to say, but whatever they might have expected, she still managed to surprise them with her next sentence.

'Yesterday, Morris asked me to go to the video shop for him. This might come as something of a surprise to those of you who know him well—'

'Goodness me, a trip to the video shop. How shocking!' Shiny giggled and spluttered.

Clarrie ignored the glances being exchanged around her and continued, 'Until last year he refused even to have a television in the house, but then he had a change of heart and became addicted to quiz shows and American talk-shows like *Donohue* and *Oprah*. Then six months ago he decided to buy a VCR. It didn't bother me that Morris had finally decided to accept modern technology – in fact, I was quite pleased. I like watching films. It was still weird, though, to see him become a TV fanatic. He always used to insist that staring at a screen for hours on end must at the very least destroy your eyesight, if not your brain cells as well. But then Morris has changed a lot in the last couple of years. We both have.'

'I can vouch for that. Each time we see you you're a little more mad than the previous time,' muttered Tilda.

'So, anyway, last week Morris went down with a nasty dose of 'flu. I don't think I've ever seen him so ill. For the first few days he just lay in bed all feverish and delirious, sleeping and sweating and muttering to himself. But yesterday he was a lot better. His temperature was back to normal and all the horrible shaking had stopped. He said he was tired and weak, but otherwise he was all right. He lay on the couch with a bottle of lemonade and a box of tissues and decided he'd like to watch some videos.'

'Can I just ask if this story is actually leading anywhere?' asked Alex. The others were spellbound, if only because nobody had heard Clarrie speak more than about five words at a time before.

'He wrote a list,' she continued, ignoring Alex. 'A list of the films he wanted to watch. He said he thought he'd be laid up for at least another couple of days so the list was quite a long one and very specific: Derek Jarman's *Caravaggio*, James Bond – *The Spy Who Loved Me*, *A Streetcar Named Desire*, *Dr Zhivago*, *The Godfather Part II* and *Star Trek II – The Wrath of Khan*. Oh, yes, and *The Wizard of Oz*, of course.'

'An eclectic selection, certainly,' said Cruella.

'He said it had to be these films in particular. He insisted that I'd have no trouble finding them – that he'd seen all of them in our local video shop. So I took the list and off I went. Now, it takes about fifteen minutes to walk to the local video shop. You can rent videos at the newsagent's at the end of our road but I knew there was no point in looking there – they only ever have a small stock; a few new releases and some soft-porn movies – definitely none of the films I was looking for. The proper video shop is quite good. It's part of a national chain. It has some big racks at the front full of new releases but then it also has lots of other racks with particular types of films – like "foreign" or "comedy" or "tear-jerkers". I found *Caravaggio* in the "art films" section and *The Wizard of Oz* in "children's". The "classics" section was pretty good – I found *A Streetcar Named Desire* and *The Godfather Part II*. But that was all. I asked the man about the other films and he said *Dr Zhivago* was out on loan (he seemed quite surprised about this) but that they didn't stock the James Bond film any more because they're on telly all the time and to his knowledge they had never stocked the *Star Trek* film . . .'

Shiny yawned loudly at this point and Kitchener glanced at his watch, but Clarrie was undeterred. Her expression had become purposeful, and she directed a fierce glare at the dinner guests. Tilda was staring wearily at her empty dish. Alex's face wore an expression that lay somewhere between incredulity and contempt.

'The man suggested I tried a different shop – Moviemania. He said they're owned by a film buff rather than a huge conglomerate and that consequently they have a wider range. Unfortunately the shop was a couple of miles away. I said my sick husband was waiting for the videos and he told me there was a bus. He was quite helpful, really. I decided I'd wait for this bus for ten minutes and no more – if it didn't come in that time, I'd go home.'

Alex was clearly becoming agitated. 'Fascinating though this story is, Clarrie, I think we might—'

But, surprisingly, Cruella wanted to hear the rest of the story. 'Let her finish, Alex.'

He shrugged and mumbled something incoherent.

'Anyway, the bus came after six minutes so I got on and went over to Moviemania. It was much bigger and better stocked than the other shop. There was a whole section called "Bond" and I found *The Spy Who Loved Me* straight away, although a girl who was standing nearby tried to tell me I should get a film with Sean Connery as Bond instead of Roger Moore. Then I found *Star Trek II – The Wrath of Khan* on a shelf called "Final Frontiers", but I just couldn't see *Doctor Zhivago* anywhere even though I spent a long time searching. I went up to the woman behind the counter and she told me that the manager was quite idiosyncratic – apparently he hated David Lean films and refused to stock any of them in his shop. This had never been a significant problem because hardly anybody was interested in renting David Lean films. I asked her if she had any idea where I could get hold of *Doctor Zhivago* and she suggested I try the video section of the local library. She said if I couldn't find it there then I probably wouldn't find it anywhere.'

'Clarrie dear,' said Tilda, in clipped tones, 'has anybody ever told you that the secret of good storytelling is in knowing which bits to leave out?'

'Don't be so impatient, Tilda,' said Cruella. 'I'm finding this all quite fascinating. It's like listening to a psychological case study or something. Do go on, Clarrie.'

'It took another three-quarters of an hour to get to the library. I had to catch the bus back as far as the first video shop and then there was another fifteen-minute walk. While I was walking I started to think, *Why am I doing this?* It isn't like me to go chasing all around town just to find a few videos – and it isn't like Morris to spend so long thinking about what films he wants to watch and then to ask me to go and find them all for him. I started to realise just how much we'd both changed since we first met and it was really quite alarming. It was like I could suddenly see our whole shared past mapped out. Most of what I could see was good: art college, the opening of the first gallery and the time we spent building it up together . . . the early days when we were getting all the press attention and serious artists were starting to come up North because they'd heard how good we were. And then I thought about the bad times: the gallery going bust and the decision to go to Italy for a couple of years and then the tragedy with Indigo and everything . . . and coming back to England, picking ourselves up off the floor and setting up the second gallery – it could never be like the first one, not now.'

'Hold on a second.' Alex had found an opportunity to cut in.

'What was "the tragedy with Indigo"? What are you going on about?'

Clarrie turned wide-eyed to look at his confused face. 'Oh, yes, of course. You don't know, do you. Indigo was our child. She died.'

'What child? This is absolute bullshit!' He tried to get to his feet but the Hammock reached across to put a calming hand on his arm and he slowly sat down again.

'Not . . . possible,' said Tilda. She was clutching her throat with one hand and gripping the edge of the table with the other.

'Clarrie dear, I think you'd better explain yourself,' said Cruella, helpfully.

'Yes. It happened when we were in Italy. That's why you both never knew. We had decided to make a clean break from the past – you know that much. It was mainly because Morris was so gutted about the gallery. I don't think anyone in the family was especially worried when they didn't hear from us for two years; we were always the weirdos, the black sheep.'

'It's true, they did disappear for two years,' said Tilda, looking around at the others.

'And while we were in Italy, I had a baby.'

Tilda caught her breath. The Hammock's hand crept back to Alex's arm.

'She was a beautiful baby girl. I wanted to call her Red because I love the colour so much but Morris insisted on Indigo and I quite liked the name, so Indigo it was. Anyway, it didn't really matter what her name was in the end because she died after only three months. It was a cot death.'

'Oh, Clarrie, why didn't you ever tell me?' Tilda gushed. 'To have to keep a thing like that all to yourself! Maybe I could have helped. Maybe we could have helped each other.'

'Tilda, don't.' Cruella spoke sternly. 'Carry on, please, Clarrie.'

'Well, there isn't much to say about Indigo. She wasn't around very long. But she's the reason we came back to England and set up the second gallery.'

'But Morris is my *brother*. I know him – he would have told me!' Alex was clearly in anguish and the Hammock tightened her grip on his arm.

'You don't know anything about Morris *or* me!' Now Clarrie

was the angry one. 'You've never taken the trouble to ask us anything about ourselves, neither of you. You're both far too wrapped up in your own private little dramas – and the rest of you are just as bad. I know about you, I know about you all!'

The clocks have stopped, thought Tilda to herself. It's all over. The night is as still as can be and it will never end. We're all stuck here together and we can't move, we can't break out of it. My feet are made of stone and my arms are useless. I can't hear the traffic or the birds. I want to sleep but I can't force my eyes to close. They hurt.

Clarrie was still talking.

'When I arrived at the library I was still thinking about my marriage to Morris and how we'd both changed so much, and I had half a mind to dump all my videos in the nearest bin. But then I thought that would be a bit silly and pointless, and since I'd already gone to so much trouble, I decided that I might as well check to see if the library had a copy of *Doctor Zhivago*. And, guess what? They did – in a section labelled "Epics". I wasn't actually a member of the library so I had to join and this was quite a lengthy process. I had to show them two sorts of identification with my address on and fill in forms, but it all went smoothly, and soon I was leaving with the video – with all the videos Morris wanted – and I suppose I felt quite pleased with myself.'

'We're *still* hearing about these bloody videos!' Alex shook his head in disbelief. He looked as though he wanted to punch Clarrie.

'And on my way home, I realised. The thing is, I don't know why I didn't realise *earlier*.' She paused, enigmatically. 'In fact it only hit me in a coherent way as I put my key in the front door. It was *totally* unlike Morris – even the changed Morris – to send me to fetch this list of videos. His new telly habit was quite indiscriminate, you see. He shouldn't really care *what* I brought back from the video shop.'

Alex groaned. 'Why should anyone care what you brought back from the video shop!'

'I think on an unconscious level I already knew. I already knew how depressed he was, and how much worse he was getting. That's why I was willing to run all over town for him looking for his films – because I had to do *something* to help him.

And I knew – as I opened the front door – that he'd compiled this particular list of videos because it would take me a long time to find them. It was a way of getting me out of the house, you see, for as long as it took.'

'For as long as *what* took, Clarrie?' Cruella's voice was gentle.

'For as long as it took him to slit his wrists and bleed to death in the bathroom.' Clarrie shrugged helplessly, smiling sadly across at Alex.

There was a roaring in Clarrie's head. She couldn't hear anything, feel anything, she could barely see. She was toppling backwards on her chair, falling down, down, grasping handfuls of table-cloth, which only slid away with her. She was leading her army of crockery, cutlery, glasses, candlesticks and condiments – they followed her like good soldiers, all the way to the floor, where they clattered and splattered their way to a halt. They lay around her, wounded and bleeding; some of them spread themselves across her – spoons and the stems of wine glasses coming to rest in her lap, morsels of bavarois settling in her ears and hair, the great white table-cloth with its stains and smears shrouding her body, and her legs spread wide – straddled over the horizontal chair which now had a broken leg.

She put a hand to her jaw, to the place where she had felt the impact of Alex's fist – her mouth was hanging open and she tried to close it. She wondered if she had lost any teeth. There was a numbness in her cheek and everything inside felt very large. She could feel she was drooling – was it saliva or blood? Was her jaw broken? She tried to smile and said, 'Ow.'

'Grab him!'
  'Stop him . . .'
  'Oh my God!'
  'Alex darling . . .'
  'What the hell . . .'
  'Roger, *do* something.'
  'That's right. Sit him down.'
  'Undo some of his buttons.'
  'What the hell . . .'
  'Closed fist. A slap is one thing, but—'

'Shush. Get him some water.'
'Nasty shock.'
'Tilda? Come on, love, don't just sit there.'
'What the hell . . .'
'Tilda honey, he needs you.'
'I need a cigarette.'
'Gentlemen just don't—'
'Shush.'
'. . . never seen anything like it.'
'What about *her*?'
'Fuck *her*.'
'Alex darling, are you all right.'
'Bloody stupid question.'
'Let him be for a minute.'
'Maybe some fresh air.'
'What the hell have I done?'

'Good heavens!' Disbelief, disgust and fatigue had room to live together in Brian Thackston's face, nestling cosily in folds of flesh and skin, while Christina's face was only big enough for fear.

'Brian, I think I'm going to faint.'

'No, you're not. I've had quite enough of your crap for one evening.' He shook her anxious hand away and stepped forward, broken glass crunching beneath his foot. 'Carnage,' he muttered, as he looked down at the spread-eagled Clarrie. 'Chaos,' he said to the blank-faced Tilda, still seated at the table. 'Crikey,' he continued, for want of a more dramatic 'c' word, as he squinted and blinked at the little huddle surrounding Alex.

'Coffee?' said Pauline, as she put her head round the door.

Coffee

❦

Cancelled, due to unforeseen circumstances.

Departure

'What are you doing?'

Clarrie was annoyed at the interruption. She looked up at a pointy face, twinkling eyes and a goatee. 'Sketching. What does it look like.'

'Only, you're not really supposed to sit on the floor.'

Clarrie thought it best to ignore this. 'Would you mind moving, please? You're blocking my view.'

The man seemed a little uncomfortable now. He crouched down beside her. 'I'm sorry. I'm not going to stop you sketching, but you'll have to go and sit in the café. You can't sit on the floor. That's the rule.'

Clarrie squinted at him. His face was all vertical lines. There didn't seem to be any horizontals. 'What's your name?'

'My name?'

'Yes.'

He shrugged. 'Morris. I'm sorry but you're going to have to move.'

She was puzzled. 'But I thought this was an Arts Centre.'

He smiled and for the first time his face was horizontal. 'Well, yes, of course it is . . .'

'For Art. For the doing of Art,' Clarrie insisted.

'More for the looking at Art, really.' His voice was apologetic.

'Not for the doing of Art?'

He put his hand on her shoulder, the left one. It had a pleasant firmness to it. 'Look, I just work here. It's just a job.'

Clarrie had seen him somewhere before, she was sure of it. 'Are you at the art college?'

'Yes.' He withdrew the hand. 'What's your name?'

'It's a funny place, the art college,' said Clarrie. 'They don't like me sitting on the floor there either. I'm Clarrie.'

'Is it you that does all those red paintings? asked Morris. 'The big ones?'

'That's right.'

He was grinning now. She could see his teeth, little and shark-like. 'They're kind of wild.'

'Yes,' said Clarrie. 'They sit on the floor whenever they want to.'

He laughed. 'You're funny.' He tried to get a look at her sketch pad, but she held it close to her chest. 'Oh, go on, let me see,' he said.

'No.' Clarrie held it even closer. 'It's private.'

'Please yourself,' he sniffed, clearly offended. His face closed up.

Clarrie found she wanted the face to open again. 'Oh, all right,' she said. 'Just a quick look, though.' And, with shaking hands, she lowered the sketch pad for him to see.

'Morris!' came a male voice, some distance off. 'Morris, where are you? I need a hand.'

'I've got to go,' he said, standing up and brushing himself down. 'I'm supposed to be helping Doug Wittham set up the exhibition. He doesn't like me. I'll be out of a job if I'm not careful.'

She sighed as she watched him become vertical again. 'I bet you have the loveliest curve at the small of your back. I'd like to touch it. I'd like to draw it.'

Clarrie slurped noisily and dabbed at the place where her mouth had once been with a dishcloth. The cloth was drenched, and covered in dark red patches. Clarrie was amazed at how much blood was flowing from her. She had become a machine churning out vast quantities of red – although this was nothing to the red that Morris had manufactured on the floor of their bathroom. She tried to speak the word 'red' aloud, but it came out as 'wurr'.

The sensations she was currently experiencing in the left side of her face were most interesting. She could feel with her hand that her cheek was enormous – bulbous like the stomach of a pregnant woman, and growing larger by the second. The skin was taut over the swollen flesh. Perhaps when the swelling went away she would be left with stretch marks. Inside the mouth was something of a mess. There was a sea of liquid which was trickling steadily away down the side of Clarrie's face and into the dishcloth. A second stream glugged down the back of her throat, forcing her to gulp now and then, followed by further slurping. Clarrie made feeble attempts to explore the inside of her cheek with her tongue, trying to check that her teeth were all present and correct – but the tongue had become a chunk of foam rubber too large and spongy to be of any use, and she was forced to give up. At least there was no significant pain. That would probably follow in the morning.

'Nobody's ever hit me before,' she said to the Clay, as he came out through the back door to join her, although it sounded more like, 'Ngohysh ejer hick ngee gehore.'

'Have this,' he said, handing her a polythene bag full of ice cubes and sitting down beside her on the step with a certain difficulty and much huffing and puffing. He wore an expression of concern. There was also a suggestion of anger, which Clarrie felt wasn't directed at her.

'Hold it against your face,' said the Clay, seeing that she had begun to play with the bag and was sliding it between her fingers.

Clarrie obediently pressed the ice to her left cheek, with a slight wince.

'Disgraceful, that's what it is,' said the Clay – although whether he was speaking to Clarrie or merely to himself she couldn't be sure.

'No matter what the circumstances . . .' he continued '. . . keep it there, Clarrie, that's it. I know it's a case of the stable door after the horse has bolted and all that, but we really should try to get that swelling down.'

'What circumstances?' she said, with slight bubbling.

'Eh? Oh, what I mean is that a man should never hit a woman – not ever! It's unforgivable, that's what it is.'

'Unforgivable,' murmured Clarrie, lost in thought.

'It's true the circumstances were extreme – I know he lost control, wasn't himself – but still, a man should never hit a woman.'

They were silent for a moment, and Clarrie listened to the breeze rustling the trees. 'What will I do?' she said, almost before she knew what she was saying. 'Woc wiw I goo?'

'I don't know, love.' The Clay sounded compassionate. 'You're in a bit of a mess, aren't you.'

Clarrie sniffed. 'My life was with Morris,' she said simply.

'Well, of course it was. He was your husband.' The Clay shifted slightly, trying to get comfortable on the cold hard concrete of the step.

'Alex will help me,' said Clarrie in a small voice.

The Clay sighed. 'I don't think you can count on that, love. He has plenty of his own problems.'

'Alex will help me,' she said again.

'How did we not *see* it?' The Clay seemed to be talking more to the trees than to her. 'How did we not realise that something was wrong? It should have been obvious to us all – doubly so to Alex and Tilda! Nobody behaves like . . . we should have twigged, that's all.'

'Twigged?' said Clarrie. (Kwigge.)

'Never mind, love.'

'What are they all doing?'

'You mean, Alex and Tilda and everyone?'

'Mmm.'

'Well . . . it's a difficult thing for them to accept, you know. I think Alex has been trying to phone your house. I suppose he's hoping that Morris will answer the phone and that it'll turn out you've been telling stories.'

'Morris isn't there.'

'I know, but I think Alex has to check that out for himself. It is his brother, after all. As for the others – well, I think Tilda's pretty upset. Some of them are clearing up the mess in the dining-room. I expect my wife has found somewhere to lie down. She's a bit under the weather, as you know.'

A few doors down a dog was barking. Its deep 'woof' was quickly joined by some frenzied yapping and something somewhere started to howl.

'Morris liked dogs,' said Clarrie, sadly. 'Do you have one?'

'No. Christina's allergic.' His eyes continued to search the night sky as the barking died down. He seemed not to want to look at her while they talked. Perhaps he was too embarrassed – perhaps the sense of shame he felt on behalf of his fellow man went too deep.

'Do you love your wife?' asked Clarrie.

'Eh?' This time he did twist around to look at her. 'Yes, of course I love her. She's not the easiest of women, it has to be said. But we've been together for years. She knows me better than anyone else. I've never strayed, you know, in spite of what she might think. I wouldn't do that to her.'

'Morris was the only person who really knew me,' said Clarrie. 'And now he's left me on my own.'

'Why are we here?' asked Clarrie, as Morris brought two cups of rosehip tea over to the table and sat down.

'What do you mean, Clarrie? Why are we on the planet? Why are we in this country? What?' He looked irritated and tense. 'Must you be so damn cryptic all the time?'

She reached for her tea. 'Why did you bring me here?'

Morris closed his eyes for a moment and seemed to be counting under his breath. Clarrie wondered if this was a cue for her to go and hide behind a sculpture.

He opened his eyes again, and they had a coldness about them. 'Well, for one thing, I want to see that Czech animation. And for another—' he was clearly exasperated '—can't you guess?'

'Guess what? Is this a game?'

Morris's forehead turned into a field, freshly ploughed into lots of straight lines. His bald head was a hill rolling away into the distance.

'We met here, didn't we. We met here, Clarrie.'

'I don't like it here,' she said. 'They don't let me sit on the floor.'

Morris grabbed both of her wrists so suddenly that Clarrie caught her breath. He held them tightly. 'My darling, I am trying to remind myself of the way I felt when we met. Of the way you filled me up with sunshine . . .' He let go of her hands. 'I want some sunshine now.'

'You want sunshine?' Clarrie was puzzled. She wiggled her fingers to make sure her wrists were still working.

'Yes, I do.'

Clarrie glanced around her, at the various grey-looking people in the café, drinking tea and eating quiche. An old man was having difficulty chewing a crust; a sullen, sunken-faced woman was nibbling at carrot cake while reading a newspaper, a scrunched-up tissue poking out of her sleeve; A thin boy with acne was stubbing out a cigarette in his coffee dregs.

'You won't find any sunshine in here,' she concluded. 'Shall we go and get some tickets for this animation thing?'

Tilda had never thought of herself as being good under pressure, but it seemed she could be extremely efficient when the pressure was somebody else's. It was as though she could see the pressure concentrate itself in Alex's chest like a small football and then radiate outwards until he was surrounded by a red pressure-aura. She watched him dialling and misdialling Morris's number again and again, coolly observed the way his hands shook as he clutched at the receiver, heard the fear in his voice as he pleaded, '*Answer*, damn you! Answer!' And felt increasingly distant from it all.

I hope he *is* dead, she thought to herself, and then felt her neck flush with a deep hot guilt. But after all, one can't control one's true gut feelings. They have a life of their own. She was entitled to feel anything she liked about this just so long as she didn't inflict her feelings on the grief-stricken Alex.

What was the point in pretending to be upset about the death of someone she'd never even liked? She could be honest with herself about it now in a way she never had been when Morris was alive. Being rid of him once and for all would be like having a verruca burnt out – your foot might be a bit sore for a while but soon it would be fully healed and you'd stop getting that nasty digging and pressing sensation when you walked.

She had tried to like Morris, especially when she first met Alex's family and was keen to make a good impression. She had been too nervous at the time to really know how she felt about them and it was only a year or two into the marriage that she allowed herself to realise and acknowledge what an irritating bunch they were. She had heard it said any number of times that you can choose your friends but not your family, and Tilda thought this was even more true of your partner's nearest and dearest – in the case of your own family, you had grown up with them, got used to them, learned to tolerate and understand, been shaped by them. But when you got married you acquired this unwanted second set whom you neither chose nor understood. Alex's father was now a nicotine-stained, stuttering old man who spent most of his time tinkering with his car and had very little to say for himself, while Alex's mother liked nothing better than to sit for hours on end in her ancient kitchen that smelled of cat and boiled vegetables, staring out of the grubby window at her enormous shit-encrusted bird table.

Thankfully, Alex found their company just as tedious as Tilda did and they soon settled down to visiting the Stones only once a year (for not more than three days), and having them down to stay twice a year (for not more than a week). Come to think of it, Tilda supposed someone was going to have to break the news to them about Morris – but, after all, it could wait until tomorrow when Alex would be in a better state.

Tilda had gradually learned to accept the visits to Alex's parents as being irksome but unavoidable, like catching a dose of flu in the winter. But Morris was a much more problematic figure. He was important to Alex in some obscure way that she as an only child could never fully comprehend.

Time spent with Morris was harrowing for Tilda – she never knew what effect it would have on Alex. Sometimes she would find herself looking on while the brothers locked horns in a blazing row after one of them had made some unfortunate and tactless remark. At other times they would be all over each other, drunk and tearful and hugging and pathetic. Alex would return from visits to Newcastle brimful of infuriating smugness or dismal self-loathing, very rarely anything in between. And it had all got so much worse when Morris married Clarrie. Alex had been convinced that Morris only married her out of a desire to ridicule the whole idea of marriage, to heap scorn on a way of life which Alex had embraced with seriousness and idealism. Tilda had tried briefly to befriend Clarrie for Alex's sake, but it was little more than a gesture. From the moment Tilda first clapped eyes on her she knew they were from different solar systems, and Alex, for once, understood. When Morris and Clarrie disappeared to Italy for two years, it had been a huge relief, even for Alex. (If only it wasn't for baby Indigo . . . No, mustn't think about that.) And now that Morris was dead, the relief would be even bigger. Yes, this was real. He really was dead.

Alex was still dialling the number, but Tilda knew he would not get an answer.

'What's happening?' Judy stuck her head around the door.

Tilda shrugged. 'He's trying to call Morris.'

'Oh.' Judy came right into the room, and together they watched Alex dial the number three more times.

'Maybe he should call the police,' Judy whispered to Tilda.

'What?' Alex slammed the receiver down. 'What did you say?' His eyes were wild, crazed-looking.

'Alex darling, I think perhaps you should call the Newcastle police.' Judy laid a supportive hand on his shoulder, and he shook it away.

'And why would I want to do that, exactly?' he spat. 'The person I need to speak to is my brother.'

'But Morris might be dead,' Tilda blurted out before she could stop herself.

'Don't you dare say that!' Alex dialled the number again, and then threw the phone onto the floor in a frenzy. It landed with a crash and the familiar expressionless words, 'The number you have dialled has not been recognised.'

'Morris is not dead,' said Alex, tears glimmering in his eyes.

Judy moved swiftly into her habitual role of supporter and caring friend. 'Of course he's not dead. We all know that that mad little bitch has concocted this whole ridiculous story for reasons best known to herself – if she even has a reason, that is. But in order to prove that the little whore is lying, we should call the police and establish once and for all that there is no body.'

She laid her hand on Alex's shoulder again, and this time he didn't shake it off. Slowly she led him over to the couch and made him sit.

'You're right. You're absolutely right,' he said, and his voice had become calm once more. Tilda and Judy exchanged relieved glances.

'Tilda,' said Judy, 'perhaps you could make the call.'

Clarrie and the Clay were thrown suddenly into a flood of light as the back door opened and Cruella clacked out, flustered and purposeful, tripping on the hem of her dress as she stepped down to stand in front of them. Her face wore a grim expression but was somewhat flushed. There was something about her – something in the way she moved or a kind of aura – that suggested excitement. Cruella was enjoying herself.

'The silly little bitch has made it all up,' she snapped, hands on hips in a self-righteous stance. 'Haven't you, Clarrie?'

'What?' said the Clay. 'Do you mean to say Alex has spoken to Morris?'

'Not yet, but I'm sure they'll be speaking to each other soon.'

Clarrie stared blankly at Cruella.

'Why did you do it, Clarrie? What has Alex ever done to deserve this?'

She continued to stare blankly, and said nothing.

'Now hold on a minute, Judy.' The Clay dabbed with a handkerchief at his damp forehead. 'Let's just get this straight, shall we? You say Alex *hasn't* spoken to Morris—'

'No, he hasn't.' Cruella kept her gaze on Clarrie. She spoke to the Clay but seemed to want to freeze him out. Her impatient tone implied this was none of his business. 'There was no reply from Morris's house, so we called the police. And guess what?'

'What?' said Clarrie, deciding to join in.

Cruella crouched down so that she was at the same level as the two seated on the step, and looked Clarrie straight in the eye. She licked her lips before speaking. 'They didn't know anything about it. There hasn't been a suicide,' she finished with relish.

'Clarrie?' The Clay's large face creased up in consternation.

'What?'

'What the hell are you playing at?' said Cruella. 'What could you hope to achieve by telling poor Alex that his brother has committed suicide?'

Clarrie frowned, but frowning hurt her face. 'Nothing,' she said.

'But you admit that you're a liar?'

'Steady on, steady on,' spluttered the Clay. 'There's no need to be aggressive. The poor girl needs help.' He dabbed at his forehead again. 'And I must say, I think I need a bit of help myself. This is all just too much!'

'Don't you have anything to say for yourself, Clarrie?' Cruella stood up again. It seemed her knees were bothering her.

'No.'

Cruella kicked out in anger at the concrete step, startling the Clay with her ferocity.

Clarrie found herself wishing she was a bird, able to fly away and leave this mess far behind. As a child she had often dreamed of flying. Her dreams were not, as you might expect, of soaring through the sky high above the town. Instead she had dreamed on many occasions of being able to float up to the ceiling in the lounge of the house where she grew up. The lounge had been full of shelves, and Clarrie simply wanted to be able to see what was kept on the top shelf – the one that was too high up the wall to come within the field of vision of a small child. As she floated upward in her dreams, she would discover all manner of interesting things up there: pirates' treasure, fairies, toys that could speak, bag upon bag of brightly coloured sweets . . . The dreams stopped when she grew tall enough to see that the shelf was empty.

'Clarrie,' tried the Clay, 'this is a serious matter. You just can't go around saying these kind of things and thinking there will be no repercussions. You're going to end up alienating everyone who cares about you. Now, tell us where Morris really is. Has he left you? Is that what this is all about?'

Clarrie laid down her ice bag. The ice was thawing through it and her hands were a mess of bloody water. Her face had stopped bleeding, which was slightly disappointing. 'Morris is gone,' she said wearily.

'So he has left you,' concluded the Clay, softly.

'And who can blame him,' snarled Cruella. 'To think what that poor man has had to put up with!'

'Judy—'

'No, I'm sorry, Brian. You're being too nice. This little liar gate-crashed Alex and Tilda's dinner party, determined from the start to make trouble. And, by god, she's succeeded, hasn't she!'

'Judy, surely you can see the girl needs help.'

'I'm not a liar,' whispered Clarrie.

'No, love. But you're not very well, are you.' The Clay tried to smile, but the effort was too much.

Now Clarrie was the one to snap. 'I'm not a liar. Morris *is* dead.'

'Not according to the police,' said the Clay.

Clarrie got up. 'But I haven't told the police!' she shouted in exasperation. 'I came here to talk to Alex, but Tilda had people coming for dinner so I couldn't. I wanted Alex to be the first to know.'

Heidi's dress was ruined. At the moment when Alex's fist made contact with Clarrie's jaw and she fell backwards, dragging the table-cloth with her, everything had stood still for a fraction of a second. Heidi had seen her full glass of red wine hovering at a ridiculous slant and her half-eaten dessert leap from its dish – she'd had time to think *three thousand pounds*, the retail value of the dress – before the wine and the dessert rushed forward to embrace her, along with some molten candle wax and a few items of sticky cutlery.

Now, as she scrambled around on the dining-room floor, scooping up edible matter and broken glass with her delicate manicured fingers and throwing it into a dustbin liner, kneeling in bavarois debris, she felt strangely empowered.

I don't give a shit, she realised. About this dress, this awful mess, about Tilda, even Alex. Poor sad Alex. Nothing touches me.

She ran a sticky hand through her hair and smiled to herself. 'Clive?' She twisted around to look at her husband, who was stacking dishes with an expression of disdain on his face, gingerly picking his way around the table, trying his best to keep his suit unmarked. 'Can we go away somewhere? Somewhere like – I don't know – some remote little island miles from civilisation. Somewhere we can be on our own – just you, me and Max. Could we do that? Honey?'

'What?' Clive shook his hands as though the stickiness would simply fall away. 'Heidi, I really don't think this is the time or the place to be thinking about our summer holidays, do you?'

She was irritated. How lacking in vision he could be sometimes. 'I'm not talking about holidays. I'm talking about living. Just living. Without all this crap.'

Clive sighed audibly. 'Darling, you're drunk. Let's just get this mess cleared up and then we can go home and sleep. I don't think I've ever been so tired in all my life.'

'You don't understand, do you?' Heidi huffed, licking something congealed from her finger. 'You never do.'

'No, of course not, dear,' Clive muttered sarcastically. He stood up, brushing down his trousers, picked up a pile of dishes and stalked off to the kitchen.

'That's men for you,' came a slurred voice. Heidi turned to see that Christina Thackston was slumped on the floor in the far corner of the room, her eyes closed and her legs splayed so that a lacy petticoat and some sort of substantial white underwear were visible. 'We women know about the spiritual side of life,' she said with a hiccup. 'While they're stuck on the physical plane.'

With a start, Heidi jolted back to herself. Clive's right, she thought. I must have had a few too many.

She stepped across the room to pull down Christina's skirt so that it covered her legs. 'Let's try to preserve a little dignity, shall we?' she said, sharply. 'God knows it's been a difficult evening.'

In the kitchen, Roger was arguing with Pauline.

'I've never been treated like this before, never,' she was saying. 'Nobody's ever told me to fuck off just for offering to bring in the coffee.'

'This is not a normal dinner party,' tried Roger.

'You're telling me! They're mad, the lot of them. Raving bloody mad.' And she folded her arms to emphasise the point and her own obvious superiority to the occupants of this raving bloody mad household.

'I think perhaps you should go home,' suggested Roger.

'I'm not leaving till I get paid.' Pauline stuck out her chin much as a two year old might. Roger thought she might stamp her feet if this discussion went much further.

'How much?' he asked in withering tones.

'Fifty quid is what we agreed,' said Pauline. 'But now I'm thinking seventy might be more appropriate.'

'Seventy pounds for an evening's waitressing!' Roger was astounded.

'I've had a lot of abuse tonight,' said Pauline. 'Not to mention having to deal with that mess.'

Roger hadn't actually noticed her taking part in the clearing up process at all, but couldn't be bothered to say so.

'Mr and Mrs Stone are having a traumatic time,' he said after a moment's stony silence. 'I'm sure they will arrange payment as soon as they can. But you have to understand that these are extreme circumstances.'

'Extreme circumstances, my arse! I know my rights,' said Pauline, and barged past him heading for the living-room.

'No you don't!' Roger grabbed her arm.

'Get off! You're hurting me.'

'Where do you think you're going?'

'I'm looking for Mr Stone. I want my money.'

'Wait. Come back to the kitchen.' Roger wondered why this role always fell to him. In a house full of moneyed people, he would be the one who would have to get out the cheque book and smooth things over. Thinking back over the years of his marriage to Judy, he could see nothing but a sea of cheques.

Pauline followed him back, and waited patiently while he fetched his wallet, chin now withdrawing into her face. He thought her face rather unpleasant – there was something of the weasel about it, and something of the lizard.

As he drew out his cheque book, she shook her head.

'Oh, no. I'll have cash, please. That was the arrangement I had with Mr Stone.' The chin was back again.

Roger swore quietly to himself and peered anxiously into his wallet. There were only two notes in it – a twenty and a ten. 'A cheque's going to have to do,' he said.

'No. If that's the best you can do, I'll wait to speak to Mr Stone. And I'll be giving him a piece of my mind, you can be sure of that.'

'What's the problem?' said Clive, coming in with a stack of dishes. 'Are you being difficult?' he asked Pauline, with a directness that Roger found quite disarming.

'This gentleman is expecting me to leave without being paid.' Pauline made the word 'gentleman' sound like the worst kind of insult.

'That just isn't true,' Roger blustered. 'I was quite happy to give her a cheque. She wants cash – seventy pounds in cash to be precise.'

'Eighty,' corrected Pauline. 'There's an extra tenner gone on now for this hassle that you're giving me.'

'Quite the little entrepreneur, aren't you,' said Clive. 'Well, we aren't the sort of people to make a fuss over a small matter like this, are we, Roger?' He smiled brightly and reached into his inside jacket pocket. 'At least, I'm not. Roger here is a little strapped for cash, apparently. But Uncle Clive is a man you can rely on when times are hard.' He drew out a bundle of notes, counted out three fifties and tucked them casually into the front of Pauline's blouse. 'Oh, yes, Uncle Clive has enough dosh for everyone.' He turned a sharp look at Roger, who swallowed silently and tried to clear an obstruction from his throat. 'As a certain Mrs Marshall knows only too well.'

The minute hand of Alex's Rolex (sadly a fake) was moving with agonising slowness, while the second hand ticked away with a kind of ineffectual regularity that made him want to smash the watch against the marble mantelpiece, smash it over and over as hard as he could until the glass shattered and the tiny springs inside scattered into the hearth. He didn't do it, of course. Instead he sat on the very edge of the armchair nearest the phone, staring intently at it – willing the minute hand to shift itself just that little bit faster. God, these police were slow. You'd think it would only take them a couple of minutes to get a car over to Morris's place – after all, this was about a body, wasn't it? Surely there must be hundreds of eager young constables in panda cars just desperate to get to see a real corpse after all the noisy neighbours and drunk drivers and street brawls they must have to deal with on Saturday nights? It had been a good ten minutes now, and still the police hadn't called back.

Tilda was chattering nervously away to Judy Marshall. 'I'm going to have to get that dining-room carpet cleaned,' she was saying. 'I can't imagine it will ever be the same again.'

'Sit down, darling,' Judy said, one eye on Alex, who was rocking himself gently and clearly unaware that he was doing so. 'Alex darling, you're rocking like a mad person,' she said. 'I suggest you try to stop.'

'Shut up,' he replied, without looking at her. 'I wish you'd leave.'

'Alex!' said Tilda.

'And you can stop your doe-eyed caring sharing butter-wouldn't-melt shit,' he continued, still keeping his eyes on his watch.

'He's distressed, Tilda, he doesn't really mean it.' Judy settled herself on the couch beside her and enfolded her in a motherly hug.

'What makes you think you know what's going on in my head?' said Alex. 'You think you know everything.'

'Judy's only trying to help,' said Tilda, muffled by her friend's grip. 'Everybody's trying to help. They're all out there now, clearing up.'

'Yes, and while they've all been clearing up and helping, she's been here with us, sticking her nose in as usual.'

'It's all right, darling,' said Judy softly as Tilda seemed to be about to continue the defence.

'You're always there when there's trouble, aren't you,' Alex continued his tirade. 'You just *happen* to be there. You're like some bloody great vulture, swooping down on people's troubles, pecking the bones clean.'

The thought of bones and corpses must have been too much for him, and he fell silent.

'We're all done. The dining-room's clear, and Clive's got rid of Pauline.' A gust of strong perfume entered the room with Heidi. She'd obviously been trying to drown out the smell of booze and fish and bavarois. It went straight to the back of Alex's throat.

He looked up at her. He'd turned almost cross-eyed with staring at the watch, and for a moment there seemed to be twelve of her faces, all of them shimmering and perfect, with a large second hand ticking infuriatingly past them and a minute hand that stood stock still. He tried to smile at her but it didn't come out right. Then the suddenly alien sound of the door bell chased away his smile and sent him into confusion. He put his hands over his ears.

'I'll get it,' said Judy and Heidi at the same time.

'Alex – it's the police,' called Clive's voice from the hall.

Clarrie was alone in the garden, and glad to be alone. They were wearing her down, these difficult people, at a time when she needed all of her strength. Even the Clay, bless him, was too stupid behind the compassionate façade to understand anything she said. He'd now gone off to check on his wife – possibly being alone with Clarrie had become too much for him. Possibly he thought he'd had to bear that particular burden for just a little too long. Clarrie didn't mind – the feeling was mutual. She'd had quite enough of slogging away in her attempt to get him to see clearly.

The grass was like cold wet hair under her bare feet as she slowly crossed the lawn. It was like walking around on the top of somebody's head. The night air was chilly enough to distract her from thinking about her swollen face. She threw back her head (with a certain amount of pain) and saw that the moon was full, as round and full as a big yellow zit on the freckled face of the sky. If she reached up her arms, perhaps she could squeeze it, and golden moon-juice would rain into the garden. She sat herself down, cross-legged, at the very centre of the lawn, taking time to commune with her round yellow friend. If she howled like a dog, would it howl back to her? Would it show her that she wasn't really alone in the world? She took a deep breath, filling her lungs to capacity, paused to gather sufficient momentum, and then let loose a long low sound that came from somewhere deep in her stomach, a sound that carried with it all of her pain and her fear and her loss and disappointment – carried them out of her body and into the air around her, leaving her empty and tired. She felt the sound echoing around the roof-tops, bouncing off window-panes, rustling through the trees and waking all of the dogs for miles around, prompting them to begin a chorus of barks, yaps and accompanying howls. She bowed her head in respect, taking an in-breath that sucked all of the pain, fear, anger, grief and disappointment back into her withered body, filling it once more. And when she finally lifted her head, she realised that she was no longer alone. A man was standing under the cherry tree a little way off, and he was carrying a baby.

'Morris?' she squeaked.

Alex was standing in the water with the waves lapping up to his insubstantial belly, forcing him to take little gasps of breath while he sobbed and peed into the sea. He was watching his brother swimming away. Now he could barely see Morris except for the top of his head, bobbing up and down in the distance, like one of those floating things – buoys – that stop boats from bumping into sharp rocks. Only buoys are tied down under the water, and Morris was floating free. Now he couldn't see Morris at all.

He wished he could follow his brother, wished he was older and stronger and able to swim. But at the same time he hated Morris, hated him for blatantly disobeying orders and casting himself on to the elements all because of some mad idea about a magic cave.

There was always some mad idea. The gallery was a half-baked notion if ever there was one, and of course Alex turned out to be right when he said it wouldn't last more than a few years. In fact, he was pretty sure that's why Morris had headed off to Italy – because he couldn't bear to hang around to hear Alex gloating.

And then it was like the cave all over again. When Alex finished his gloating he began to wonder if he was missing something. How could Morris just throw in the towel and head off into the sunset with his loony of a wife? Two whole years they were gone – two years of utter hedonism while he scrimped and saved and worked his arse off. And then Mum and Dad worried just like that time on the beach: *Where is he, Alex? He must have told you, at least, Alex. Is he ever coming back, Alex? Why is he doing this? Alex, why didn't you stop him?* Oh, yes, it was just like that day on the beach; Morris the dreamer followed his dream *again* while Alex, the sensible one, took the blame and picked up the pieces for the *favourite* son. So when did Alex even *have* a dream, let alone follow one? The closest he'd ever come to hedonism was his pathetic attempt to leave his wife for another woman, and look where that had got him!

And then, unexpectedly and without explanation, Morris and Clarrie appeared one day on the doorstep. They were silent about Italy, just saying that they were back and needed somewhere to stay for a week or two while they sorted themselves out. They seemed to believe it was perfectly acceptable to disappear for so long and then reappear as though they had never been away, saying nothing about what had happened. It was an odd time, to say the least, but they were an odd couple. Clarrie was sketching all the time with red biros – she barely stopped throughout the visit, you could hardly get a word out of her. And Morris – well, he was quiet too, not at all his usual self. Positively wan, in fact. One evening he had knocked on the door of Alex's study:

'What do you want, Tilda?' This had been Alex's first opportunity in days to be alone and he didn't want anyone bothering him until dinnertime, which shouldn't be for another hour at least.

'It's me – Morris,' came the voice from the other side of the door. 'Can I come in for a minute?'

Reluctantly, Alex closed the thriller he was reading, slipped it into a desk drawer and pretended to be deeply immersed in the papers in front of him. 'All right, come in.'

Morris slid nervously into the room, rather as a cat might, closed the door behind him and then just stood awkwardly, saying nothing, looking down at the carpet.

'Well, don't just stand there. Sit down.' Alex gestured at the spare chair.

'Thanks.' Morris sat, his hands wedged firmly under his legs, and continued to look at the floor. 'I know you're busy,' he added. 'I didn't want to disturb you but I thought it might be my only chance to get you on your own.'

Alex felt his interest rising. He couldn't even remember the last time his brother had wanted to be alone with him. Was he about to confide some dark secret? He leant back in his chair, picked up a toothpick and began distractedly to dig about in his molars.

'Nice study, this.' Morris gazed absently around him. 'Comfortable. Functional.'

'Yes,' said Alex. 'I find it so.'

'Do you mind if I have a cigarette?' asked Morris, producing a battered half-empty packet from his shirt pocket.

'Go ahead,' said Alex, surprising even himself. He pushed a china coaster across the desk to serve as an ashtray.

'Cheers.' Morris lit up with a shaky hand. 'How's work? You seem to be doing well. You have a sort of prosperous look about you.'

'Do you mean I'm getting fat?' said Alex, lightly.

'God, no.' Morris half laughed, half coughed. 'No, I mean you look happy, confident – you know.'

'Yes, I think I do know.' Smoke was getting in Alex's eyes and he waved it away. 'Things are good, I guess. Life is good.'

'Glad to hear it, glad to hear it,' said Morris, tapping ash onto the coaster.

'Little pre-dinner Scotch suit you?' asked Alex, opening a cupboard.

'Now you're talking, bro, now you're talking.' Morris looked suddenly brighter.

Alex splashed Scotch into two tumblers and passed one across to his brother. This was becoming more interesting by the second. When did Morris ever bother to make small talk?

'Tilda seems in pretty good shape, too,' said Morris.

'She's fine,' said Alex, and waited.

Morris sipped from his Scotch. 'Lovely stuff. So warming. I've always thought drinking Scotch is rather like drinking fire. Single malt, I take it?'

'Naturally.'

'Look, Alex,' Morris cleared his throat. 'The thing is . . .' He trailed off.

'Take your time, Morris. Take your time.'

'Yeah. Cheers. Well, the thing is . . . things aren't going too well for us right now, for me and Clarrie.'

Alex leaned forward on his chair. Morris caught his eye briefly before returning his gaze to the carpet.

'Italy?' said Alex.

'Yes.'

Alex thought back over the last few days. There had been a discernible weariness in Morris and Clarrie, where usually there was an excess of energy that drained everyone around them. They were edgy with each other and with Alex and Tilda. Clarrie was continually bent over her sketchbook, and when Alex tried to take a look at what she was drawing, she slammed it shut and told him to mind his own business. Tilda had been complaining all week about their antisocial behaviour, and asking him when they were planning to leave.

'Want to tell me about it?' he asked, all sympathy and understanding.

'No.'

Alex found he was disappointed. He reached for the Scotch bottle but Morris put his hand over his glass.

'No, thanks. I've had enough for now.'

Alex poured some more Scotch into his own glass and replaced the cap.

'I don't want to talk about Italy,' continued Morris. 'Italy's done, finished. There's no point in dragging it out and going over and over what's been and gone.'

'Sometimes it helps to talk.'

Morris shook his head. 'The past isn't the problem. The problem is *now*. What are we going to do now?'

'So you want to chew things over with me? You want my advice?' Alex picked up the toothpick again and returned to his favourite molar.

'No. Look, stop jumping the gun. Just listen for a minute,' said Morris. He got up from his chair and crossed to the window, turning his back on Alex. 'Wonderfully golden, that tree out there,' he said. 'Isn't autumn beautiful?'

Alex was irritated. Was Morris trying to wind him up as usual? 'I hate autumn,' he said. 'Everything dies.'

'That's what Dad says,' said Morris. 'You're quite like him, you know. In all sorts of ways.'

'And you're like Mum,' said Alex, crossly.

Morris chuckled. 'I suppose so,' he said. 'That's why I need your help. You're the practical one, the one who's got his feet on the ground.'

Alex softened. He'd never before heard his brother express this in such generous terms. 'What can I do for you, Morris?'

His brother turned back to face him, perched on the edge of the window-sill. 'I've lost everything, Alex. Everything except Clarrie. We were wrong to go off to Italy, I see that now. We were running away. I'm not like you. When the gallery folded, I couldn't bear to hang around. I thought it would be better to move on, start afresh. And Italy's such a beautiful country . . .'

'So what did you do over there?'

'Oh, this and that. Enjoyed the wine, the olives, the *gelati*. It doesn't matter now.' He drew another cigarette out of the packet and flicked his lighter.

Alex snapped his toothpick in two.

'I have to start again, Alex. From square one. From further back than square one – square minus one or something. I want to stay in Newcastle, make it work for me again. It's my home, the place where I'm known – for whatever that's worth. I built up my reputation there, I met Clarrie there.'

'And does she want to stay in Newcastle?'

'She doesn't care much about places. She just wants to be with me.'

Alex thought about how Tilda had reacted when he had once – and only casually – floated the idea of moving house.

'Do you have a plan?' asked Alex.

'Yes, I do, actually. I want to start a new gallery.'

Alex chuckled. He couldn't help himself. 'Are you serious? After what happened last time?'

'Yes, of course I'm serious.' Morris was clearly annoyed. 'I think I'll have that Scotch after all, if you don't mind.'

Alex reached for the bottle and poured a small amount.

'Thanks.'

'Morris, what makes you think that it would be any different this time from the way it was before?'

'It just would be. Don't smirk at me!'

'I'm sorry.' Alex worked to suppress his laughter. 'Go on.'

'The only problem before was *me* – my attitude,' said Morris. 'I got bored, frustrated. I thought that running a gallery was too pedestrian – too much like something *you'd* do.'

Alex felt his mouth twitch but he let the comment pass.

'I guess I was jealous of Clarrie, jealous of artists and what they can create. I felt I was just a glamorised shopkeeper. But now I've tried out other things – I've done my bit of playing around – and I've realised that what I was doing with the gallery – well, it was important in its own way. I was a kind of enabler, a protector. I was doing my bit to shape the future of the visual arts.'

'Oh, please!'

'I know that sounds pretentious, but don't dismiss what I'm saying. I'm being honest with you.'

Alex nodded. 'Sorry.'

'The gallery went wrong because I stopped working at it, putting energy into it. I switched off and just went through the motions. And so it died.'

Alex let a moment pass to make sure Morris had finished. 'And so this time your heart is fully in it. You're going to put your *all* into this gallery – make it the kind of success that your last one deserved to be but never actually was?'

'That's right.' Morris looked pleased, happy that his brother had understood.

'And that's what you're going to tell the bank manager, is it, Morris – when you go to ask him for a loan? "Please, sir, I've changed, really I have. It won't be like last time because this time *I really want it to work*." Jesus, Morris, if you could only hear yourself!'

'I *knew* you were going to react like this.' Morris drained his glass and banged it down on the desk. 'I knew I shouldn't come to you, but Clarrie said—'

Alex started. 'Clarrie said what? What did she say?'

Morris breathed deeply, visibly trying to calm down. 'Nothing. She said nothing. Look, I know a bank manager wouldn't take this seriously. I'm not stupid, I know how it sounds.'

'Then what?'

'That's why I need help from someone who knows me well, who will believe I can make this work.'

'Oh, no. You're not serious.' Alex felt his heart flutter. He looked at Morris and found his eyes locked into a kind of pleading, beseeching gaze. 'No way! No bloody way!'

'A hundred grand,' said Morris quietly. 'I need a hundred grand to get this off the ground. I've done my research, I've done my maths. What I need is one hundred thousand pounds.'

Look at that face – screwed up tight like a six year old who doesn't want to go to school. Alex has made himself as small as he can possibly be. He grips his own arms as though there is an invisible strait-jacket preventing him from letting them go. His knees are tucked up to his chin – or rather he is bent so that his chin is almost on his knees – and he rocks back and forth, back and forth. There is a kind of mania about him. He has shifted away from the room, away from the rest of them and into an interior world that is clearly not a comfortable place to live. They sit and stand around him, and stare, not knowing what to do. His face is becoming more and more red, and there is a tension in his neck, a rigidity in his grip, as though he is exerting pressure from within – pushing at something. He looks as if he is trying to force out a giant turd.

Tilda wants to help him, but doesn't know how to. 'What can I do?' she whines to Judy Marshall, who stands beside her, calm and contemplative.

'Nothing,' says Judy, whose gaze is fixed on Alex. 'Let him be.'

They can still hear voices in the hallway. Roger and Clive have gone to see out the smart, besuited and bouffant D.I. Darnley and her ridiculously young male sidekick, the gangly D.S. March. Darnley and March delivered their bad news with admirable professional compassion. They have clearly perfected their manner of empathic aloofness – Darnley spoke in a low, soothing voice. She delivered each sentence slowly and carefully, waiting and watching for the impact of her words on the assembled group, while March remained quiet – the subordinate whose function is perhaps simply to provide support to his superior – a kind of understudy who would be ready to step into the breach on that rare occasion when Darnley's words might fail her.

They kept it simple, sticking to the bare facts. Two Newcastle policemen had been sent over to 152 Bishop Terrace, where they rang the doorbell several times. When there was no answer they tried peering through windows without success, and finally went down a side alley in order to climb over the back wall and see if they could enter the house from the rear. As it turned out, the small kitchen window was not locked and they were able to force it open and climb in.

They repeatedly called out the name they had been given – Mr Stone or even – Morris – as they wandered through the empty rooms of the ground floor. Very little furniture – not what you'd call homely. The house was quiet and cold.

They climbed the stairs, glancing with minimal interest at the large canvases lining the walls. Not really what you'd call proper paintings – merely blotches and daubs of red. Perhaps they were supposed to be modern. These paintings were everywhere; hardly an inch of wall space had been left bare.

'This place is spooky,' said one of the policemen, with a slight shiver, as they peered into a bedroom which was entirely purple except for the inevitable red paintings. He picked up a framed photo of a thin bald man in a dinner jacket. He was grinning, a glass of champagne held aloft in his right hand, his arm around the shoulders of a small puzzled-looking woman with a mop of curly hair.

'Jesus Christ!' called his partner from another room, and there was a sound of retching. 'Get the chief on the radio. He's in the bath and he's not pretty.'

Of course, Darnley did not say all of this. She didn't tell the assembled group about the blood – there had apparently been a lot of it, mingled with bath water. She didn't speak of the discussions she knew were going on in Newcastle regarding the possibility that this man may not have taken his own life. She would leave that to D.C.I. Johnson and his people to do once the brother had a chance to get his head around it all. She was not, after all, the investigating officer – merely the bearer of bad tidings. In a short while she and March would feel that the right moment had come for them to leave. And with any luck there would be enough time to stop off at her flat for a quick shag before they returned to the station.

'I understand Mr Stone's wife discovered the body,' Darnley had said.

'That's right. Clarrie,' said Tilda.

Darnley nodded. 'And she's here?'

'Yes. Somewhere around.'

'She's in the garden,' said Brian Thackston. 'She's in shock, I think. Hasn't been making much sense, if you know what I mean.'

'I see.' Darnley and March exchanged an enigmatic glance. 'She'll need to go with you to Newcastle in the morning,' Darnley continued. 'She'll have to make a statement. A necessary formality, you understand. I don't think we need to speak to her just now.'

She stood up. 'We'll be off. You should go to bed,' she added to the unresponsive Alex. 'Try to get some sleep.'

He snorted and said nothing.

'Inspector Darnley,' said Judy. 'Could I just ask – well, was there a note?'

'Yes.' Darnley nodded at March, who drew out a notebook

from an inside pocket, and read in a flat voice: '"C I love you red M".'

Tilda tries to banish the blood from her head; splatters of blood, puddles and pools, blood up to the waist so she would have to wade through it carrying a redundant mop and bucket. And somewhere, in the midst of it all, bobbing and floating like a dead fish – Morris's bloated body.

She reaches out for Judy's hand and finds it, cold but comforting to hold on to.

'Come back,' sobs Alex, and rocks harder.

Judy's grip on Tilda's hand tightens as Tilda half moves to get up and go to him, and then hesitates.

In a flurry of hair and perfume, Heidi is across the room and perching on the arm of Alex's chair. His head is pressed to her chest and his arms reach around her as he cries into her cleavage. Her hair falls forward concealing both her face and his. 'I love you,' he cries.

Tilda feels as though she has been stung by a wasp. There is a sharp pain in her stomach followed by total confusion as he repeats, 'I love you,' once more. But then she realises that he is talking about his dead brother. Of course he is. Still, she should surely be the one to comfort him now. She shoots an annoyed look at Judy, who seems to be avoiding catching her eye.

'What I need is one hundred thousand pounds.'

That should have been the end of the matter, but it wasn't. When Alex had finished laughing at Morris's presumption and, frankly, sheer stupidity – and when Morris had left the study, shamefaced, saying, 'Let's just forget we ever had this discussion, shall we. I clearly made a mistake' – when Alex was alone with his thoughts, his laughter died down and vanished, and he took from his desk drawer a sheet of paper, a pen and a calculator.

'Morris, have you got a minute?' Alex found his brother alone in the kitchen, peeling potatoes for the Sunday roast.

'As I'm sure you know, I have a great many minutes.' Morris didn't look up from his peeling. 'If I could only roast my minutes as I'm going to roast these potatoes – cook them in oil and dish them up to be devoured – well, then I might be a happy man.'

'Mind if I sit down and talk to you?'

Morris shrugged. 'It's your house. You can sit where you like, say what you like . . . although I suppose it's Tilda's house, really. Perhaps you'd better ask her permission.'

Alex pulled up a chair and sat down. 'I've been thinking.'

'Well, there's a thing.'

'I've been thinking about our discussion the other night.'

'What discussion? I don't remember having a discussion with you.'

Alex sighed. 'Look, you did rather spring it on me, you know,' he said. 'It's a lot of money you're after. How did you expect me to react?'

'Like I said, I don't remember any discussion.' Morris put down the potato peeler and sucked a cut finger.

'The problem for me,' Alex tried again, 'is that I don't quite buy your explanation of why the gallery failed. Sure you lost interest, but it's more than that.'

'Look at that.' Morris held his cut finger out for Alex's inspection. 'Who on earth manages to cut himself on a potato peeler?'

Alex ignored him. 'I think the reasons for the gallery's failure were there right from the start.'

Morris picked up another potato, frowned. 'What do you mean? My gallery was successful for years.'

'Success is relative,' said Alex. 'Of course it was successful if you consider success to mean that it didn't make much of a loss for the first few years. But did your gallery ever make a profit? I don't think it was ever a truly commercial enterprise.'

'Well, if you put it that way—'

'I don't think you'll ever make a real commercial success of a gallery run in the way you used to run that place.' Alex knew he had Morris's attention now.

'So how would *you* run a gallery, Alex? What would you do differently?' There was contempt in Morris's voice, but there was also interest.

'Let me think.' He pretended to mull over the problem. 'To begin with, I wouldn't exhibit work as a favour – not for friends and not for my wife.'

'I didn't do *that* many favours . . .'

'I also wouldn't display work by artists who were looking for their first break – their first real exhibition.'

'But that's a very important part of what I used to do,' protested Morris.

'I'd only have shows by established artists,' continued Alex. 'People with international reputations.'

Morris smiled. 'And how would I get those sort of people to take me seriously, eh? They aren't interested in displaying in galleries like mine—'

'Exactly.'

'—and I'm not so sure I'm interested in them. They're not the point.'

'Morris, you've got to set your sights higher,' said Alex. 'You can't just *play* at business, you have to take it seriously.'

'Like you?'

'Frankly, yes.' Alex pulled his chair closer. 'Before you start building, you need to lay your foundations. In this case, that means making the right contacts, doing your homework on marketing and publicity. Get a good PR firm on board – it's essential. Make yourself known to the advertising men, the big private collectors – come down to London and I'll do what I can to get you introduced to the right people. Find out who the London galleries are showing – go along to the private views and see if you can talk them into exhibiting in Newcastle as well. Get the right premises; it's no good having some out-of-town warehouse like you did last time – you need to be in the right part of town in the right kind of building. Have a really flash launch with all the art journalists there. It'll cost but in the end it'll pay off . . .'

'Alex, this just isn't me.' Morris was massaging his temples as though he had a headache.

'It's going to have to be you. You'll need to do all that and much more. You want it to work, don't you?'

'One hundred thousand pounds.' Morris picked up the peeler again and started work on the last potato. 'I think my soul is worth rather more than that.'

'Actually I think you'll need two hundred thousand, at least,' said Alex. 'That is, if you're going to do it properly.'

Alex couldn't really afford to lend Morris two hundred thousand pounds. In fact, Alex couldn't afford to lend him one hundred thousand pounds. But an opportunity had presented itself that was just too good to miss: it was Alex's chance to control Morris. He tried to tell himself that he was doing this out of a genuine altruistic desire to help his brother, and yet he knew that wasn't his true motivation. At his wedding reception, Morris had asked Alex whether he wanted to be like Morris or whether he wanted Morris to be like him. The question had unsettled Alex, made him uncomfortable. It was a touch too perceptive. At the time he hadn't known the answer, but now he thought he did. Throughout his life he had secretly wanted to be like Morris. As a child, he'd wanted to be included in his elder brother's games, his vivid imaginary world. As an adult he had envied Morris's spontaneity, unpredictability, his refusal to compromise. But something shifted on the night Morris asked for the loan. Which brother had power over the other now?

Morris would get his loan – even if it meant that Alex had to take out a loan himself – but Morris would have to play things Alex's way. Alex would be the not-so-silent silent partner.

In fact, when Morris accepted the loan, Alex was strangely disappointed in him. Somehow he'd expected Morris to throw the offer back in his face – had even wanted him to. His big brother wasn't so big any more. He'd shrunk down to human proportions. And then he shrank still further.

The gallery started well and continued better. The first year produced profits that far exceeded anything Alex had anticipated or hoped for. The second year was better still. But as the gallery grew, Morris shrank in equal proportion. Alex began to hate himself for what he had done, and hated the fact that he still took pleasure in it.

Alex had made a success of his brother, but had he also destroyed him? Morris shrank so small that he disappeared inside his business suit; you'd need a magnifying glass to find him. This suicide, this awful event that Alex had tried to block out, tried not to believe in even while he knew it was true . . . this suicide was Morris's bid for freedom. He'd cut himself loose and gone swimming away, leaving Alex forever unable to follow.

'Morris?'

'Eh?'

The voice was all wrong. Clarrie strained to see him clearly through the dark. He was moving, walking towards her.

'Morris?' she said again, but this time more quietly. She tried to get up, feeling light-headed. The world clouded over for a moment in a swarm of coloured dots, and then her vision became clear once again.

'Is this the Stones' place?' the man asked. He was standing in front of her now. Silly of her to think it could be Morris, even for the briefest moment.

'Yes,' she said. The baby was sleeping in his arms. It was a pretty baby – peachy, fair and angelic, like a baby from a soap advert. Not like poor Indigo. He hoisted it up slightly. It didn't stir.

'Nice baby,' she said and looked at the man's face. He was much younger than Morris. Young and blond. Blue-eyed. Good-looking, Clarrie supposed, in a conventional sort of way. Perhaps the word handsome was most appropriate. He was like Prince Charming in *Cinderella*. He smiled, showing even white teeth.

'Yeah, he is,' said Prince Charming, and then added hastily, 'He isn't mine, though.'

'Oh,' said Clarrie. 'That's a shame.'

'Not really,' said the prince. 'I'm a bit young for all that.'

'Yes,' she said, distracted. A thought had come into her head. 'How did you get into the garden?'

'Back gate was open,' said Price Charming. 'Just walked right in. Thought I might have the wrong house, though. Houses look so different from the back.'

'So do people,' said Clarrie. 'And from the inside, too. They're very different from the inside.'

Prince Charming laughed. 'Houses or people?'

'Both,' said Clarrie, irritated.

Prince Charming looked her up and down, inquisitively. 'Aren't you cold?' he asked.

Clarrie shrugged.

'Your face is all messed up,' said the prince, noticing for the first time.

'I know,' said Clarrie.

'How did it get that way? What's going on in there?' He looked uneasy, uncomfortable.

'What do you want?' she asked, ignoring his questions.

'I'm looking for someone,' said Prince Charming.

Clarrie shivered, beginning to feel the cold. 'Did you hear me howl?'

'That was you?' The prince chuckled. 'Jesus, you've got a pair of lungs on you.'

'Yes,' said Clarrie, pleased. 'Who are you looking for?'

'Clive Stilbourne,' said Prince Charming, and his charming smile shrank away. 'I need to speak to him.' The baby let out a noise that was a kind of cross between a sigh and a gurgle.

'He's inside,' said Clarrie. 'They're all inside.'

'Well, goodness gracious.' Judy Marshall quickly converted a look of horror into a surprised smile.

They faced each other across the kitchen table. An edge of irritation entered Judy's smile as she overcame the initial shock. 'I came out to look for a light,' she said, reaching for the ignition on the gas stove and bending to light a cigarette from the blue flame. 'What are you doing here, Saul?'

'That's a very bad habit,' he said.

'What, smoking or lighting fags from a cooker?' Judy drew deeply on her cigarette. 'Baby Max, I presume,' she said, reaching a finger out to stroke the baby's cheek. 'He's quite fat, isn't he?'

'Where's Clive?' Saul asked, with a hint of impatience.

'Oh, darling, you mean you aren't here to see little me?' Judy's tone was mocking. She sat down at the table and crossed her long legs, lounging back against the wall.

'Why would I have any interest whatsoever in seeing you?' said Saul, regarding her with obvious contempt.

Judy assumed a hurt expression. 'Sweetie, how cruel of you! It really wasn't so long ago that you were only too glad to while away a quiet afternoon with Auntie Judy.'

'Sorry, I just don't need the cash these days,' said Saul, tossing back his blond hair.

'Uncle Clive keeps you nicely in pocket, I suppose,' Judy sneered.

'Let's just say I don't want for anything,' said Saul. 'And certainly nothing you could give me.'

Judy shifted in her chair and looked down at the floor. 'Well, you've picked a great moment to visit,' she said, at length. 'We've had the police here this evening.'

'The police?'

'Yes. That delightful creature in the garden has just murdered her husband . . . Yes, I did say murder. The husband was Alex Stone's brother. She's saying it was suicide, of course, but then she would say that, wouldn't she.'

Saul sat down slowly on the chair across from Judy and shifted baby Max into a different position. 'Are you making this up?'

'Now why would I do that?' Judy sipped from her glass of gin and tonic and placed it down on the table.

Saul immediately grabbed it and drained it dry. 'I'm out of here,' he said, quietly.

'I think that would be wise, really, all things considered,' said Judy, bowing her head. 'Perhaps whatever little drama you've come round to create could wait for a more tranquil evening. You'll never get the attention you deserve if you make a scene now.'

'No, I mean I really am out of here. I'm leaving.'

'Leaving your flat? Leaving London?'

'I'm leaving, period. I'm going back to Australia. I've had enough.'

Judy raised an eyebrow. 'And you've come to say good-bye.'

'That's right.'

'When are you going?'

'Tomorrow,' said Saul.

Judy looked searchingly at his open face. 'Do I detect a decision made in haste?'

'I called the airline tonight. Late cancellation – picked up a cheap ticket. But I've been thinking about it for a while.'

'I call it running away,' she said.

Saul smiled. 'No, you've got it wrong. That's what I was doing when I came to England. Now I'm going home.'

Judy nodded slowly and stubbed out her cigarette on a nearby plate. 'He'll miss you,' she said.

'I know. I'll miss him too.'

'Oh, please!' she snorted.

'No, I will,' Saul said quietly. 'I love him, you see. That's probably not something you'd understand.'

'So what is this, some kind of sacrifice? You're *doing the decent thing*, are you?' she mocked.

'That's right.' Saul got to his feet. 'You see, I'm also quite fond of this little fellow.' He glanced down at Max. 'And he's not fat. He's perfect.'

In spite of herself Judy found she was strangely touched. So much so that moments later, when the hall was filled with guests putting on coats (there had obviously been a communal decision that it was time to leave), she wanted only to help the Australian.

'Saul!' Heidi's surprise couldn't have been more complete. 'What's going on? Is something wrong with Max?' She fluttered over like a cumbersome mother hen, and swooped on her baby, whisking him away from Saul and holding him close. Max, inevitably, woke up and began to wail with escalating volume, his perfect little face contorting into an ugly snarl.

Christina Thackston, who had just been roused from her slumber in the dining-room and collected by her indefatigable husband, found that Max's ceaseless cries were just too much for her. 'Make it go away!' she whined, her face pressed to Brian's lapel. 'Make it stop.'

'Heidi darling,' said Judy, now at her most brusque and efficient. 'Let's get Max upstairs away from this crowd and calm him down. I think he needs changing, judging by that stench. They won't have any nappies here, of course, but perhaps we could improvise with a towel or something.' She began to guide Heidi out of the kitchen by the elbow.

'But I don't understand,' protested Heidi. 'What's going on? Why is he here?' She twisted round to look at Saul, who was staring at the floor, his floppy blond fringe shielding his eyes. 'Clive?' Her husband was looking strange – pale, unwell even.

Finding inspiration, Judy bent to whisper conspiratorially in Heidi's ear. 'Saul's in trouble, poor lad. He's been pouring his little heart out to me in the kitchen. It was too much for him to be alone with Max tonight. He's got a girl pregnant, you see, and he's terrified, just *terrified*. He needs money. He's desperate. Clive was the only person he felt he could turn to. He thinks of him as . . . as an older brother. Let's give them a few minutes to talk – alone. Come on, sweetie.'

Heidi's eyes were wide with amazement. 'My God, Judy. I . . . I had no idea,' she whispered. 'Of course they must be alone. Saul's quite right to turn to Clive, you know. Clive's really very fond of him.'

I was born at the wrong time, thinks Judy to herself. *I would have been a great person to have around in a war. I am a composer and an orchestrator. I create and I arrange. I know how to make things happen, and I know how to destroy. I never miss my target.*

'Clive, why don't you take Saul into the dining-room?' she called back over her shoulder. 'I think you'll find it's empty now.' Impulsively, she gave Saul a little wink. He looked most surprised. Judy liked to surprise people.

Roger opened and closed his mouth like a fish as his wife pushed past him with Heidi and Max, making for the stairs.

'Not now, Roger,' she warned, barely looking at him.

But he had seen the wink, and didn't like it. Not one little bit.

Clarrie was sitting on the grass under the cherry tree deep in thought when the Clay came trudging across the lawn looking purposeful. She was thinking about the enduring nature of trees, of the things that trees must see. She considered the cherry tree, pondering the fact that it had watched Tilda grow from a tiny child into a woman, seen her parents shrivel up like ageing prunes and finally disappear. And what had it seen before the arrival of Tilda's family? This house was very old and at one time grand people would have lived here with their servants. This innocent-looking tree had probably witnessed arguments and illicit courtships, had probably heard the solitary confessions of many an anguished soul; it held within its bark all of the secrets of all of the residents of this house. If you extracted a sample of sap from this tree and analysed it under a microscope you would discover that it was entirely composed of molten secrets.

The idea developed further. Trees were living things, able to observe and carrying somewhere within them a record of what they had seen – this much was clear. Perhaps, then, wooden

furniture, which had been cut and carved from these silent
observers, also had a life of its own – was also able to witness.
Maybe the table on which they had eaten this very evening had
groaned inwardly under the weight of the memory of all the
dinner parties held on it. Maybe the bed on which Alex and Tilda
made love – or didn't make love – took voyeuristic pleasure in
their activities. Perhaps the wooden towel rack in her bathroom
at home had watched Morris slowly bleed to death – no, this
couldn't be right. It was impossible that furniture was alive. It
was composed of lifeless fragments. To suggest that furniture was
able to see and remember would be like imagining that random
limbs – arms and legs which had been hacked from the body –
were able to continue a life of their own. Yes, this idea was a
silly one. She had better discard it.

'Clarrie, come back into the house now. You're going to catch
your death if you sit out here in the cold all night.'

'Catch my death,' she mused, staring at the Clay's large feet.
His shoes looked expensive. Italian leather, no doubt. Clarrie
wondered if shoes were alive and could see – after all, they had
come from the skins of cows and cows were living things. But
what about plastic shoes . . .

'Did you realise the police were here?' asked the Clay.

Clarrie shook her head slowly.

'They've been to your house. They found . . . they found
Morris.'

She shuddered. She didn't like to think of strangers in her
house, poking around among her things, eating sandwiches
around her husband's body, treating him disrespectfully. 'I was
wrong to come here tonight,' she said eventually. 'I should have
stayed with him. He shouldn't have had to be there alone,
waiting for them to come.'

With difficulty, the Clay crouched down next to her. His shoes
creaked and he winced with the effort. 'Listen, pet, it doesn't
matter now. Do you understand? It doesn't matter. He's gone.
And, well . . . maybe you should have called the police, but
that doesn't matter either, not really. It's all in hand now, all
in hand.'

Clarrie squinted at his well-meaning tired face, and imagined an enormous hand descending from the sky, scooping

them up and carrying them away somewhere. 'Whose hand?' she asked.

The Clay sighed and pretended not to have heard. 'Clarrie, what I'm going to say now – well, it's important, and I want you to remember it.'

Clarrie thought how funny it was that this man could decide his words were important and should be listened to while her own were unimportant and should be ignored.

He began delving into his inside jacket pocket and produced a small card, which he held out for Clarrie. Obediently she reached out and took it, and stared at the swirling gold letters that spelled out Brian's name.

'I want you to keep that card somewhere safe,' he said. 'And if there's a time when you find yourself in a difficult spot—'

'Difficult spot,' murmured Clarrie.

'Yes – well, if you do find that . . . that you're in some sort of trouble, or that you just aren't coping – somehow – well, please call me. I feel sort of involved—'

Clarrie wondered why this man might be feeling involved with her life. She didn't feel involved with his.

'—and I'd like to help.' He smiled a sad little smile, and Clarrie could see that he really did mean what he was saying. She didn't understand why, but that wasn't really the point. She thought she'd better humour him so she smiled back.

'You'll have to go to Newcastle tomorrow with Alex and Tilda, and the police will want to talk to you,' said the Clay, watching for her reaction with some anxiety. 'It won't be pleasant. It might be a really horrible experience. And you're not exactly in the frame of mind to be dealing with that kind of thing. Alex – well, frankly, he's in a bad way, that much is clear. If you need someone there to look out for you, you just call me, OK? Will you do that?'

Clarrie nodded. 'Thank you,' she said.

The Clay smiled again, a kindly sort of smile, and reached over to give her hand a little squeeze. 'I'm going to be off now,' he said. 'I've got to get Christina home.'

He stood up, slowly and with a pained expression on his face. 'Well, goodbye then,' he said with a shrug.

'Bye,' said Clarrie, watching him trudge back to the house.

She looked again at the card, which lay in the palm of her hand. Clearly the Clay was a man who liked curly calligraphy, not really her cup of tea. The card was far too ornate with its marbled background and three different kinds of font.

A sharp breeze rustled through the branches of the cherry tree, and Clarrie threw back her head in order to feel it on her face, sharp and refreshing.

The breeze lifted the card from her hand and carried it away into a flower bed. Clarrie had already forgotten its existence.

Three cars were heading off down the Marlsham Road. Two were black cabs and the third was a beautiful Mercedes sports car in deep blue. At the lights, one cab turned right, the other turned left and the Mercedes drove straight on.

'Saul should have come in the taxi with us,' said Heidi Stilbourne. There was no reply from Clive, who was unusually quiet. But after all, thought Heidi, what was left to be said at the end of a night like this? 'We should have made him come with us,' she tried again. 'He's got *miles* to walk.'

Clive stroked the forehead of his sleeping son. 'He wanted to walk. He's got a mind of his own.'

'Did you two have a good talk?' asked Heidi, after a pause.

Clive gave her a look that was edgy. She felt she was wrong to have pried. She wished she hadn't said anything.

'Poor Alex,' he said.

'Did you give him any money?' asked Heidi, unable to stop herself.

'*Alex*?'

'No, Saul, of course.'

'Shhh. Keep your voice down or you'll wake Max.'

'Don't be ridiculous,' said Heidi. 'Cars always put him to sleep. Remember when he was a new-born and we used to have to go driving around in the middle of the night to get him to shut up and fall asleep?'

'I remember,' said Clive with a smile. 'Somehow it was always my turn.'

'That poor cow,' said Heidi, as the taxi lurched around a corner.

'She's lost her baby and her husband. I wonder what's going to happen to her?'

'She'll probably end up in the loony bin.'

'Clive!'

'Which way now, guv?' asked the cabby. 'Shall I go by Grey Street or Witcham?'

'As you like,' said Clive. 'Either will do.'

'Alex will have to identify the body, won't he?' said Heidi with a shiver.

'Or Clarrie,' said Clive.

'Maybe Alex will want to do it. It might be good for him to see the body. It helps the grieving process, I think. It's much better to face reality head on than to hide from it.'

Again the taxi lurched. 'Hey, watch it,' Clive said to the driver. 'We've got a baby back here, you know.'

'Sorry, guv.'

'I've been thinking about what you were saying earlier.' Clive turned to look at Heidi.

'What was I saying?'

'You know – about going away.'

'Oh, that.' She dismissed it with a wave of her hand. 'Don't worry, I was being silly. I didn't really mean it.'

'No, I think you were right.' Clive was animated now; eager. The sullen silence was over. Heidi couldn't decipher the meaning of this behaviour.

'Maybe we *do* need to get away somewhere – some place fresh and new. All this stuff tonight, it just makes me think what a fucked up country we live in.'

'Yes, but . . .' Heidi was at a loss for words. Surely he wasn't serious. What about her business and his job? What about their home; their friends? 'Where would we go?' she said, eventually.

His eyes were shining in the dark. 'Well, I thought . . . how about Australia?'

Christina's sleeping head was heavy against Brian's right shoulder. The shoulder was beginning to ache, but he didn't particularly mind. Christina was always something of a dead weight, but it was a weight he was long accustomed to. Without her, his life would be awfully light.

'Had a few too many, has she, mate?' asked the cab driver.

'Don't worry, she's not going to throw up,' said Brian in a tired voice.

'No, mate, that's not what I meant – not at all. Just making conversation, that's all. No offence.' He sounded hurt.

'None taken,' said Brian. The driver was about the same age as him, and was also a large man. Brian noticed a picture of a pretty woman with peroxided hair and two boys of about nine or ten. Twins? 'Those your wife and kids?'

'Yeah, that's right. It's an old photo, though. Sean's fourteen now and Mike will be sixteen in April. Got any of your own?'

Christina was snoring slightly. Brian shifted his shoulder to try to jolt her into stopping, but she snored all the louder. 'No,' he said. 'She can't.'

'Oh, I'm sorry to hear that,' said the cabby, trying to catch Brian's eye in his mirror.

'It's OK,' said Brian. 'It was a problem at one time but we've got over it. You just go on, don't you. It's all you can do.'

'That's right, mate. Couldn't agree more.'

'It's been a terrible night,' said Brian. 'You wouldn't believe it if I told you.'

'Try me,' said the driver. 'I like a good story.'

'Nah,' said Brian. 'I'd rather not.'

'Suit yourself.'

'Take the next on the right,' said Brian.

Christina murmured something inaudible and sighed in her sleep.

'I don't know what I'd do without you,' whispered Brian, reaching to touch her cheek.

'Get out of my fucking way,' snapped Roger Marshall and honked his horn uselessly at the double-decker bus that was rumbling along in front of the Mercedes.

'Why so aggressive, darling?' said Judy. 'We're not in any great hurry, are we?'

'I want to get home,' said Roger, without looking at her. 'I want to sleep.'

'Well, there's not much point in getting angry with a bus, is there, sweetie? Your anger won't get us home any faster.'

Roger saw his moment and roared past the bus, going straight through a red light.

'I'd quite like to get home alive, darling,' said Judy.

Roger gripped the steering wheel hard and remained quiet.

'She killed him, I know it.'

'Oh, yeah? And just how do you *know it*?' Roger all but choked on the words.

'It's obvious. That note – "I love you red" indeed! Morris didn't write it. That girl's obsessed with red. She probably murdered him just to get a look at all the blood. She might even have hung around to do a few sketches.' Judy examined her nails as she spoke, hunting for chips in the varnish. She was so calm, she could have been talking about the price of beef. 'Then she panicked, of course, and ran away.'

'You'd better watch who you say those kind of things to.' Roger darted her a fierce glance. 'This isn't something to gossip about.'

'Christ, if I can't speak my mind to my own husband, then who the hell can I talk to?' Judy was laughing, but her laugh was hollow and forced.

'Why do you have to make everything nastier and dirtier than it already is?' Roger's voice shook and he flinched as Judy reached over to lay her hand on his knee. 'You don't know the first thing about Morris. He's been a depressive as long as I've known him. He topped himself – he's always had it in him.'

'What a fascinating idea,' cooed Judy, 'that one can carry suicide around inside oneself like an extra kidney or a gallstone or something.' She giggled.

'This is no laughing matter,' said Roger, slamming on the brakes and swearing as the traffic lights ahead turned red.

'There's humour in everything,' said Judy, lightly.

The lights turned green and they lurched forward again. 'Oh, yes, you laugh at everyone, don't you,' said Roger. 'Especially me.'

'Darling, you're so manly when you're angry!'

He felt an impulse to hit her hard in the mouth. 'I saw you wink at that boy.'

'What boy?'

'You know – that boy. You winked at him.'

'I did no such thing!' Judy appeared outraged. 'And anyway, what if I did? What does it matter?'

'How could you blackmail our friends? What kind of a woman are you!'

'Darling, don't be absurd!'

'I know what you're doing. Clive as good as told me himself.'

Now Judy seemed to be hurt. 'And you take his word over mine? I'm your *wife*, Roger.'

'Yes, you are, God help me.'

'Clive Stilbourne has never liked me. Yes, it's true, and you know it. And he tried to seduce me once, did you know that?'

She was doing it again – he knew she was. He could feel himself calming down, inwardly digesting her words. He wanted so much to be able to believe her. And yet . . . He steeled himself. 'I thought you said he was into men.'

'Oh, he likes both. He's highly sexed, or so he told me. He has a large . . . appetite.' Judy smiled.

'And that boy? The baby sitter?'

'Oh, come on, Roger. Lighten up. Shagging the baby sitter is a time-honoured tradition, isn't it.'

'And what about you? Have you indulged in that particular time-honoured tradition?'

'Well, what do you think.' Judy reached over to tweak his moustache.

Alex wandered randomly through the empty rooms of his house. Ha, *his* house indeed! It had never really been his and it never would be. It was Tilda's house. He passed through the hallway and began to mount the stairs, sipping wearily from the glass of Scotch in his hand. He supposed it was helping to deaden the frenzy of pain that he'd been feeling. Or was it just his body's natural defences closing off the avenues of hurt that ran through him like rivers? Either way, what he felt now was an awful numbness.

He didn't know what to do with himself. What did people do when they'd heard of the sudden death of a loved one? Should he sit in a darkened room wearing funeral garb and weeping? Should he be practical; make lists of all the things he would have to do over the next few days? Should he be calling his parents – who were presumably sleeping peacefully in blissful ignorance . . . Ah, sleep. It would be the right thing to do, but how did one sleep at a time like this?

From the top of the stairs he heard the sound of the back door being opened and closed, noises of bare feet slapping over the quarry tiles in the kitchen. The guests had all gone, hadn't they? Clarrie! He'd completely forgotten about her. She'd been in the garden all this time and now she was back – looking for him? He couldn't face her at this moment. She would want to talk to him, to share their loss. How could he stand to look at her swollen bruised mouth and listen to her incoherent rambling nonsense? No, not just yet. The footsteps were getting closer. She was heading into the hall. In a few seconds she would appear at the foot of the stairs, gazing up at him where he stood leaning against the newel post; gazing expectantly, reproachfully, waiting for him like some sort of angel of death.

No, he couldn't deal with this now, not yet. He shrank back into the shadows, put his empty glass down on the carpet, and slipped off his shoes. He moved noiselessly across the landing and mounted the next flight of stairs, treading in time with the steady comforting tick of the old grandfather clock. As his hand closed around the handle of the bedroom door, he found he was almost praying that Tilda wouldn't be in there. Still, all things considered, she would be easier to face than Clarrie at this time. Tilda was the lesser of two evils.

'What are you doing?'

Tilda jolted at the sound of his voice and then continued folding clothes into a small suitcase.

'Tilda?'

'Packing, darling. We don't know how long we're going to have to stay there, do we?' She stepped around the bed to close the wardrobe, brushing past him.

'Will you stop that.'

She opened the underwear drawer and counted out knickers onto the bed. Silk, cotton, lace. Mostly white. Tilda wasn't fond of coloured underwear and disdained black unless it was worn under a black dress.

'What?' She reached for his underwear drawer. White cotton boxers – all identical – all bought by Tilda.

'Just stop packing, will you. I have to think.'

He sat wearily in her mother's old green armchair – the chair Tilda had refused to allow him to dispose of when they took over the house.

'Of course you do. That's why I'm packing. You can't be expected to do it but one of us has to be practical.'

Seven pairs of knickers, seven pairs of boxers. Enough for a week if necessary. Surely they wouldn't be in Newcastle for much more than a week? How long did these things take? They could always buy more underwear if they ran out, she reasoned.

'I said stop, damn you!' he shouted.

'Alex!' She was appalled at his unreasonableness, but tried to calm herself. He could hardly be held responsible for his behaviour at a time like this. 'I'm sorry,' she said. 'You're not yourself.'

'I *am* myself.' He was on his feet, grabbing her arm, and his fingers dug painfully into the flesh. 'Why do you say I'm not myself?' His eyes were unblinking. The grip on her arm tightened. 'I *am* myself,' he said again.

'Darling, I – I only mean . . .' she spluttered.

'Oh, what's the use.' He dropped her arm abruptly and turned away from her, sitting down on the edge of the bed.

She felt she was going to cry, and busied herself with his sock drawer to hide her tears from him.

'I don't want you to come with me,' Alex said slowly, deliberately.

'What?' A black sock fell to the floor and Tilda allowed it to stay there.

'You heard.'

'I'll look up the number of the Stafford Hotel,' Tilda said brightly. 'You know, the one where we stayed when Morris and Clarrie got . . . married . . .'

Her voice trailed off limply and she bit her lip as she realised what she had said. Alex didn't move. He made no response whatsoever.

'Or we could stay somewhere else,' she continued. 'We should try to get some sleep and then set off first thing. It shouldn't take more than a few hours. There won't be much traffic on a Sunday morning. And Clarrie had better come too, of course.'

The thought of being confined in a car with Tilda and Clarrie was almost more than Alex could bear. And it would certainly take more than a few hours to drive to Newcastle. 'I can't think about this now,' was all he could find to say.

'But, darling, we *have* to think about it, hard though it is.'

'You're really in your element now, aren't you.' Alex was irritated. It was becoming impossible to be in the same room with her. Perhaps he shouldn't have tried to run away from Clarrie after all.

Tilda decided to ignore that comment. 'We have to go up there. You heard what Inspector Darnley said. Somebody's going to have to . . . And the police will want to talk to Clarrie.'

'Shut up about Clarrie.' Alex's voice was tired and flat. 'I'm sick of all this stupid speculation. I'm sick of all the whispers that have been going on in this house, and I'm sick of being surrounded by people. Including you.'

Tilda retrieved the sock with a shaking hand. 'So you don't want me to come with you.'

'Eu-bloody-reka!' Alex pulled off his shoes and eased himself onto the bed. He lay back against the pillows with his right arm thrown against his face, hiding his eyes.

'Don't shut me out,' said Tilda. 'I'm here for you. I love you.' The words surprised her as they emerged. It was as though someone else had spoken them, but she felt they were the right words. She folded another sock with momentary satisfaction.

He grunted.

Sheltering beneath his arm, Alex travelled back to the day when Heidi announced she wouldn't leave Clive for him. He relived the sense of hopelessness, remembering how he had lain down on the same bed in more or less the same position as today, hiding under his arm. He had felt then as though his whole body had turned to pulp, like a heap of rotting vegetables. His limbs were a couple of rancid aubergines – he didn't have the strength to move them, or even to wipe his face and his nose when the tears started to roll. He just lay, crying into his hair, thinking about how Heidi had made him feel, for a brief time, as though he was really worth something. He had lain there in this way for many hours while the room became dark around him. And eventually Tilda had come in, believing herself to be alone in the house – and screamed when she saw him. Afterwards she explained that for a second she'd thought he was lying dead on the bed. And then she began asking questions, which he chose not to answer.

Still sheltering, he travelled further back, to a day when he was thirteen years old, sitting on the edge of the bath, staring at himself in the mirror while he pressed the flat of the sharpest kitchen knife against the inside of his left wrist. He pressed lightly at first, so that he could hardly feel the blade – and then a little harder. He wanted to see his wrist open out and the blood begin to appear. Would it spurt or merely seep slowly? He dropped the knife, his wrist still intact, letting it clatter onto the lino. He had only wanted to know what it felt like when you decided to hurt yourself. Did his mother ever notice the scars on Morris's arms when he wore short-sleeved T-shirts? Did his father ever wonder why Morris liked to wear all those bits of material tied around his wrists? It seemed that Alex was the only person who could see.

'I'm frightened,' Tilda realised aloud.

'Frightened of what?' said Alex, from under his arm.

'Of *her*. Of all this.' Tilda laid a sock down and perched on the edge of the bed, reaching for Alex's foot to hold. The foot flinched when touched, and Tilda turned hurt eyes on her husband.

'You know I don't like my feet to be touched,' he muttered.

'Sorry.'

'There's no need to be afraid of Clarrie.' Alex realised this was true even as he said it. Clarrie was no angel of death. She was nothing more than a lost soul, a woman still reeling from having lost everything she valued. What was there to be afraid of except for the marks left on her by his own violence? If Alex was to fear anyone, he should fear himself. And perhaps Judy Marshall, that evil meddler, the one to ask about suicide notes, the one to whisper the word 'murder' – oh, yes, he had heard her. 'Judy Marshall is poisonous,' he said, 'and she's determined to inflict her poisonous thoughts on everybody else.'

'Darling!'

'Be sorry for Clarrie if you like, but don't be afraid of her. She hasn't done anything wrong. She's just a fool.'

'Is that why you hit her, then?' Tilda longed to pull his arm away from his face and make him look at her. 'Because she's a fool?'

'Shut up.'

'None of us knows what really happened,' said Tilda. 'We can't know for certain until after the inquest.'

'Inquest?'

That finally made him sit up.

'Well, of course. There's bound to be an inquest.'

'Oh, Jesus!' Alex flopped back. 'This is a private matter. Clarrie didn't kill him. He killed himself. Oh, God, there'll be press and everything, won't there!'

Tilda reached back to rub his foot again, trying to soothe him. 'We'll face it together.'

'No.' Alex drew his feet away. 'Get off me. I can't stand people touching my feet.'

'Seems like you can't stand me touching you at all.'

'My brother is dead!'

Give him time, Tilda told herself. Don't push him. But somehow she couldn't help it. 'I'm not just talking about tonight. You never want me to touch you.'

'I can't discuss this now.' The arm went back across his face.

Tilda got to her feet and walked through to the bathroom, angrily kicking her shoes into a corner. The fluorescent light above the mirror was harsh, lighting up what seemed to be a thousand lines and wrinkles, fissures and cracks. Her own face was conspiring against her. She started taking pins out of her hair, letting them drop into the wash-basin. She searched her scalp for grey hairs as though checking for headlice.

'You don't want to me touch you. You don't want me to go to Newcastle with you. Just where exactly do I fit into all of this?' Her voice was shaking.

'You don't,' came sullenly from the bedroom behind her.

'So Clarrie's going with you but I'm staying at home? Me, your *wife*. And what about your parents? Who's going to tell them?'

'You can, if you like.'

Her hair was wiry against her neck. Her scalp itched unbearably. She ran her fingers through her hair like combs, letting her nails scrape hard against the scalp. The itching grew worse, making her want to tear at her hair and rip it out. 'I don't want to argue with you, Alex, but you're not being fair.'

'Fair? What's fair?'

'Why are you doing this?' Tilda swung back into the bedroom.

'Tilda, I can't be the way you want me to be,' he said simply. 'I know you want me to cry on your shoulder and tell you I love you and all of that, but I just can't. That's not how I feel.'

'Well, what am I supposed to do!' She was on the bed now, astride his legs. She hissed her words over his face and globs of spit flew from her mouth as she spoke, hitting him in the eyes.

'Do what you like. I don't care.' He was limp, expressionless.

With difficulty, she lay down next to him, her head on his chest, making the bed shake as she shifted awkwardly. He made no move either to draw her to him or to push her away. She could hear his heart beating steadily, his stomach gurgling as he digested. The sounds of his body functioning as normal were enough to make her want to slap him.

'I want to make love,' she said softly. 'I want you to make love to me.'

He said nothing. His stomach made a kind of creaking noise but otherwise he was silent.

'I want *you* to make love to *me*,' she said again, beating a fist against his chest to emphasise the words.

'I can't.' His words vibrated in her head. She felt the sound of them.

'You mean, you won't. You won't even try, will you?'

'I don't want to.'

More tears were oozing forth from her eyes, falling on his shirt, making forlorn little damp patches.

'I think I'd rather die.'

Alex knew he meant what he said. Her head was unbearably heavy on his chest. It made him think of the heaviness that had lived inside him the last time he had succeeded in making love to his wife. Such a long time ago. Did the word 'succeeded' really apply? They had been to Clive and Heidi's for the evening and they had both had too much wine. Tilda had been shrill and ridiculous all night, or so he remembered. She had been laughing loudly at the wholly un-funny jokes of the insipid little squirt seated next to her, while Alex breathed in the scent of Heidi's hair as she sparkled gloriously on his left. This was before anything had happened between himself and Heidi, of course. It was awfully delicious to be so close to her yet unable to touch her. He was forced to content himself with trying to see down the front of her blouse and imagining the delights he would find there.

When they got home at the end of the evening, Tilda was still giggling. Playful but unalluring. She had buzzed around him while he took off his clothes and failed – in his drunken state – to find his pyjamas. Had she hidden them while he was in the toilet? In bed with the lights off, he wanted to be left alone, but she was all over him, writhing like a lizard and clawing feebly. To his dismay he found he had an erection, and there seemed no option but to work it away inside her.

Being inside Tilda that night was like being trapped inside a dark dank cupboard, pushing at a door that wouldn't open and gasping for breath in an atmosphere devoid of oxygen. He couldn't even bring himself to try to pretend he was with Heidi. Instead he thrust away like a tired carpenter unable to cut through a stubborn piece of wood with a blunt saw – until he finally managed to force out a minute quantity of sperm with a titanic effort that left him feeling empty and alone.

He shuddered at the memory.

'You'd rather die than make love to me?' Tilda retreated, weeping. She half sat and half flopped onto the floor, lolling back against the wall, her face in her hands. 'That is without doubt the most horrible thing you've ever said to me, do you know that?'

'Yes,' said Alex.

'Aren't you going to apologise? Aren't you going to say you didn't mean it? That you only said it because of what's happened tonight – that . . . that you love me but you aren't able to show it just now because . . . because you're impotent? Aren't you going to say any of those things?'

She looked as though she might be about to get on her knees and beg. He hoped very much that she wouldn't.

'I can't tell you I'm sorry because I'm not. I can't say any of the things that you want me to say because they aren't true. I don't have the energy to lie.'

Her lips grew tight and her tears dried up. 'Oh, yes? One of those things is true, that much I know!'

He sighed. 'You're talking about my impotence, I suppose.'

Her fists were clenched but she didn't seem to know what to do with them. 'Alex, you may not be able to face up to your problem, but that doesn't mean you don't have one.'

'But I'm not really impotent. I just can't do it with *you*.'

There was no hint of malice in Alex's voice, but that only seemed to make it worse. Tilda didn't like the feeling that was growing inside her – the feeling that both she and Alex were out of control. She couldn't believe that he had really spoken those words, and neither could she feel she was in any way responsible for her own.

'You can't do it with me,' Tilda said slowly. 'Is it my fault then? Is it something I've done wrong?'

'No,' said Alex after a moment's hesitation. 'It's me.'

Tilda had never felt so helpless, so ineffectual. And then another thought came to her – one that she didn't like one little bit. 'You can't do it with *me*. And it's not my fault. You say it's . . . you. You've been doing it with someone else, haven't you.'

He didn't answer. He didn't need to.

Had Tilda known all along? She thought now that she had. Of course, she hadn't allowed herself to know it. It had been hidden away like a Christmas present waiting for the right day to be opened. Now she was holding the parcel in her hands – beginning to unwrap it – but already knowing what lay inside from its familiar distinctive shape.

'Who is she?' She spoke the words slowly, knowing they were words that had been spoken by thousands of millions of other pathetic wives. She could almost hear their voices echoing around her.

'It doesn't matter,' he said.

'Yes it does. It matters to me.'

'Nobody you know.'

And now Tilda could hear the voices of thousands of millions of lying cheating husbands. 'How long?'

He was shifting uncomfortably on the bed. 'A while. It doesn't matter. It's over now. She's married and it's over. You don't know her.'

'I'm . . .' Tilda searched for a word to describe how she felt. 'I'm crushed.'

'I didn't mean to crush you.'

'Well, you *have* crushed me.' He was so remote. She wanted to make him hurt the way she was hurting, but she knew she didn't have the power to do so. 'I've slept with someone else too,' she said at last, realising that she was indulging in the childish game of tit for tat.

'Was it good?' asked Alex, his eyes closed, his face placid.

Tilda was entirely lost for words. Did he care about her so little? They weren't a couple of schoolgirls swapping stories about their first sexual exploits. They were man and wife. She struggled to think of what to say. 'It was escapism,' she began, moistening her dry lips with an even drier tongue. 'It was something I did because my life was so – so empty. I wanted my husband to love me and to make love to me. I wanted a baby to fill my days, to nurture and care for – to be the precious thing that *I* had produced. I just . . . *wanted*. I still want those things, you know, even now. I built up a fantasy as a kind of consolation, and I tried to make that fantasy a reality. And it worked for a while. Yes, it was good. And then it was awful.'

'I'm sorry.' Alex's voice had changed. His eyes were open again and he was looking at her with something approaching compassion. Or was it pity?

'Was it like that for you too?' Her voice was a little too eager.

'No,' said Alex. 'I loved her. I still love her. But she doesn't want me.'

'You bastard!' Tilda was darting around the room now, zipping about uselessly like a demented bluebottle. She wanted to hurl things at his head in the manner of angry wives on film – frying pans, plates, anything – things that smash, things that do damage. That was what you were supposed to do at moments like this, wasn't it. But she wasn't the kind of person who could treat her belongings with such disregard. Half-heartedly she reached into the suitcase and flung a few pairs of boxer shorts at him.

Realising how ridiculous this token effort was, she stopped and stood still, breathless, arms hanging limply at her sides.

He brushed the boxer shorts away and got to his feet.

'Where are you going?' she asked, as he opened a cupboard and extracted a pair of trainers.

'Newcastle.' He bent to lace the trainers. They looked absurd with his suit and cravat.

'Now?'

'Yes.'

'But you can't.' She felt a flutter of panic in her chest. Her hand flew to her throat, as it always did.

'Excuse me,' he said, pushing past out of the doorway, not even looking at her.

She followed him down the stairs onto the first-floor landing. She clutched feebly at an arm, but he shook her off as though she were an insect. She felt too weak to do more, and stood gripping the banister, watching him descend.

Clarrie was sitting on the bottom stair, fully clothed once more in her jeans and jumper. She twisted round to look at him, and gave a contorted grin with her swollen mouth. (It was really quite alarming to see how swollen her mouth was.) She got to her feet to let him past and followed him as he walked across to the front door.

'You can't drive the car – you're drunk!' shouted Tilda, her voice hoarse and thin.

He was opening the front door.

'You'll get yourselves killed on the road,' she persisted, her knuckles turning white from the force of her grip on the banister. 'Or you'll kill someone else.'

'We'll be fine,' called Alex, holding the door open for Clarrie.

'When are you coming back?'

Alex did not reply. He stepped out after Clarrie. The sky was turning pink – the new day was arriving.

'Will you call me when you get there? Please?'

He did look up, though only briefly. She couldn't read the expression on his face. But then again, perhaps she had never been able accurately to read what he was thinking and feeling. He nodded, curtly, before the door slammed and they were gone.

*   *   *

The house was so large. Tilda had never before experienced it as large, in spite of the fact that 'huge' and 'enormous' were words frequently used by visitors when she gave them the tour. She sat down on the stairs and realised how silent it was. It was as though all those people hadn't even been here last night. She was still a little girl sitting on the stairs, trying to catch the comforting sounds of her parents' voices carrying up to her from the living-room when really she was supposed to be in bed. But now there were no voices. As she sat and listened, the silence gave way to all those sounds that lay beyond silence: the tinkling of the chandelier, the ticking of the grandfather clock, the roar of the boiler firing up as it came on for the morning, followed by the gurgle of radiators, birdsong, car engines, the occasional creak of the house, even the sounds of her own regular breathing. How dare these sounds continue as though all was normal! Did they not know that everything had changed?

Tilda got to her feet and began to walk down the stairs. If she had a child, she would go to its room now and peep in at the door, quietly, so as not to wake it. She would gaze with love at its sleeping face. Clarrie had been a mother, however briefly. She had given birth, she had held her baby in her arms, she had peeped in at her sleeping child in just this way. In spite of herself, Tilda felt jealous. Clarrie might have lost her child but she had known what it was like to have one – she at least had memories.

Tilda wondered if it was too early to phone Judy.

'I'm sorry I hit you.' Alex held the passenger door open for Clarrie, who got in without replying. 'I said, I'm sorry I hit you.' He got into the driver's seat, rubbing his hands against the cold.

'That's OK,' said Clarrie, realising this was what he needed to hear.

He put his keys in the ignition and started the car. 'Would you like the radio on?' he asked.

'No, thank you,' said Clarrie.

'Oh,' said Alex.

Clarrie then understood that it was Alex who wanted the radio on. 'I've changed my mind,' she said. 'Put it on.'

He smiled, briefly, and switched on Radio 4.

'Where are we going?' asked Clarrie.

He looked at her rather oddly. 'Newcastle, of course.' He twisted around to see clearly as he reversed the car out of the driveway.

'Are we going to see Morris?' she asked, puzzled.

He seemed startled. 'I suppose so. In a way.'

'Good.'

They drove onto the road, and a car behind flashed them. Guiltily, Alex switched on his lights, rubbed his eyes and yawned. 'I tell you what,' he said. 'Once we get out of London and onto the motorway, we'll stop off for some breakfast. Would you like that?'

'Yes,' said Clarrie, automatically.

'What I'd give for a good strong coffee!' said Alex.

'Yes.'

He looked at her again, puzzled. 'How are you feeling?'

'OK.' She was knitting her fingers together as tightly as she could and then releasing them, over and over again. 'Did I do the right thing?' she asked. 'Coming here, I mean. Was it right to come here?'

'Yes,' said Alex. 'You did the right thing.'

They turned right at the end of the Marlsham Road. The traffic wasn't too bad.

Clarrie squinted, and Alex turned into a blue glass bottle. She preferred red ones, given the choice.